Carolina Harmony

MARILYN TAYLOR McDOWELL

Carolina Harmony

Delacorte Press

Published by Delacorte Press
an imprint of Random House Children's Books
a division of Random House, Inc.
New York

Delacorte Press and colophon are registered trademarks of Random House, Inc.

Visit us on the Web! www.randomhouse.com/kids

Educators and librarians, for a variety of teaching tools,
visit us at www.randomhouse.com/teachers

Library of Congress Cataloging-in-Publication Data is available upon request.

ISBN 978-0-385-73590-2 (trade)—ISBN 978-0-385-90575-6 (lib. bdg.)—
ISBN 978-0-375-89199-1 (e-book)

The text of this book is set in 12-point Goudy.
Book design by Trish Parcell Watts
Printed in the United States of America
10 9 8 7 6 5 4 3 2 1
First Edition

For my mother, Irene Mae McDowell,
in remembrance of her grace, faith, and unyielding strength

The catbird took flight. It sailed over a wide expanse of
mountain peaks and lush valleys, over the green of summer
leaves and the winding trails of clear mountain streams.
It flew over cabins tucked in the hollers. It flew down over
pastureland, down over corn patches and fields overlaid with
the green leaves of sweet potato plants. Wings flapping,
talons taking hold, it perched on a branch low in the tulip tree,
getting an open view of the farmyard. It watched the dog
suddenly rise up on its haunches and chase the cat, which
scurried into an opening between the weathered gray boards
of the barn. The bird flapped its wings and flew again, over
the chickens pecking in the dirt, over the sheep grazing in
a meadow of grass, and over a long winding path,
where a girl was running.

Chapter 1

JULY 14, 1964

Carolina ran, a hot sharp pain stabbing at her side. The path stretched out before her. Tears threatened. She shoved them away, pressing on with fierce determination, sneakers pounding the dirt. Her breaths pulsed hard, fast. Arms pumped. A leg lifted. A leg pushed off. The stitch in her side tightened. She winced. Each gulp of air burned in her throat.

The farm path was well traveled, hollowed deep with ruts and potholes that still held last week's rain. Carolina skirted a length of tractor tracks filled with mud slick as grease and felt stickers tear across her legs as she sprinted through the weeds alongside the hickory trees. She cut through the pasture, frightening the sheep. They trotted away, bleating, but the sound was a distant echo in Carolina's ears, their cries drowned out by the thumping beats of her heart and each gasping breath. The sun scorched her nose. Her cheeks throbbed from the heat. She had to squint to see the silo and the barn. *Almost there*, she told herself. *Almost there*.

She reached the back of the barn and squeezed through an opening at the base of gray ragged boards, falling into the mare's stall. It was black as night. *Hurry!* She pushed her arms in front of her and felt the wooden rails of the ladder.

Grasping the sides, she climbed ten rickety steps to the ground floor. Sunlight filtered in from an opening high in the hayloft, illuminating flecks of dust in its path. She brushed against hay bales stacked high, nearly to the roof. Scrambling over the rusted tractor, she tripped and bumped against a line of shovels, rakes, and pitchforks. She heard them clattering onto the floorboards behind her as she burst back into the light of day. Black and red speck-led hens squawked and scattered in the barnyard as her feet beat past them.

Her eyes darted from one place to the next—the gar-den, the porch, the henhouse. She caught the scent of freshly mown hay, so strong she could taste it. Across the yard towels hung on the clothesline, damp and limp as the humid air. She saw Miss Latah's skirt moving behind a sheet, saw her reach down into the clothespin bag and reach up to pin the strap of Mr. Ray's long-legged overalls.

Carolina went to yell, but only a hoarse whisper came out.

She gulped in air. She forced a scream.

"Help!"

Miss Latah looked up. The overalls slumped to the side as Miss Latah rushed across the grass toward her.

"Carolina, what is it? What has happened?" asked Miss Latah.

"Mr. Ray . . ." Carolina choked out words between gasps. ". . . In the field . . . under the tractor . . . hurt real bad."

Miss Latah's forehead creased for a moment, fear written all over her face. Her eyes held Carolina's with a fierce intensity. Carolina thought they'd like to bore right through her. Miss Latah squared her shoulders.

"Come with me," she said.

Carolina willed her legs to run again and followed Miss Latah across the yard toward an old pickup truck with round green fenders.

Miss Latah cupped her hands at her mouth. "Lucas!" she called out.

Carolina slid onto the seat at the same time that Miss Latah leaned on the horn.

"Here he comes," said Carolina.

Lucas came into sight between rows of orchard trees. He sailed over the split-rail fence, his hand barely touching down on the post, and sprinted toward them in long even strides. Carolina pushed the door open as the tires rolled forward. Lucas leaped onto the running board and hurled himself up, crashing against Carolina as he hit the seat. The smell of his sweat filled the cab. His T-shirt was damp and stuck with bits of field grass.

Miss Latah pushed the gas pedal to the floor.

"Where's the fire?" Lucas asked. It was an expression he used when someone was suddenly in a big hurry.

Miss Latah didn't answer. She sped around the barn, the truck rattling and screeching. Carolina bounced up and bit her lip as the truck crashed into a rut and made a bang so loud it sounded as if the axle had broken in two. Then they tore down the path, alongside the pasture, down under the shade of hickory trees, and on toward the creek. The slatted boards of the bridge rumbled as they crossed. They were headed toward the back fields.

Carolina wondered how long it had taken her to run this same distance. She wondered how long it took a man to bleed to death. She dragged her arm across her forehead. Her sweat turned the red-clay soil on her arms into tiny beads like blood, and as she stared down at them, she recalled the events leading up to the accident.

They'd been having so much fun. Mr. Ray was telling stories with hilarious endings, contorting his face into the silliest expressions as he acted out one character after another. She'd gotten to laughing so hard she had to hold her belly. Even Mr. Ray was bent in two. All the while, he was teaching her how to drive the tractor.

Mr. Ray said it was not too late to turn this hillside into a field of cabbages, and then he went right into a story about a family of cabbage heads. That got Carolina laughing all over again. They made each other hungry talking about spicy cabbage relish and a crock full of sauerkraut. They agreed they would have a plentiful harvest come October. Mr. Ray said it was certain to be hard planting in this field, what with the rise and all, but you had to make the best of what you were given and appreciate the blessing. Carolina figured Mr. Ray to be the most thankful man she'd ever met.

He let her hold the steering wheel and then he showed her how to use the clutch. Her heart swelled with his praise—*"You're a good learner. Aye, you're a natural."* She drove at a slow and even speed, dragging the wooden stoneboat over the plowed field. After a while, Mr. Ray hopped down to the ground and let her drive all by herself.

Carolina felt on top of the world as she looked down from her perch on the tractor seat, holding that big steering wheel in her hands. Mr. Ray walked alongside in the furrows, picking up rocks in the overturned soil that were bigger than his fist and tossing them up onto the stoneboat. She steered the tractor around a large boulder. Mr. Ray began working at dislodging it. As the distance between them grew, she heard him yell, *"Drive the length of this row and then stop."*

Carolina figured she'd show Mr. Ray what a good driver she was. She knew she could turn the tractor around. Why, it would be simple. Didn't he say she was a natural? She shifted gears and pressed her foot on the gas, heading up the rise. She heard Mr. Ray holler and she hollered back, *"I can do it!"* Then everything went wrong at once.

A jerk, a bang, the tractor rising, her hands leaving the steering wheel as if a force was pulling it away from her, and out of the corner of her eye, she saw Mr. Ray running as fast as he could.

She remembered how strange it was, how at the moment when she flew off the seat, it was as if she was floating in slow motion. First she saw sky, then mountain peaks, then trees and hill and field. She remembered the scream dying in her throat as she saw the underside of the tractor, thinking she was about to be crushed. But before her back hit the dirt, she was caught in his arms, yanked away, just about thrown. She landed with a solid thump. It knocked the wind out of her. She lay still, as if she'd been struck deaf and dumb. She remembered staring up at the soil caked between the wide ridges of the tire and seeing a cloud floating in the blue sky above it. Finally, she rose onto her elbows, uncertain whether ten seconds or an hour had passed.

That was when she saw Mr. Ray.

His eyes were closed as if he was sleeping, as if he was . . . No, she wouldn't let herself think that.

She crawled across the dirt quick as a spider. She shook him gently. "*Mr. Ray, Mr. Ray, wake up.*" He made not a sound. He lay still as a stone. "*Mr. Ray, Mr. Ray, please wake up.*" She saw the blood seep through his skin, saw a slow trickle make its way across his forehead.

After that, all she remembered was running. *Get help!* Every other thought in her head moved out of the way.

Miss Latah downshifted, and as she did, the blue cotton fabric of her skirt brushed Carolina's leg. Miss Latah's jaw was set tight. The space between her knuckles was stretched tight on her brown hands as she gripped the steering wheel. Regret was welling up in Carolina's heart and filling her throat like a lump of wet sand.

"There he is!" yelled Lucas.

Across the field, the tractor was turned on its side like an uprooted tree after a bad storm. The stoneboat had skidded deep into the plowed ground. Mr. Ray was leaning back against it. He was slouched like a rag doll, but still he was sitting up.

He's okay! Mr. Ray's not . . .

Carolina pushed the word away.

She took a deep breath and let it out slow.

He's okay.

Her worst imaginings faded. She gulped the lump down but didn't dare try to talk. She had to squeeze her eyes shut to shove the tears away.

Mr. Ray's left arm hung limp and lifeless at his side, but he reached up with his good arm and gave them a tired wave. Then Mr. Ray went and smiled. Carolina thought the wheel of the tractor looked like a big fat halo hanging over his head.

Miss Latah slowed the truck to a crawl and stopped. Both doors opened at once as Miss Latah and Lucas jumped down from their seats and ran up the rise across the bare furrowed ground. Miss Latah kneeled before Mr. Ray, checking him over from head to toe. Lucas reached down and picked up his father's cap. He knocked the dirt off by hitting it against his leg and then took his place at his father's side, shifting his weight from one foot to the other. Inside the cab it was hot as blazes, but Carolina was frozen to the seat.

She saw Miss Latah look up and say something to Lucas that made him sprint back to the truck. Carolina looked through the window and saw Lucas grab a thin slab of hickory board out of the truck bed. She watched him run back to his mother and saw the way Miss Latah placed Mr. Ray's arm on the board, using it as a splint.

Carolina figured Miss Latah could mend Mr. Ray as good as a nurse, maybe even a doctor, even though her learning had not come from any university. Miss Latah was Cherokee. The gift of healing had been passed down to her by her grandmother, who'd taught her how to cure all manner of sickness using herbs and roots. It was doctoring that knew what nature provided, and it seemed to Carolina like something magical. She'd heard about certain older folks who could draw a burn out of the skin or suck the whooping cough out of a baby. Lots of mountain folks, all kinds, still believed.

Miss Latah reached behind her head. As she pulled away her scarf, her long black hair spilled across her shoulders like a shining silk shawl. Miss Latah used the yellow daisy-print scarf for a bandage, wrapping it securely around Mr. Ray's arm and the board. When she was finished, she sat back on her heels and rested her hands in her lap. Miss Latah and Mr. Ray smiled at each other. It was that special smile that always made Carolina feel happy inside.

Miss Latah took the cap from Lucas. She placed it lopsided on Mr. Ray's head. Then she leaned forward and kissed him—right on the lips. Lucas stared down at his work boots. Carolina couldn't help grinning at his sudden bashfulness.

She climbed down from the cab when Miss Latah and Lucas were helping Mr. Ray to his feet, and as they were walking toward her, a memory of them filled her mind, as vivid as a picture.

> *Golden light streaming from the heavens*
> *and grasses bending in the breeze.*
> *An angel with black flowing hair*
> *was holding a basket and twirling around,*
> *filling her skirt with wind.*
> *Another angel had thrown a berry into the air*
> *and was catching it in his mouth.*
> *A third angel, wearing bib overalls,*
> *was playing the fiddle*
> *as if a spirit had hold of his hand.*

Carolina smiled, remembering how she'd thought she was dreaming and how she'd thought she was seeing angels. Her heart got tender as she remembered the feel of Miss Latah's warm strong hand wrapped around her own and the comfort of somehow knowing she had finally reached a safe place.

That had been two days after the Fourth of July. She'd awakened in their meadow as scratched-up and scared as a lost pup. Including today, she'd been hiding out on the farm for nine days. Carolina was holding a secret wish that she could stay.

"Carolina, go ahead and hop in the back," said Miss Latah, "Mr. Ray needs some elbow room."

Feeling sheepish and full of shame, Carolina raised her eyes to look at Mr. Ray. Darkened hairs stuck to his ear. A trail of dried blood stained his cheek. He caught her eye.

"Don't fret, child," he said. "I'll be good as new in two shakes of a lamb's tail."

He lost his balance then and leaned on Miss Latah for support.

"Guess I'm a bit light-headed," he said, pulling off his cap and running his hand over his straw-colored hair. A thick clot of blood matted a clump of hair to his scalp. Carolina saw the swollen bump on his forehead. It was already turning purple.

"Hop in the back now. Go ahead," Miss Latah chided her.

Carolina climbed up and over the back of the truck, stepped over some wood and fencing wire, and sat on a bale of hay. Lucas eased down next to her, draping an arm over the bale and stretching his long legs out in front of him.

"What happened?" he asked.

"We were clearing the field . . . going along fine . . . tried to turn the tractor around . . . the rise didn't seem so steep." She fumbled for words, thinking a puny "I'm sorry" wouldn't amount to a hill of beans. "It tipped right over," she said, shrugging, and then blurted out, "I ran back fast as I could."

"You ran all this way?" Lucas turned his head, his eyebrows lifted in disbelief.

Carolina nodded.

"Well, shoot. You're just one surprise after another."

She felt a strand of hair pull away from her lip as he tugged one of her long braids. Carolina forced a weak smile. She was relieved that he wasn't angry, that he didn't blame her. Lucas pulled a blade of grass from the bale, stuck it between his teeth, and sat back to enjoy the ride.

Carolina bumped and swayed, the dry hay tickling her bare legs as Miss Latah drove slow and easy over the ruts on the tractor path. Leaves of young saplings brushed Carolina's arm as the truck crossed back over the bridge. Two black flies settled beside her on the bale of hay. She brushed another one off her leg, and as she lifted her eyes she saw a catbird take wing from a buckthorn branch. She watched it fly over the fast-moving water of the creek and disappear into leaves and branches on the other side.

Carolina reached up and felt the wood carving she wore as a pendant. She rubbed her finger over its wings and its tail, feeling where her daddy had made the cuts and where he'd sanded it smooth.

> "I've a present for you, Carolina.
> It's a catbird, case you couldn't tell."

She remembered that clear June night when they were camping up near Grandfather Mountain.

> "Lift your hair so I can tie a knot in the cord."

She remembered leaning into the crook of his shoulder and gazing into the night sky with the campfire crackling and blazing before them.

> Balls of white fire trailing ribbons,
> streaked across a black sky.
> Told Daddy what Miss Ruby said
> about shooting stars,
> how they were angels lighting the way
> for souls on their way to Heaven.

Carolina rubbed the tip of her finger over the catbird's beak. Her daddy had carved it open, as if it was singing.

The truck lurched forward as Miss Latah shifted gears and turned onto another tractor path that was two long lines of dirt worn away by tires and a hump of grass growing down the middle. They drove between two wide fields, lush with the green leaves of sweet potato plants. Carolina could see the farmhouse. White paint was peeling and the porch was crooked, but it looked peaceful set down in the clearing. Next to it the tin roof of the barn was colored with patches of orange rust. It was sagging and showing its age, but up close it looked real pretty, with white daisies and pink hollyhocks blooming against the barn board.

Beyond the barn, cream-colored ewes and lambs dotted the hillside pasture, and beyond that the Blue Ridge Mountains of North Carolina rose up in all their majesty. Carolina was used to hearing mountains referred to by name, as if folks had grown as attached to them as family. There was Peach Knob, Cattail Peak, Pumpkin Patch Mountain, and Little Yellow. The Great Smoky Mountains were farther to the west, with Cherokee names like Nantahala and Cohutta. Carolina looked to the mountain that rose up beyond the pasture. Her gaze rested on the very top.

Miss Latah pulled out onto the paved country lane and drove a little ways alongside a split-rail fence that zigzagged beside a small meadow. Sadie was grazing. Lucas had brushed the horse's coat yesterday until it shined, and Carolina had combed every burr out of its mane and tail.

At the sign that said HARMONY FARM, they turned in and Miss Latah headed down the long dirt driveway to the house.

A breeze moved over the scarecrow that was propped up on a pole in the center of Miss Latah's vegetable garden, causing its shirtsleeves and pant legs to flutter. Carolina admired her handiwork: the colorful patches she'd sewn onto the brown pants and raggedy flannel shirt. She especially liked the straw hat she'd placed on the scarecrow's hay-stuffed pillowcase head. She'd found the hat half-buried in the barn. The mice had chewed holes in it, but Scarecrow didn't mind a bit. The shirtsleeves hung from two sturdy twigs that were its arms. The fabric moved in the breeze along with the dried gourds that hung from each arm. The dried seeds inside the gourds made a sound like a baby's rattle every time the wind got hold and shook them.

Yes sir, that scarecrow was doing a right fine job. In the garden, pole beans had reached the tops of six-foot stakes. Tomatoes were ripening in the sun, so heavy they were bending the plant stems. Miss Latah was spending many a morning canning tomatoes and putting up dilly beans. Once, when Carolina was helping, Miss Latah gave her a wink and said, *"A taste of summer is mighty fine when winter winds start blowing."*

Carolina had nodded her head and put on a smile, feeling her heart fill with all sorts of wants. She wanted to believe she could stay the winter, go to school, decorate a Christmas tree, and do all the things a girl does when she's part of a family. Miss Latah spoke as if it could be so, yet

Carolina feared the sheriff would learn of her whereabouts long before winter set in.

Most days, it was easy to pretend it was real, that she was part of the Harmony family. But it wasn't real. All this pretending was binding up her heart; the little lies she was telling were setting down roots and growing through her veins like thorny vines. Truth be told, she was just hiding out.

The only real family she had left on this earth was Auntie Shen.

"Auntie Shen, you are the best grandma any mountain girl could ask for." Those were the very words Carolina would say every morning before running out to play. They worked like a magic charm. Auntie Shen would look up from rolling out biscuits and there'd be sparkles dancing in her eyes. It made Carolina's heart soar, as if it had wings.

Carolina was missing Auntie Shen something terrible. She had hardly gone a day of her life without seeing her. Auntie Shen's hands were the first human hands she'd ever felt. They were the hands that had held her as she tumbled out into this world, the strong and wrinkled hands that had tenderly passed Carolina to her daddy and then to the waiting arms of her mama.

Carolina loved hearing her birth story. Auntie Shen loved to tell it.

"It was 1953, the last night of a hot, hot August. A wild thunderstorm was brewin'. Wind blowin' so, leaves near tore off the trees. Near about midnight you burst into the world. Your eyes blinked open the same moment a lightnin' bolt ripped

the sky in two. You screamed your lungs out. Law, law, it was like you were callin' for the thunder, because jest then a mighty crack opened the heavens and sent a rumblin' in the clouds so loud I thought cannonballs were rollin' down the mountains. It shook the house."

Auntie Shen loved to tell stories, and she told Carolina lots of them—stories of the old mountain ways, stories of Carolina's daddy when he was young, and stories called Jack Tales about a boy who wasn't very big but sure had his wits about him. Why, that boy Jack could outsmart giants.

Auntie Shen told the story of how she'd come to be a mother to Carolina's daddy, told how his real mother had been her dearest friend and how she'd died young. Before her friend passed on, Auntie Shen had made her a promise that she would raise the boy, and she'd held true to her word.

Carolina could never have imagined that Auntie Shen would raise her too. As Auntie Shen helped Carolina pack up her clothes, she spoke about being strong and having faith and trusting that Carolina's mama and daddy and baby brother were in Heaven. *"I 'spect the Lord wants me to stay true to my word a might longer, and it's a blessing to me. I don't think I coulda beared it, if'n He'd taken all of you'uns."*

Carolina and Auntie Shen had made out fine, helping each other get through that first year after the funeral. Neighbors helped them too, giving them rides into town and bringing firewood up to the house. When a family slaughtered a hog, some of that meat always showed up on their table.

It wasn't fair that they'd been forced apart. Carolina's anger burned hot as a hornet's sting every time she thought about it. She could hardly get her mind away from it.

Those do-gooder church ladies
had no business
walking up the path to Auntie Shen's
as if they were paying a visit
and then
talking among themselves
as if I was nothing but a porch post.

"Left here all alone."
This one looked at me with sorrowful eyes.
"To fend for herself."
This one clucked her tongue like a chicken.
"Dire situation."
The third one shook her head.

They said Auntie Shen was too sick to come home,
said the hospital was keeping her.
It felt like they'd thrown a bucket of ice water
over me.

They said the hospital had rules about visitors.
Twelve years old and up, they said,
and here I am almost eleven,
which everybody knows
is standing right up straight next to twelve.

Carolina thought about how the church ladies went on and on that day, talking about children needing supervision, about rules and laws concerning children who had no parents or relatives to care for them. Carolina had stayed real quiet waiting for them to get to the part about who was going to take her in.

"Families around here have too many mouths to feed already," they said.

"Can't be taking in a stray."

A stray?

Carolina had to clamp her teeth together and swallow hard to keep those tears from rising up in her eyes.

That was when she began to understand Auntie Shen's complaining about modern ways moving in and threatening to destroy the mountain traditions she lived by. Auntie Shen said it used to be that mountain folks helped each other out, plain and simple. Now there were so many rules and laws, everything was getting ruined.

Miss Latah pulled the truck around the barn and parked near the house.

"Go ahead and play," Miss Latah said, and then gave Carolina that soft look. "It'll be all right."

Carolina jumped down off the tailgate and ambled across the yard to the tire swing. Holding on to the rope, she jumped, swinging her legs up to straddle the tire. She rested her head against the rope, watching Miss Latah and Lucas steady Mr. Ray so that he could step up onto the porch. The screen door made a loud squeak and a bang as it shut behind them.

Stepping backward until only the toes of her sneakers touched the grass and the tire was pressed flat against her rear end, she looked over at the silo standing at the end of the barn. It was taller than the roofline. Carolina liked to imagine it was a sentry, guarding the Harmony family by day and watching over them by night, always on the lookout, keeping harm at bay.

Holding tight to the rough twisted hemp with her calloused hands, she pushed off. She let her body fall as she drifted on the sway, her gaze climbing up through the branches to a cloudless blue sky. Sunlight flickered through green leaves. Her memories were like that. They came and went like little flashes of light.

> *Red hairs shimmering in Daddy's itchy beard.*
> *Mama smiling so pretty*
> *at me pulling a bouquet of violets out from behind my back.*
> *Caleb's soft little face*
> *rubbing against my cheek.*

They're gone. Carolina pulled herself up quick as the mean thought snapped into her head. There was no sense wishing, and no sense crying. No amount of either would make things go back to the way they were. It had been a year and two months since the old green Rambler careened off the Blue Ridge Parkway during a sudden storm. Word had it they'd skidded right off the road, right off the mountain, right over the edge, where the only thing holding them was sky.

At the funeral, grown-ups said, *"You're a lucky one."* Carolina still turned those words over and over in her head, trying to make sense of their meaning, and wondered, *Is the lucky one the one who dies or the one who's left behind?*

Chapter 2

A BASKETFUL OF SECRETS

"I expect we won't be home until after dark," said Miss Latah.

Miss Latah smiled and laid her hand gently on Carolina's cheek. "There's a sweet potato pie set on the counter made fresh this morning. You and Lucas go ahead and help yourselves to it. Don't go hungry, now."

Carolina watched the dirt clouds coming up from behind the truck as Miss Latah and Mr. Ray headed down the drive and turned onto the road. She wondered if Mr. Ray would be wearing a white cast when he got home from the hospital. One of the boys in her class had broken his arm once. He let his friends write their names all over it. That cast looked as if it had been painted blue by the time he had it taken off.

She caught sight of Lucas heading toward the barn. He reached up and gave her a casual wave, as if to say *you know where I am if you need me*. It was that lazy time of evening, between dinner and suppertime, when she and Lucas could do what they wanted instead of tending to chores. She figured Lucas was going to take advantage of his free time by fussing with the engine in that rusted tractor. That didn't interest her a bit.

The hound dog was sound asleep on the porch. Every now and again he'd whimper and his feet would twitch as if he was chasing a rabbit in his dreams. Carolina didn't have the heart to wake him.

Carolina dragged her hand along the wire fencing that bordered the sheep pasture as she hiked up the grassy slope. A gentle breeze tumbling down from the mountain brushed over her bare arms. She walked through a stand of loblolly pines and dogwood trees, and then she was in a meadow full of wildflowers. Tall broom sedge and horseweed scratched against her legs as she walked, leaving a thin trail where her steps had been.

The silence was broken by the *con-ka-reeee* of a red-winged blackbird. She watched it sway with the reed that it was perched on, and then her eyes fell on an opening at the wood's edge. It was calling to her.

The air smelled sweet as she strolled along the sunny path bordered by masses of hay-scented ferns. She climbed up and around clusters of boulders, holding on to saplings to pull herself up. Dappled sunlight caused leaves to shimmer and flecks in the stone to sparkle like flint. She came upon a scattering of tiny mushrooms with bright red centers, what Auntie Shen called jelly cups, and her thoughts harked back to a happy time.

"Carolina, look at all these wild strawberries I picked."
Auntie Shen couldn't wait to show me.

I must have had frog's eyes, I was so excited.
"It's jelly-making time," I said.

Auntie Shen smiled.
"And don't that make me happy."

And we peered into her butternut basket,
gazing at what was to be the first jar.
Carolina Sunshine
is what she'd write on the label,
just like every year,
because the first jar is mine.

Carolina
because that's my name, and
Sunshine
because the berries held summer's first sparkle.

Carolina's heart sank at the memory. *No jelly making this summer. Guess the birds can fill their bellies. Auntie Shen's pantry is filled with empty jars covered in cobwebs and dust. If Auntie Shen hadn't gotten sick, we'd have made all the strawberry, raspberry, and blackberry jams by now and would be searching for ripe blueberries.*

Carolina followed the path as it dipped down into deep shade, where a stream was making music. Its waters trickled over rocks and pebbles, bouncing and splashing and flowing on. Chipmunks ran along the ground and ducked into tiny spaces beneath fallen logs. The path had been getting harder and harder to follow, and now at the base of a rock-strewn clay ravine there was no path at all. Washed out from many rains, it looked as if the earth had been sliced open.

Finding handholds and planting her feet in deep crevices she climbed, higher and higher. Her shirt was nearly soaked through with sweat by the time she reached a small plateau.

Carolina looked around her. Wildflowers trailed through mountain laurel. A cluster of white flowers called Indian pipes stood on end. *It sure is pretty up here*, she thought. Carolina held out her arms and felt a cool breeze blow over her.

She was close to the summit. Here the birches were shorter and stout. Thick branches, knotted and twisted, spread low to the ground. Fat white trunks grew so close to round moss-covered boulders, it looked as if they'd become one.

Gnarled branches fed Carolina's imagination with visions of fairies and gnomes, what Auntie Shen called the little people. Carolina weaved around thorny underbrush, and there before her was a massive outcropping of rock ledge, flat as could be, jutting out of the mountainside.

Standing in the middle of that great ledge was like looking out over the whole world. Green treetops covered a rugged land. The mountains sloped down and rose up again, forming hollers and coves. In the western sky, rays of celestial light fanned out from beneath a bank of white clouds. The sight caused her to wonder about Heaven.

In the distant view, fog was settling like new snow. It swirled around blue peaks that rose and fell like many round-topped triangles. The mountains went on and on and on, fading into wavy lines that looked as if God had colored them in with the side of a light blue crayon. Carolina figured the ocean must go on and on like this too, and her thoughts drifted to her friend Mattie. She wondered what Mattie was doing right now.

Mattie was still her best friend, even if she did go and move all the way to the Atlantic Ocean, even if they hadn't seen each other for a whole year. Mattie was the funniest girl she'd ever met. Just thinking about her made Carolina chuckle out loud.

> *Laughing like hyenas,*
> *we ran out the front doors of our school,*
> *happy we had only one more week to wait*
> *and fourth grade would be over.*
> *We wouldn't have to wear dresses anymore.*
> *We could shuck our shoes and run barefoot.*

Carolina remembered that day exactly. It was June 5, 1963, and it was Caleb's second birthday. Carolina was going camping with her family up near Grandfather Mountain to celebrate, even though it was a school night. A meteor shower was predicted, and that was enough for her daddy to give permission.

The whole family was down by the road, waiting for her.

Her daddy was reaching into the engine of the old green Rambler. Her mama was scurrying around the wide trunk of a green-leaved maple tree, chasing Caleb, who was squealing with laughter. Auntie Shen was standing at the edge of the road. The handle of a basket was draped over one arm, and her other arm was raised high in the air. She was waving like crazy with a happy grin on her face.

Auntie Shen had a window seat
and so did I.
Caleb was tucked in between,
and the breeze was pulling my hair right out of my braids.
Daddy zoomed along the Blue Ridge Parkway
so close to the sky
it was as if we were flying.

Daddy was keeping a beat with his fingers
on the steering wheel
and singing along with Bob Dylan
on the radio
until the static got loud
and Mama turned it off.
Auntie Shen started to sing a ballad
that she called a love song.
Mama hummed along
and Caleb cooed and shook his head of curls.

Then I sang.
I used my best voice,
singing the song Auntie Shen had taught me,
the one that was born in her heart
the day I was born.
I was giving it to Caleb now.

"Little bitty angel
sent from above,
all the stars of Heaven
could not equal this love.
I'll care for you, little angel,
till the stars call me back home.
Little bitty angel,
my precious little love."

That was the happiest day of my life, Carolina thought.

She rested her chin in her hands. She gazed out over the landscape from her perch high on the ledge. She saw a waterfall in the distance. From here it looked no bigger than her thumb, no bigger than a berry.

She thought about what Mr. Ray had said to her before he and Miss Latah headed off to see the doctor, how he'd said it was a miracle that they weren't killed when the tractor tipped over. Here she'd gone and caused him to get hurt, but instead of being angry, he was thankful for the blessing. Mr. Ray and Miss Latah seemed to find the good in everything. Carolina wondered if they'd still see the good in her if she admitted she'd been telling stories instead of the truth. It was like carrying a basketful of secrets, and it was getting heavy.

Carolina raised her eyes and spoke to Heaven just on the wishful hope that an angel might be looking down.

"I miss you, Mama," she said.

The weight of the wood carving she wore as a pendant caused it to pull away from her chest, and it dangled in the air, attached to the leather cord that was tied at the nape of her neck. She held it in her hand, rubbing her thumb around it, remembering the night of the shooting stars, when she'd known exactly where she belonged.

> *Caleb's hand was wrapped around my fingers.*
> *Daddy had his arm around Mama.*
> *Auntie Shen was poking a stick in the embers.*

> *Daddy whispered in my ear,*
> *said how happy he was*
> *that all his angels were beside him,*
> *right here on Earth.*

That was the happiest day. The very next day, June 6, 1963, was the saddest.

In the middle of writing *Cardinal* on the line next to *State Bird*, Carolina had heard a light knock on the classroom door. With her head down but her eyes up, she watched the school nurse whisper to her teacher. She glanced over at Mattie, who was chewing on the eraser of her pencil and staring down at her paper as if she was trying to burn a hole in it. Carolina quickly put her eyes back onto her paper as her teacher walked down the aisle. Her teacher took the pencil out of Carolina's hand. Carolina opened her mouth to protest but saw her teacher place an index finger on closed lips and motion for Carolina to follow. The nurse was waiting in the hall.

"Am I in trouble?" Carolina whispered.

"Come with me, dear," the nurse said.

The nurse's white shoes made a soft patter as they walked down the hall.

"I wasn't cheating," Carolina said.

"Of course you weren't, dear," said the nurse.

Thoughts raced through Carolina's mind. *Did Julie tell on me and say I put the chicken head in her desk? Did Tommy Gentry tell the principal I gave him a black eye?* She was still mad at him for cheating at kick ball. She wouldn't say she was sorry. They couldn't make her.

The principal was seated in a little room all his own at the back of the office. He sat up tall behind a wide desk, his hands clenched together on top. His broad shoulders, wide neck, and short crew cut made him look stern. Even though he'd always spoken to Carolina in a friendly voice, she felt her back stiffen. The nurse stood aside, quietly patting a handkerchief to her eyes.

"Carolina," he said.

The principal made a sound like a cough as he cleared his throat.

"Carolina," he began again, "there's been a terrible accident."

Even though his voice was calm, the news he delivered struck hard, hit her like a wild wind, spinning her world into a whirlwind of confusion that then lay in ruins, as if a hurricane had ripped clean through.

Chapter 3

RAIN A-POURIN' DOWN

It didn't seem right for God to be laughing at a funeral. Couldn't He see that all these neighbors had come to pay their respects? Couldn't He see they were trying to mourn? God continued on His merry way as if nothing was wrong. He flung open flower petals, red and yellow and purple, and let them dance all over the hillsides, pouring forth their sweet fragrances like tea at a church picnic. Here at the funeral, soft voices sang a mournful hymn while in the branches above them songbirds chirruped lilts and trills. It didn't seem right.

Carolina couldn't look at the men and women who had gathered. She couldn't bear for them to look at her. She would not look at the deep holes dug into the dark ground or the tombstones all lined up, leaning over from old age. She stared at the sky. White billowy clouds floated in the blue like puffy cotton balls. She saw puffy white horses and puffy white dragons. One cloud took the shape of an elephant. She watched as it slowly transformed into an old man with a long nose. As the wind carried the cloud across the sky, she watched it transform into a flying angel with long hair flowing behind her. The angel cloud moved in front of the sun, and for a few moments, a five-pointed star adorned her robe.

Auntie Shen had said that somewhere beyond the clouds, beyond the stars, beyond the planets, was a place called Heaven. Carolina had believed this when she was little. She took it for truth, same as the sun is yellow and the grass is green. But now she *had* to believe it was true. Her mama and daddy and baby brother just had to be in Heaven. She stared deep into the skies and imagined a pretty place with magical streams and golden fields, where everyone was happy all the time and would be forever. She tried to imagine her mama with angel wings. Deep within, she thought it sounded more like a tall tale, and she was troubled by a nagging question that asked *Is it really true?*

She stopped praying that day, the day of the funeral. After the principal told her about the accident, she had prayed like crazy. She'd prayed it wasn't true. She'd prayed they were only hurt. She'd prayed for God to make them better.

Carolina figured God must have turned His back on her. She couldn't figure out what she'd done to deserve it. Finally, she decided to ignore Him too.

Auntie Shen nudged Carolina when the minister said, "Let us pray."

Carolina lowered her head and stared at her feet.

When the minister finished his prayer, the funeral service was over. Carolina felt Auntie Shen grab her hand and give it a gentle squeeze. Carolina wanted to squeeze back, but it seemed all the strength had drained out of her. She watched the mourners walk away, friends and neighbors setting off on footpaths that led home. Farther down the hill, along the edge of the dirt road, engines were revving up in beat-up cars that belonged to the men her daddy had worked with at the sawmill. Auntie Shen said they'd taken the day off, without wages, so they could pay their respects.

Mattie's grandma came to pay her respects too. Mattie called her Grammy. Everyone else called her Miss Ruby. She lumbered over on her wide ankles, leaned down, and wrapped her arms around Carolina and spoke softly into her ear. "The good Lord has taken them home." Then Miss Ruby began to rock with Carolina, who was still deep in Miss Ruby's arms. Miss Ruby's voice cracked as she spoke, "Jus' remember, your baby brother's spirit still lives in your heart. You jus' call him up when you miss him."

Miss Ruby straightened herself up. "Mattie said she was sorry you'uns couldn't say good-bye. She said the last days of school weren't the same without you. She said she'd be missing you."

Carolina knew she'd be missing Mattie too. At the time she needed her most, Mattie had to go and move. Her father moved the family away to the other side of the state, all the way to the Atlantic Ocean. Seemed he'd found work there.

Carolina nodded her head. A lump had grown in her throat and she couldn't talk. Miss Ruby exchanged a few words with Auntie Shen about holding on to faith, and then she slowly walked away.

"It's time to go home," said Auntie Shen.

Carolina looked over. She was nearly even in height to Auntie Shen, almost eye to eye. She nodded. Home was with Auntie Shen now.

Two gravediggers stood off to one side. They were respectfully staring at the toes of their shoes, having laid their shovels facedown on the grass beside them. Carolina held Auntie Shen's hand a little tighter as they walked past.

They made their way up the steep mountain path, a path too narrow and rugged for a car, but that didn't matter, because Auntie Shen didn't own a car anyway. Carolina's mama used to say the path was a short mile down and ten long miles up. Finally they reached a rambling house without a speck of paint on it. Auntie Shen said her grandfather had built it long ago from logs he'd hewn by hand into planks, and she'd never known anywhere else. She was born here and said she'd be happy to die here too.

Sixteen cats greeted them. Most of the cats and kittens came and went so frequently that Carolina barely had time to name them, but some had made themselves to home. Caesar was prancing across the railing and Mittens was sound asleep on top of a rusted milk pail. Felix gave them a quick glance before darting behind the springhouse.

Carolina and Auntie Shen laughed when they saw Pickles; he was drinking the last of the rainwater in the bottom of a wide Mason jar. The glass magnified his head so he looked like a cartoon character. After that there wasn't any laughing at all.

Inside, the kitchen table was full of food that friends and neighbors had brought by. There was Miss Ruby's strawberry-rhubarb pie, a bowl of potato salad, and a pot of beans made by the ladies from Auntie Shen's church. Pickled pigs' feet floated in a clear glass jar. There was even a plate of deviled eggs. Carolina always reached for these first whenever the church had a potluck supper, but today she couldn't make herself hungry. Auntie Shen said she was all worn out and wouldn't be able to eat a single bite. She took to bed.

The house was silent. Carolina wished these rooms were filled with company, but Auntie Shen had refused everyone, saying she wished to be alone in her time of grieving. They were respectful of her wishes. Carolina felt she should do the same. She had never thought much about not having aunts and uncles or cousins, until now. The big, dark, empty silence grew around her until it threatened to swallow her up.

On the third morning after the funeral, Carolina was awakened by a bad dream. She lay in the feather bed, thinking about how her "sleepover" bed would be her everyday bed from now on. The lavender-colored curtains on the window were the ones her mama had stitched for her room back home. Auntie Shen had taken them down and hung them up again in this room. Carolina moved them aside and pressed her face to the glass, expecting to see the morning mist.

The stars were twinkling! She quietly slipped out from beneath the covers, stepped over a cardboard box she hadn't unpacked yet, and entered the hallway. She listened to Auntie Shen's rhythmic breathing and quiet snores as she tiptoed past her room, and then she quietly lifted the door latch. She wanted to see the sun come up.

Patches of purple and yellow Johnny-jump-ups bordered the path that wound down the hill from the porch steps. Carolina stepped over them and headed up the slope, bushwhacking through the trees. Light from a half-moon lit her way.

She climbed until she reached her favorite spot in the bald, a magical forest garden where rhododendrons and mountain laurel encircled the grassy area, protecting her from the wind. The blooms had passed already, but soft pink flower petals carpeted the ground. She sat down, pulling her knees to her chest, and stretched her nightgown down over her toes.

On most mornings fog was thick and hazy, but today she had a clear view of the stars. The Big Dipper was there, and Cygnus the Swan, and so was Cassiopeia. Constellations were like pictures in the sky, and each one had its own story.

From the time she could fit neatly in the center of her daddy's lap, Carolina had listened as he told of people who lived in faraway places, all around the world, and they all had their own account of how the constellations came to be. He said they passed their myths and legends down from generation to generation, and now he was passing stories down to Carolina. It seemed in all lands, eyes were turned toward Heaven. Carolina imagined an invisible thread stitching together all the stars in the sky, wrapping up the whole wide world in a sparkly quilt.

Carolina stayed to welcome the morning. The sky turned a soft blue, and then only Venus, the morning star, glistened above the eastern horizon. It faded away too as the forest got back its colors in many shades of green. White clouds appeared, and a gentle wind moved through the tops of trees. Songbirds whistled jubilee. Woodland critters scurried and scampered along branches and through thickets. Insects chewed under decaying logs. The whole mountain was wide awake, filled with sounds of the new day.

As she meandered back to the house, she plotted a way to get Auntie Shen out of bed. Ever since the day of the funeral, Auntie Shen had hardly done a thing but stay buried under her quilt, staring out the window. Carolina decided she would tell her that Pickles wasn't eating and that he looked sickly. It was only a little fib, and she convinced herself that she was only telling it for good reason.

Her scheming was interrupted by the smell of sweet bacon fat. She was surprised to see the kitchen door wide open. She could hear the sizzling and spitting in the pan as she stepped onto the porch. Auntie Shen called out to her.

"Beautiful morning to set to work," she said.

Auntie Shen lifted strips of bacon with a long fork, flipping them from the black iron skillet onto thick biscuits.

"We'll eat these later this morning when our stomachs start growling," she said.

"Auntie Shen, why do you call them cat's-head biscuits?"

"'Cause of their size, that's all," said Auntie Shen. She laid three thick bacon strips inside the second biscuit she'd cut in half.

"Well, it might be good to keep your voice down," whispered Carolina, moving her eyes this way and that so as to call Auntie Shen's attention to the cats and kittens in the room.

Auntie Shen followed Carolina's furtive glances, a peculiar look on her face, and then she began to laugh. It started out small and then built up. She got to laughing so hard, she had to set herself down in a chair. Just as it seemed she was near to done, the laughter would get going strong again. By the time she was finished, she was all out of breath.

"Carolina," she said, "I jest love ya to pieces."

She handed Carolina a sturdy split-oak basket.

"Working is the best way to keep your mind off things," she said.

Carolina held the basket while Auntie Shen began filling it with glass jars of jelly and jam and honey. The pantry shelves were lined with them, as well as pickles made from last summer's cucumbers. They filled as many baskets as could be lined up in Carolina's rusty red wagon. Pieces of Auntie Shen's artwork were gathered too and carefully laid out in a wheelbarrow. Carolina pulled the wagon and Auntie Shen pushed the wheelbarrow and they set off, heading down to the main road.

Carolina eased her wagon over the rocks in the path, careful not to let it topple over. Auntie Shen had to hold on tight to the wheelbarrow so it wouldn't take off without her. It was a cloudless summer day, and Morning Glory Jelly Stand was going to open for business, as it had every summer that Carolina could remember.

Auntie Shen said the stand was a good way to earn money for extras, things she couldn't grow, such as sugar and fabric and nails. All through the summer, it set on the roadside as pretty as a patch of wildflowers, catching the eyes of tourists headed eastward to Boone. They would close it up when the first killing frost came and the weeds blackened and yellowed. During the winter the stand seemed to creep back into the woods, lonely and barren, buried under snow and ice. The wooden structure was greatly weathered but sturdy. On this sunny morning it looked downright joyful. The sun shone on the metal roof, and patches of pink sweet William bloomed all around it.

Carolina helped tie on a gingham-print awning and put out the sign:

Wildflower Honey
Mountain Crafts
Jams and Jellies—Homemade

Auntie Shen stood on the opposite side of the road with her hands on her hips and a broad grin on her face.

"I'd say this stand is right invitin'," she said.

Carolina smiled and nodded in agreement. These were the exact same words Auntie Shen spoke at the start of every season.

Carolina took one jelly jar at a time out of the baskets and set each one securely on the wooden shelves. Blackberry jam, apple jelly, and raspberry preserves were soon lined up in neat rows, glistening in the sunlight like amethyst jewels. Everything had to be just so, and Carolina had learned long ago how particular Auntie Shen could be. She'd been her helper since the summer she turned six.

"Customers won't buy from a stand that doesn't look cared for," said Carolina.

"That's a fact," said Auntie Shen.

Each jar had a pretty label that said *Homemade on Blue Star Mountain*. Carolina looked at her own handwriting on the jars that she had helped Auntie Shen set up last summer. Her penmanship was so much better now. She remembered how long she had stirred the deep purple liquid. She'd thought her arm would fall off from all that stirring, but Auntie Shen wouldn't let her stop, saying, "Jelly don't like to be left alone. Turn your head and it'll be ruined."

They decorated the stand with Auntie Shen's paintings of wildflowers, birds, and woodland plants. She'd made fabric pictures too, in all shapes and textures, sewn from pieces of Carolina's baby dresses and her daddy's worn-out shirts and the yarn from unraveled socks. Each one had a Bible verse stitched along the bottom.

Carolina read one out loud. "'Faith is the substance of things hoped for, the evidence of things not seen.' Hebrews 11:1."

Auntie Shen smiled. "That's a good one," she said.

This was work Carolina enjoyed doing and it really did ease her mind. Auntie Shen put an arm around Carolina's shoulder and planted a kiss on her cheek.

"You got a good eye for display, Carolina."

The compliment warmed her like a ray of sunshine on a cloudy day.

They dragged out a couple of aluminum lawn chairs with red and green webbing that was fraying on the edges. They knocked the cobwebs and dirt off as best they could. Then they sat and waited for a car to drive by. Auntie Shen talked about Carolina's daddy.

"Oh, he could pull some shenanigans when he was a boy," she said.

She began the story of how she came to adopt him.

"Nothing that was legal, mind you, but he was my boy just the same," she said.

She told the story as simply as it had come to happen. "His father put on a uniform and went off to serve his country. He was never to return. We got word he'd been killed. It left your daddy's mama a widow woman."

"And that's when you made your promise?" asked Carolina.

"No, not then. It was when the sickness had taken hold and got bad and we were afeared it wouldn't let go."

"And you kept your word," added Carolina, remembering the telling of this story.

Auntie Shen nodded in agreement.

"The good Lord brought him to me, and I don't believe in questioning the Lord's ways," said Auntie Shen. "He was nine years old then, jest like you. It was 1938. All my kinfolk was still alive and I knew near every family 'at lived this side of Blue Star Mountain. I was friends with near ever'one. It was good. We were there when we needed each other. That's what mattered."

Auntie Shen brought up one happy memory after another and got them both to laughing.

"Your daddy loved to roam these hills and mountains," she said. "He ran free as a bobcat, and when it came time to work, he was almost as good as a grown man. He was drawn to book learnin' too, right from the start. I was so proud when he earned that big scholarship, but my heart broke to pieces when he went up North. Got in his head to get educated. It was a real nice college. I never did get to visit, but I have a picture, a real pretty postcard."

Auntie Shen said she supposed it was these mountains that eventually drew him back, and it was a good thing too, for it was here that he met his bride. Carolina listened without interrupting. She could tell Auntie Shen was in one of those talking spells when she needed to take her mind off things that were bothering her.

Auntie Shen told stories that had been handed down to her, stories about Scotland and stories about the hardships her ancestors endured when they made their home in these mountains. She spoke of her own memories of being a girl growing up on Blue Star Mountain.

"Roads were scarce then, travel near impossible. Families stuck together and we helped one other. If one family took sick, another family would shuck their corn. It were a lot better than today. No one ever expected to be paid, we was being neighborly," she said.

Auntie Shen helped Carolina try to pronounce a few phrases in Gaelic, a language her ancestors had spoken in Scotland.

The only word Carolina really knew was *seanmhair*—pronounced "shen-a-vair." It meant *grandmother*.

"I didn't know how to pronounce seanmhair when I was little," said Carolina.

"'At's right. I was always Shen-Bear. After a while, the Bear part fell away, but Shen stuck," said Auntie Shen with a smile. "It still tickles me."

A brand-new car with Virginia plates pulled off to the side of the road. A man and his wife and their two little children got out. The children ran to the stand ahead of their mother and father. They all looked over the jars of jellies and the paintings.

Auntie Shen leaned over and spoke kindly to the little boy. "Them jellies are set up pretty, ain't they? There's no need for rearranging."

The little boy didn't answer. He ran off to chase his sister. When he did, he knocked one of the jars. It crashed to the ground and broke open. Sweet purple jelly spilled into the dirt.

The boy's mother held his arm and scolded him. She offered to pay for it.

"Oh, it's all right. He didn't mean it," Auntie Shen said.

The family got back in the car then without buying a single thing.

"Auntie Shen, they should have paid for that. We worked hard to make that jelly, and now it's no good for anybody."

"Oh, it's not worth frettin' over."

"We should make a sign. *You Break It, You Pay For It.*"

"Now, Carolina, there's no sense in gettin' uppity. We'll have other customers."

The day did turn out to be a profitable one, in many ways. The sun shone bright and the air was clear. Many more cars passed by and many stopped to buy. Carolina learned the art of Auntie Shen's relaxed and friendly way of doing business.

The following day the rains came. It rained all day and the day after and the day after that. Streams ran down the path from their door and turned the clay dirt to mud. The ground was too slick even to walk down to the jelly stand. They were stuck inside with each other.

On the third evening they were sitting in rocking chairs on the porch. There was a wide space between them. Carolina pushed off with one foot, listening to the chair creak on the floorboards and the steady tapping on the roof. Rain fell like silver strands of tinsel. She stared out at green trees with drooping leaves.

Carolina had been feeling particularly grouchy all day long, and she and Auntie Shen had gotten to speaking cross to each other. It got so bad that each of them refused to look in the other's direction. They were trying hard to find their way to forgiveness. Carolina picked at a scab on her knee. Auntie Shen stared out into the rain. After a spell, she began to tell a story.

"I remember a winter morning when my seanmhair

spoke cross to me. She said I was actin' hateful, that I was feeling sorry for myself and that hatefulness was preventin' me from doing my work."

"What was your work?" Carolina asked.

"I was to milk the cow, but I didn't want to walk in the snow to the barn. Law, it was a bitter day. The wind was howlin' and the snow was driftin' so high you could fall into it waist deep. Oh, she gave me a talkin'-to. 'The milk cow cannot do her work if you don't do yours,' she said. So I walked to the barn feelin' that my seanmhair was as mean as a witch and didn't care about me at all. Law, I was angry. The milk cow felt my anger. I knew it because she was so full of milk but she wouldn't let down.

"She was such a pretty cow—a fawn-colored Jersey—and she turned her head to look at me. She had the longest eyelashes, Carolina. Why, she was lovely. I felt like a fool, a hateful fool. Here I was sullen and miserable, and this beautiful cow—Molly was her name—was standing there wanting more than anythin' to give me warm, sweet, delicious milk. My hateful feelings turned soft and got me to smilin', and her milk flowed into the bucket."

Auntie Shen was quiet for a moment, then continued.

"It seems small in the retelling, but it was an important lesson for me. I learned that nothin' had changed. The wind was still howlin' outside, and the snow was still blowin' through the cracks in the barn walls. Sweet Molly was givin' me her milk, and my seanmhair was in the kitchen baking bread for me. Nothin' had changed, 'cept me. My eyes had new sight. I was holdin' somethin' beautiful in my heart.

"I remember the steam risin' up from the milk bucket. Her milk and my tears flowin' together. It was difficult carryin' the bucket back to the house without spillin', but I did it. My seanmhair hugged me, and I remember it was a sweet feelin'."

Auntie Shen sighed, then said, "Those memories give me peace."

They sat silent for a long time, moseying around in their own thoughts. Rain tapped on the roof. Rain pattered in deep puddles.

Finally Carolina said, "I would carry a million milk buckets if it would bring Mama and Daddy and Caleb back."

Auntie Shen spoke to her with a strong voice.

"Hear that wind a-howlin'? See that rain a-pourin' down? Sometimes in life, we must walk headlong into a fierce wind though rain beats upon our faces."

Auntie Shen's rocking chair creaked back and forth.

Carolina moved her chair right up close so the arms of the rocking chairs were touching, feeling the last remnants of anger wash away.

"Don't you fret," said Auntie Shen. She reached over and gently patted Carolina's knee. "The sun always shines again."

Carolina watched Auntie Shen gaze into the darkening day. Tears gathered in Auntie Shen's deep wrinkles and flowed down her cheeks in tiny rivulets. Carolina reached over and patted Auntie Shen's hand, burying her own tears into a place deep inside.

Chapter 4

AND THE SUN SHONE DOWN AGAIN

Barely a month had gone by since the day of the funeral. Auntie Shen was picking black raspberries at the edge of the woods. Carolina's attention had turned to a whole passel of newborn kittens in back of the springhouse. They were mewing softly and cuddling up together on a cushion of old rags that Auntie Shen had thrown out. Carolina was on her hands and knees, taking a peek at the little critters. Their eyes were barely open. They were wriggling about and nosing for their mother. A glimpse of color caught Carolina's eye. Something large was moving up the path. Her first thought was *bear*.

Carolina focused her eyes on the sunny clearing down the path. She couldn't believe who she saw. Miss Ruby and

Mattie were slowly climbing the steepest part of the path. She saw Mattie stop and help Miss Ruby down onto a rock to rest. Carolina leaped to her feet, shouting.

"Mattie!"

She ran down the hill as fast as she could to meet up with them. Mattie left Miss Ruby's side and started running toward Carolina. They both had their arms out and were waking up the world with their high-pitched screaming. Carolina nearly knocked Mattie to the ground when she jumped into her arms, her legs straddling Mattie's waist.

She hopped down from Mattie and started jumping. "What are you doing here?"

"I'm staying the summer," answered Mattie, grabbing Carolina's hands and jumping along with her.

"What?" Carolina looked at her as if she'd announced she'd been to the moon.

"Mommy and Pap said I could stay with Grammy for the whole summer."

"Honest?" asked Carolina, looking to Miss Ruby, who had finally caught up to them, breathless and pressing her hand against her hip, as if she couldn't take another step.

"Oh, child, get me up to the porch, where I can set myself down," said Miss Ruby, "and I'll tell you all about it."

Auntie Shen was there waiting for them.

"I heard the commotion and come a-runnin'," she said. "Thought a body was gettin' killed."

All four of them visited, drinking sweet tea and eating biscuits with jelly. Mattie explained how her father was helping to build a bridge on the seacoast and how her mother had gotten a good job working for the phone company and how her two older brothers were living and working on a tobacco farm. Mattie talked a blue streak. Miss Ruby could barely get a word in edgewise.

"So Mommy and Pap said it would be all right if I stayed with Grammy for the summer," she said, and then she sat back and smiled so big every one of her teeth showed.

Carolina's day had started as ordinary as the beginning of a long hot walk, and now it had turned as exciting as the opening day of the county fair.

"Well, Ruby, I'd say these two will be keeping us young," said Auntie Shen.

Miss Ruby laughed and said, "If'n they don't completely wear us out first."

"Mattie. Do you want to see my room?" asked Carolina.

Auntie Shen always said there were two kinds of friends. There were the fair-weather types who liked you as long as everything was going their way, and there were the all-weather types. The all-weather friends stuck by you in good times and in bad times. They laughed with you when life was sunny and cried with you when life was full of dark clouds. Mattie was an all-weather friend. Carolina was an all-weather friend to Mattie too.

The day Mattie had stood in front of the chalkboard and the teacher introduced her to the fourth-grade class, Carolina could tell she was scared. Carolina had seen and heard the grown-ups, red-faced and angry, saying, *"Don't want no colored children in our school."* She'd heard the objections at the grocery store, at the drugstore, and even in Miss Fay's diner. Their kids were the ones sitting in the classroom with big pusses on their faces, glaring at Mattie as if she'd done something wrong. Other kids shuffled in their seats as if they didn't know what to do with all this hatred. At home, Carolina's parents were saying, *"It's about time,"* and talking about what might be. All Carolina knew was that if she was the one standing up there in front of the classroom, she'd be feeling scared too.

Carolina looked closely at Mattie's face to decide for herself if she was going to like this new girl. She decided Mattie was pretty. She had smooth skin the color of dark caramel candy, but there was something else Carolina saw, something much deeper than skin. She saw a girl who thought about things. She saw a girl who knew how to have fun.

At the same time Carolina was deciding about Mattie, she realized that Mattie was deciding about her too. When their eyes met, Mattie suddenly smiled.

Julie, the popular girl with long blond curls, turned her head and looked at Carolina as if Carolina didn't have a brain in her head.

"You're not planning to be friends with *her?*"

Julie was the teacher's pet. All the kids curtsied to her every whim. If she liked you, so did everyone else. If she didn't, you might as well be a toad croaking on the windowsill.

Carolina didn't hesitate a moment before answering.

"That's exactly what I'm planning to do," she said.

When it was time for Mattie to walk down the aisle between the desks, she did it with her head held high and sat herself down at the empty desk next to Carolina. They'd been best friends ever since.

When Mattie laughed, even the birds stopped to listen.

Carolina was sure of it. Happy laughter spilled out of her like water tumbling down a ledge of rocks, skipping and jumping and making the most beautiful music. Tears would spill down Mattie's cheeks, and Carolina would get to laughing along with her so hard and for so long that her cheeks would ache.

All summer long they traveled back and forth through the woods. Miss Ruby's cabin was tucked down in the holler, and Auntie Shen's house was high up on the ridge. By mid-July they had a well-worn path to follow. Carolina worked at the jelly stand with Auntie Shen and Mattie helped Miss Ruby with the housework and gardening, but then the day belonged to them.

Once Mattie's uncle came to take Miss Ruby and Mattie to visit family down in the lowlands. Carolina was allowed to go with them. They headed east, down out of the mountains, where the land flattened out and the sun felt a lot hotter. Along the way, they stopped for supplies. Mattie's uncle went into the hardware store and Miss Ruby went into the grocery store.

Carolina and Mattie wandered up and down the sidewalk, looking in store windows. After the long hot ride they both were so thirsty they could have drunk up a river. Carolina spotted two water fountains and ran over to one. She turned the nozzle and water flowed up in a loop. She guzzled water until it dripped off her chin and down her blouse.

"What are you waiting for?" said Carolina, water dripping down her chin. "I thought you were thirsty."

Mattie seemed to be studying her big toe sticking out of

the hole in her sneaker. Her arms hung down at her sides. Then she looked up, and Carolina saw the hurt and anger in Mattie's face and the tears making her eyes shine.

"You are blind and stupid, Carolina," she said.

Carolina followed Mattie's gaze to the signs above the fountains. One sign said WHITE and one sign said COLORED. All Carolina had seen were two fountains, one for her and one for Mattie, and now she'd gone and done a terrible thing.

"God made me as good as you," Mattie said. Her bottom lip was starting to quiver, but her fists were tight, as if she was stuck in the middle between sad and angry.

Carolina couldn't understand why people acted as if there was a right skin color and a wrong skin color. She figured it must hurt real bad to be looked at as if you'd been made wrong.

It suddenly dawned on Carolina that she'd been drinking out of the fountain that said COLORED. She stepped over to the fountain with the WHITE sign above it. She took a sip.

"The water in the other fountain tastes a lot better. Go ahead and see for yourself."

Mattie scuffed her sneakers over to the fountains. She took a drink from the fountain that said COLORED. Then she walked on over and looked up at the sign that said WHITE. Mattie had that scared look on her face like she'd had on the first day of class. She glanced to the left and then to the right. Her black braids glistened in the sun as she grabbed hold of the spigot and turned it. She opened her mouth and took a big gulp.

Mattie faced Carolina. She moved her cheeks in and out as she swished the water around, and then she spat it out in a stream, making a long wet streak on the pavement.

"Cow piss," she said.

"Told you," said Carolina.

Mattie tilted her head to the side and grinned, and Carolina knew she'd been forgiven. They skipped down the sidewalk, holding hands. A car was stopped at a traffic light, and the radio was blaring. It was playing one of their favorite songs, a tune called "Locomotion," by the Chiffons. Carolina held Mattie's waist and they danced all the way back to her uncle's car, singing the lyrics at the top of their lungs.

When they got to the car they faced each other, raised their arms, and shook their hands and bodies in a big finish. People stared and shook their heads. Carolina had a strong feeling that it didn't have anything to do with their singing. She figured it was about a white girl playing with a black girl that put those looks on their faces. As far as Carolina was concerned, the whole world could go on acting hateful because they were too stupid to see past the color of skin. She had no plans to join in.

Besides, in the mountains it didn't matter what color skin they'd been born with. They drank all they wanted from fresh streams, kneeling side by side. They waded together in the creek that ran directly behind Miss Ruby's cabin. Many an afternoon was spent dragging fishing line and dangling their feet in cool water as birds sang to them from the branches above.

Mattie would come up the ridge for sleepovers at Auntie Shen's, where they shared the feather bed. Carolina would go down into the holler for sleepovers at Miss Ruby's, where they climbed up into the loft and slept on a wide mattress on the floor. Sleepovers included lots of loud laughter. Auntie Shen was hard of hearing and so she wasn't bothered by it, but the ruckus always got the better of Miss Ruby.

"You girls hush. I'm as tired as a plow horse and I got a full day's work to do tomorrow. Now, hush!"

They would cover their mouths with the edges of their blankets and try hard to concentrate on sad thoughts. It never worked. Their giggles escaped like tiny bubbles, popping out from beneath the blankets and bouncing off the walls of the room. Somehow Miss Ruby got to snoring anyway, and they never did get in a lick of trouble.

The night they returned from the lowlands, it was too hot to go to sleep. They dragged the mattress to the long window and gazed out at the stars.

"Look real close, Carolina. You can see through the openings all the way to Heaven."

"What openings?"

"There, where the night glows. Those are the openings," said Mattie.

"You mean the stars?"

"They look like stars from here, but really they're big openings in the sky. It's like this blanket over our heads. We can peek through the holes and see the light in the room. So the sky is the blanket and the stars are the openings letting the light from Heaven shine through."

"Mattie, sometimes you have the strangest ideas. Do you really think the sky is full of holes?"

"It's full of holes because God made it. It's a holey sky. Get it? A *holy* sky," said Mattie.

"Holy Moley, I can see Heaven," said Carolina.

They both laughed so loud that Miss Ruby hollered up at them, and then they both tried so hard to stop. They had to cover their mouths with their hands. After a while, they started to feel sleepy and gazed out at the stars spread across the Milky Way and listened to the katydids chirp.

"I wonder if those stars really are openings to Heaven," Mattie whispered.

"Maybe they're angels," said Carolina.

"Grammy says slaves ran away on dark nights when the stars shined the brightest," said Mattie. "But how does a person follow stars?"

"You can read them like a map," said Carolina. "See the Big Dipper there? It's in the north sky. By morning it will be headed toward the east and standing on its handle."

"How do you know so much?" asked Mattie.

"My daddy taught me," said Carolina. "He loved stars."

"I'm sorry I called you blind and stupid," said Mattie.

"I'm sorry too," said Carolina. "I didn't mean to hurt your feelings."

Carolina slipped her hand into Mattie's, and Mattie held on tight.

"All they had to do was look up at the stars," said Mattie with a sigh.

"And they found their way," said Carolina.

Chapter 5

JUST US TWO

Miss Ruby stirred up a rich cake batter. Mattie scooped it into cake pans. Auntie Shen put the pans in the oven to bake. It was the day of Carolina's tenth birthday, the very last day of August, 1963.

Auntie Shen took her dulcimer out to the porch and sat in her ladder-back chair. Miss Ruby got comfortable in a rocking chair and started humming tunes that were familiar to them both. Carolina and Mattie had the newspaper spread out on the floorboards, looking at the ads for transistor radios and wanting them more than anything.

"You young'uns have it in your heads that things that cost money are worth more than things that do not," said Auntie Shen.

Miss Ruby nodded in agreement.

"Come use the voices God gave you," said Miss Ruby. "Come sing with me."

At first, Carolina and Mattie sang to please Miss Ruby, but after a while all that singing made their hearts light.

"This little light of mine,
I'm gonna let it shine."

"Oh yes," said Miss Ruby. "Don't singing make you feel so happy?"

Auntie Shen started playing her dulcimer, and then her foot got to tapping. Mattie and Carolina held hands and sashayed across the floorboards. It turned into a real party.

After the cake cooled, they spread pink icing on top and stuck in ten candles. Before Carolina blew them out, she made a wish that Mattie could stay for the school year, but the very next day her parents showed up and took her back to the ocean.

Three weeks into September a cold blast took Auntie Shen and Carolina by surprise. They woke to see that the greens had frozen in the garden overnight; their leaves were blackened and limp as wet rags. Carolina shivered so hard in the outhouse, she could hardly relieve herself. Auntie Shen made a fire in the woodstove and sat down to talk to Carolina about starting up in a new school. The only folks Carolina knew on this mountain were Mr. Jim and Miss Abigail, who were about a ten-minute walk away in the woods, and Miss Ruby. She hadn't met any kids.

She'd never even thought about it, since she'd spent all her time playing with Mattie. The thought of being the new kid standing in front of a new class in a new school made Carolina's stomach knot up. She changed the subject every way she could.

One day, while they were working at Morning Glory Jelly Stand, the school bus flew by. The windows of the bus were wide open, and Carolina and Auntie Shen could hear the kids shouting and laughing from inside. There was no more getting around the subject after that.

The following morning, when it was still dark outside, Carolina put on a crisp white blouse and a plaid skirt. She put her arms through the sleeves of her mama's old yellow sweater. It had orange yarn stitches all over it, holding the holes together. Carolina wrapped it around herself. It made her feel as if her mama's arms were around her, holding her close. She held her catbird pendant in her hand and squeezed it hard, as if courage would rise up through it and push these scared feelings away.

As she walked down to the main road with Auntie Shen, her school shoes pressed tight against her toenails. Carolina hadn't thought about her feet growing over the summer, since she'd run barefoot most of the time. By the time they reached the place along the roadside where they figured the bus would stop, she had a blister on the back of each heel and her toes were throbbing.

They waited. Sure enough, the school bus came rolling down the hill. It sped right by, blowing a gust of wind and dust in their face.

"Well, what do you make of that?" asked Auntie Shen.

"Maybe it's not my bus," said Carolina.

"Oh, for Heaven's sake," said Auntie Shen.

"Well, no sense worrying about it," said Carolina. "We can try again tomorrow."

Auntie Shen had her finger on her forehead and her thumb in the crease of her cheek, as if she was working her brain hard to find a solution to this dilemma.

Carolina looked up and down the road and was about to take a step across when she saw a car round the bend. It passed by, and then stopped, and then went in reverse. The woman in the car reached across the seat and rolled down the window.

"Good morning," she said.

"Good morning to you too," said Auntie Shen as cheerful as could be. A person would have thought she'd known the woman her whole life.

"Looks like you're headed to school," the woman said, speaking to Carolina.

"Yes, ma'am," said Carolina, "but the bus drove on by."

"What's your name?" the woman asked.

"Carolina Campbell," she said.

"I'd say you were in the fifth grade."

"Yes, ma'am," Carolina said. "How could you tell?"

"I've been teaching fifth grade for the last twenty years," the woman said. "Why don't the two of you hop in and I'll give you a ride over to school. I take it you haven't registered yet?"

"Registered?" Auntie Shen said, looking confused. "No, I suppose we haven't done that."

"Where are my manners?" the woman said. "Let me introduce myself. My name is Mrs. King. I'm the fifth-grade

58

teacher and assistant principal at Molly Mitchell School.
I'll help you get the paperwork filled out and get Carolina
into class. She's already missed three weeks."

"Molly Mitchell," Auntie Shen repeated. "That must
be one of them consolidated schools."

"That's right," said Mrs. King, "and it's a fine place to
learn."

Carolina's being behind all the other kids in arithmetic
lessons was only the start of her problems. It seemed as if
every other boy and girl had been friends their whole lives.
At least it didn't matter that she wore patched-up clothes
that were getting too snug. It seemed no one else in school
had much of anything either. What did matter was the
way the other kids acted toward her, as if being an orphan
was something contagious. They stayed away as if they
were afraid they might catch it same as catching a cold.

The only bright spot in her day was Mrs. King. It took
three days to get the bus situation figured out, and so
for those three days Carolina rode to school with Mrs.
King. She figured Mrs. King to be the nicest teacher in the
whole school. Mrs. King really seemed to understand
things.

As dark nights took on an autumn chill, Carolina and
Auntie Shen sat at the kitchen table while the heat of the
fire roared up the pipe of the woodstove. They studied together. Auntie Shen's old dictionary was thicker than the
family Bible, and it lay open most all the time as they
looked up vocabulary words. They made up a game called

"Spell the Best." Carolina brought home one test paper after another with a big *100%* written on the top. But try as she might, Carolina could not make sense of arithmetic.

By the end of October, Carolina had decided the best friends she'd have that year were to be found between the covers of the books that Mrs. King kept lending to her. Carolina and Auntie Shen would sit close, pulling a quilt around their shoulders, while Carolina read those stories out loud. It seemed to fuel Auntie Shen's imagination. She'd turn the kerosene lamp down low and end the evenings with a storytelling.

A few days before Halloween, nature gave them a sweet surprise. It warmed up as if it was a day in July. Auntie Shen called it Indian Summer. Butternut squash and pumpkins were growing to beat the band in the sunny patch by Auntie Shen's wild apple tree. On Halloween night, Carolina and Auntie Shen lugged all seven pumpkins to the porch and carved faces into them, throwing the innards into a pot for stewing. They lit candles inside every one.

Sitting out in the dark trees, they stared at the jack-o'-lanterns.

"Don't they look like a line of haints," said Auntie Shen.

"I can imagine that real good, Auntie Shen," said Carolina.

"Remember that *wizened* tree we came upon yesterday?" asked Auntie Shen.

Carolina smiled. Auntie Shen was using a vocabulary word.

"Remember the dried-up and shriveled spot where it had lost a branch? Didn't that look like an old woman's face? Why, I nearly expected her to go and begin us a story."

Carolina nodded. "Sometimes I see haints in the rocks too. First I see its eyes and then a nose and then a mouth as plain as could be," she said. "Haints aren't real. They don't scare me."

"Ghosts are something different," said Auntie Shen. "Now, ghosts are real. I remember a story about a haunted house that was visited in the night by a ghost."

Carolina turned her full attention to Auntie Shen's story.

"The old man had been murdered in that house, and every Halloween . . ."

Auntie Shen's voice was low. Carolina shivered, not knowing whether her chills came from the cold breezes picking up or the scary images popping into her brain. The glowing eyes in the jack-o'-lanterns flickered with fire.

Auntie Shen's voice rose. ". . . and then the old man's head fell right off his shoulders and rolled across the floor."

Suddenly and without warning, a gust of wind blew their hair. It grabbed hold of a jack-o'-lantern as if it had hands and threw it off the porch. Carolina nearly jumped out of her skin.

Auntie Shen laughed. "Land sakes, I'm scarin' myself."

"Tell me another one," Carolina begged. "Make this one really scary."

"I don't rightly think I could stop myself," said Auntie Shen.

The next day it rained hard, and the wind blew the last of the leaves off the tree branches. November's gray fog hung around nearly all month, but on Thanksgiving Day they woke to find a winter wonderland. A sheet of ice had covered the whole mountain while they were sleeping, and in the early-morning light, the trees sparkled as if they were made of crystal glass. Carolina brought out her mama's camera and used the remaining film taking pictures of the scenery.

All the fixin's for a proper dinner—the meat and potatoes and beans—were stored in the cellar house. When they went to fetch them, they discovered that the door latch was frozen tight. Auntie Shen and Carolina pounded and pried on that latch all morning, but it was no use.

They had no one to ask for help. Their neighbors, Mr. Jim and Miss Abigail, had gone to visit Miss Abigail's mother, and Miss Ruby was down in the lowlands with all her children. Carolina tried to cheer up Auntie Shen by baking cinnamon-sugar candies from pie dough, but then she got engrossed in a book and forgot all about them until the kitchen was full of smoke and the smell of charcoal pinched her nostrils. The treats had burned black as coal.

Their bellies growled with hunger and their hearts pined with lonesome feelings for family. Auntie Shen prayed for a blessing, and the day wore on. The sun shone bright and the ice on the latch melted away. Auntie Shen said it was the good Lord who had been smiling down all day. They brought up a ham and potatoes and apples. They cooked until the kitchen was as steamy as a summer day. Carolina draped a white tablecloth over the kitchen table, and they set out a meal so fine they couldn't help heaping their plates full and going back for seconds. It was long after dark before they had finished cleaning up, and they fell into bed feeling fat and happy.

On the first day of school after Thanksgiving recess, everyone in Carolina's class was given a part to study for the upcoming Christmas play. Carolina began memorizing her lines, fearful her mind could not contain them all. She read her part and Auntie Shen read all the others, each in a different voice. They practiced at the kitchen table while cutting out red and green bells from construction paper. Mrs. King had given Carolina the scraps of paper to take home, since Carolina had worked all through recess designing and stapling up a festive bulletin board for their classroom. Auntie Shen and Carolina strung the paper bells together with red yarn and hung the garland along the mantel in what Auntie Shen called the front room.

A few weeks before Christmas, Carolina and Auntie Shen decided it best to carry on the tradition of a winter's day hike searching for the perfect Christmas tree.

They tromped through a half foot of snow, hiking until the tips of their toes felt frozen to the bone, and then suddenly there it was, the perfect tree. Carolina couldn't help smiling. All of a sudden the tradition was as exciting as ever. She lay on her side in the snow and yanked that saw back and forth at the base of the trunk until she was ready to give up.

"You can do it. I know you can," Auntie Shen said, cheering her on. "Just a little more. Okay, now I'll push it."

They dragged the tree home behind them, huffing and puffing all the way. They had a time of it, trying to get it in through the doorway, but they succeeded. With a fire roaring in the woodstove, Carolina folded thin layers of birch bark and fanned them out to make angel wings. Auntie Shen coaxed butternut wood into stars. They poked a needle and thread through tiny red cranberries and made long strings of garland. That night, after Carolina and Auntie Shen had put on their nighties, they gazed upon their festive creations, each filled with a grateful heart.

Finally, the day of the Christmas play arrived. Carolina could hardly button up her sweater, her fingers were shaking so. She might have pretended she was sick, but Mrs. King showed up bright and early to drive Auntie Shen and Carolina to school. Carolina realized that Mrs. King was making sure Auntie Shen didn't miss it. When the play was all over and everyone was clapping and Carolina was breathing a sigh of relief and feeling wonderful for having remembered every line, she looked into the audience to find Auntie Shen. There she was, wearing her straw hat, clapping like crazy with tears rolling down her cheeks. Minutes later, Carolina was being hugged and Auntie Shen was exclaiming that she was so proud.

Finally, it was Christmas Eve. Carolina could see her breath in the frosty air. She looked up to the sky. She and her daddy had always peered into the stars to see if they could spot Santa's sleigh. This year, she searched Orion to see if she could spot a new star in the constellation, recalling her daddy's words. *If stars are angels, I'll be aiming for Orion. I'll stay there too, traveling round the whole Earth, looking down on everybody.*

On Christmas morning, snow was blowing through the

cracks along the windowsills. The water in the teakettle had iced up solid. Auntie Shen got the woodstove roaring with a warm fire.

"Carolina, we got us a blizzard," declared Auntie Shen.

Snow piled up deep as Carolina, huddled under her quilt, exchanged presents with Auntie Shen. Carolina's gift to Auntie Shen was two sachets, cotton cloth that she had stitched together by hand and filled with pine to make them sweet-smelling. Auntie Shen's gift to Carolina was a pair of red mittens. Each one had a red and white striped candy cane tucked inside.

All morning it snowed hard. When the storm finally subsided, the heavy white snow reached halfway up the front door.

"I 'spect we won't see another soul until spring thaw," said Auntie Shen.

Carolina was scratching her name into the ice that had formed on the inside of the window pane when she got the surprise of her life. Down the path a ways, Mrs. King and her husband were coming up over the rise. They were walking on snowshoes and dragging a sled behind them.

Mrs. King's husband shoveled snow away from the door. The kitchen filled with life the moment Mrs. King walked in. Her cheeks were rosy and she talked of having a merry old time hiking up that long hill. She and her husband shook out their hats and gloves and rubbed their hands by the woodstove.

They unloaded the sled, carrying in three big bags full of groceries. Mr. King had a bulging sack slung over his shoulder, making him look like Santa Claus. Carolina was nearly beside herself wondering what he might bring out of that sack, and knocked the cat's water dish right over with her stocking feet trying to sneak a glance. When finally he opened it, he brought out presents all wrapped up in store-bought Christmas paper. Carolina and Auntie Shen squealed as if they were sisters the same age, rather than grandma and granddaughter. Auntie Shen got a new pair of slippers and Carolina got a paint-by-number set. There were four tangerines in the sack too. Auntie Shen and Carolina held one in each hand and put the exotic orange fruit up to their noses and breathed in with their eyes closed.

Auntie Shen couldn't thank them enough for coming. She grabbed the iron skillet and started frying up some of her homemade sausage. She made a pot of fresh coffee, and wonderful smells filled the kitchen. It was a lovely Christmas.

It was well into the bitterly cold days of January when Mr. and Mrs. King snowshoed up the hill once again. Carolina thought she was in big trouble after missing so many days, but Mrs. King understood about staying home from school when you needed to keep the woodstove burning. She sat with Carolina at the kitchen table, took out her pencil, and made a list of homework assignments. She wrote page numbers next to arithmetic examples and put the notebook paper in Carolina's textbook to mark the chapter she was to work on. Then the books were put away, for Auntie Shen was setting out warm corn bread, fresh from the oven. Hours later, when the visiting was over, Mrs. King and her husband had gifts of Auntie Shen's best honey and jars of raspberry jam.

From that day on, Auntie Shen learned arithmetic right along with Carolina. Auntie Shen said she'd never had so much fun. They started a game of quizzing each other. Carolina tried her best, but Auntie Shen always won.

About the middle of March, when they couldn't stand winter any longer, a warm spring wind turned ice into running streams. In April wildflowers carpeted the forest floor. In May they strolled through rhododendron forests where branches as thick as Carolina's arms held massive bouquets of round purple balls of flowers. As if they were in a magical kingdom, Auntie Shen and Carolina laid out picnics in the dark places under the umbrella of blooms, where they consorted with fairies, or at least pretended to. They walked down into the holler to visit with Miss Ruby. Mr. Jim and Miss Abigail stopped by with their baby girl; she was already walking by herself.

In the natural rhythm of spring, Auntie Shen began to think about jelly making. She started gathering up empty Mason jars she'd been collecting and giving them a good soak in a washtub on the porch. And on a bright sunny morning, Carolina ran to tell Auntie Shen that she'd spotted a catbird.

"Well, if'n the catbird's back, I guess it's warm enough to run barefoot," said Auntie Shen. "Go ahead and kick your shoes off, if you'd like."

A week into June, the wild strawberries were as big as a child's thumb. Carolina passed fifth grade and was looking forward to summer vacation. Her report card showed she'd earned a B-minus in arithmetic. Auntie Shen tacked that report card to the bare wood wall in the kitchen, where they could admire it.

At the edge of the woods, raspberry canes had green leaves, and green berries were popping out in abundance. Vines and weeds were growing even faster, so Auntie Shen and Carolina began yanking them out, being careful not to break the stick-thin stems of the canes or pull the new berries off. In seven more days it would be June twelfth, and Morning Glory Jelly Stand would open for business. There was much work to be done.

As Carolina moved through the tall weeds, her feet were getting crisscrossed with red scratches. She brushed against stinging nettle. It did sting. It felt like a burn on her bare legs.

"Ouch! Auntie Shen, I need long pants."

"Long ants?" Auntie Shen stared at the ground around Carolina's feet.

"No," Carolina said, chuckling. *"Pants.* I need pants. I'll be right back."

"I'll be here," she said.

Carolina ran back to the kitchen. A pair of brown cotton pants hung over the chair. She hadn't stitched up the hole in the knee yet, but she put them on anyway. She found one sneaker in the corner behind the woodstove and found the other under her bed. She ran back outside, letting the screen door slam behind her.

She couldn't see Auntie Shen.

"Shen-Bear," Carolina called in a singsong voice.

Carolina moseyed up the hill, searching the edges. Then she spotted her.

Auntie Shen was lying in the grass!

Her body lay crumpled in an awkward pose. Carolina ran and knelt beside her. Auntie Shen's face had a strange look, as if one side had forgotten what to do. She tried to make words but only gibberish came out. Carolina tried to help her up, but Auntie Shen couldn't move. A wave of panic rushed through Carolina's whole body.

"I'll be right back," Carolina said.

She held Auntie Shen's eyes for a moment and then ran back to the house. She grabbed a pillow and the quilt off her bed, wishing the whole time they had a telephone like everybody else so she could call for help. She rushed back to Auntie Shen. Carolina gently lifted Auntie Shen's head and set it down on the pillow. She tucked the quilt around her sides.

"I have to get help," she whispered. "I'll run fast I can."

Carolina hesitated a moment, afraid to leave. Auntie Shen's eyes held an expression that was fierce, as if she was saying, *Get going.*

Carolina ran like a deer along the ridge. It was a narrow path across a steep hill, and the quickest way to Mr. Jim's house. She kept her eyes on the trail, sprinting over roots, stepping off boulders, hoping her feet didn't slip and send her tumbling. A prayer bubbled up and flowed out of her heart all on its own.

Please, God, don't take Auntie Shen. Please, God, make her better. Please, God, let Mr. Jim's truck be fixed.

Chapter 6

DO-GOODERS

The engine turned over on the first try, and Mr. Jim and Carolina hightailed it up the road. Mr. Jim tried to coax the truck up the mountain path, but it was too steep and too full of boulders. They ran the rest of the way.

Mr. Jim tenderly lifted Auntie Shen into his big burly arms, and he carried her all the way down to his truck. After he gently laid her down, Carolina reached across the seat and held Auntie Shen's hand. Auntie Shen's long fingers could barely move. She reminded Carolina of a bird with a broken wing.

Carolina did as she was told. She stayed behind and waited. She watched Mr. Jim's truck lean this way and that as the tires rolled over the rocks in the path. She watched until the truck turned onto the road and rounded the bend. She stayed until the only sound was wood thrushes singing from deep in the trees.

It was nearly dark when she saw Mr. Jim's red flannel shirt through the trees. He was ambling up the path with a tired gait. Carolina leaped off the porch and ran down to meet him.

"How is she? How come you didn't bring her home? What did the doctor say?" Carolina rattled off her questions, barely taking a breath in between.

Mr. Jim spoke in a soft voice. "Doc says he's got to keep an eye on your Auntie Shen. They're keeping her for the night, might be longer."

"What's the matter with her?"

"Could be something they call a stroke," said Mr. Jim.

Carolina thought about Auntie Shen sleeping in a strange bed in a big building. She figured Auntie Shen was already wishing she was home. Mr. Jim interrupted her thoughts.

"You're welcome to come to the house. Miss Abigail will have supper waiting. We can put the baby to sleep in our bed if'n you want to spend the night."

"No thank you, Mr. Jim. I want to wait here. Besides, I need to feed the cats."

Mr. Jim pulled on his beard. He scratched his sideburns. "Well, then," he said, "I'll be by in the morning."

The next day Carolina was up bright and early. She wanted to do something special for Auntie Shen, so she set about doing every chore she could think of. She swept the dirt on the kitchen floor into little circular mounds. She got down on her knees and reached the broom under the woodstove. She moved the chairs and swept under the table. She patted Auntie Shen's feather pillow between her hands until it fluffed out full. She pulled the covers up over the pillow and tugged and smoothed them out until there wasn't a single wrinkle.

When hunger began to gnaw at her belly, she crawled along the garden paths, picking radishes and tender greens, sprinkling them with vinegar and salt. The vinegar made her cough, and she wondered how Auntie Shen could stand it. Carolina decided sugar made lettuce leaves a much better meal. A bit of pork and several handfuls of raspberries filled her stomach. From her perch on the porch, she could see down the length of the footpath. She imagined Auntie Shen would soon be meandering on up, stooping here and there as she gathered a bouquet of wildflowers to set in the Mason jar on the kitchen table.

Instead it was Mr. Jim she saw coming up the path, just like he'd said he would. His truck had died again and he was fit to be tied. Carolina didn't mind that he didn't stay long, since he was in such a bad mood. Later Miss Abigail came by way of the wood's path. She was a petite woman with a high squeaky voice and long golden hair that glistened in the sun. Her baby girl was seated on her hip, and Miss Abigail was carrying a basket of sandwiches.

Carolina got to playing with Miss Abigail's baby girl, remembering the games she used to play with her baby brother, Caleb. She'd pretend to chase him and he would squeal when she got close. She'd blow raspberries on his belly and he'd cackle with laughter, bring his legs up, and then lower them so she could do it again. He'd squish her cheeks together so her lips looked like a blowfish.

Before she left, Miss Abigail invited Carolina to supper. Carolina politely said no and was glad Auntie Shen couldn't hear her saying it. Auntie Shen considered it just plain rude to decline someone's hospitality, but Carolina wasn't meaning to be impolite. It was only that she couldn't bear to leave her lookout spot on the porch.

By late evening, Carolina was looking out on a sky that was as clear as could be. An orange sun was slipping down and lighting up the western slopes as pretty as peach marmalade. Streaks of scarlet and purple painted the sky.

Light played in the clouds as darkness settled in. One by one and then by dozens and then by hundreds the stars came out, and Carolina was comforted by the whole sparkly sky; by Bootes the Herdsman, sitting and smoking his pipe; by Corona Borealis, the crown above his head; and by Cygnus the Swan, with its wings spread wide, flying along the Milky Way.

Auntie Shen always said that faith brought the sun's return each new day, but Carolina's faith was in the stars. *Sure as there are stars above*, her daddy used to say. During the day she couldn't see their light, but it didn't matter. She knew the stars were always there.

An old sofa at the end of the porch was nearly torn to pieces from the cats. Carolina decided it didn't smell that bad and dragged out a patchwork quilt that Auntie Shen had stitched together from flour sacks. She brought out her pillow too. The pillow used to belong to her mama. Carolina had taken it off her mama and daddy's bed the day she moved in with Auntie Shen. Sometimes she'd lie on that pillow and imagine her mama's soft breathing, as if they were taking a nap together.

Carolina gazed up at the stars and wondered about angels and Heaven. She drew an imaginary line with her finger from the tip of the Big Dipper's bucket over to Polaris, the North Star. She longed to see Orion. If she could see him, then maybe this sorrowful feeling would pass, this feeling of missing her daddy so much. Carolina sighed. Orion didn't live in the summer sky. She'd have to wait for him too.

She fell asleep on the old sofa and opened her eyes as night was turning into day.

Morning passed slowly. Mr. Jim was still trying to fix his truck. Miss Abigail couldn't visit long, as her baby girl was acting fussy and only walking and rocking her was going to calm her down. Again, Carolina declined the invitation to supper.

Evening lingered. Clouds rolled in and fog settled down so thick Carolina didn't see the sun set. Darkness just slowly crept in and surrounded her. For the third night in a row Carolina slept at the house alone. She crawled under the covers in Auntie Shen's bed and lay awake for a good long while.

The following day, Carolina was lying on the sofa reading *Johnny Tremain*. It was the best book she'd ever read. This book blew dust in her face, drew blood on the pages, and made her feel as if she'd fallen in, as if she was living right beside Johnny.

A little gray kitten lay sound asleep on her chest. She placed the open book on her belly and stared at nothing in particular. She was thinking about how brave people are in books. She thought about how hard it was to be brave in real life.

A soft breeze moved the stray hairs that had escaped her braids. A stronger breeze blew and the leaves of Auntie Shen's wild roses brushed against the railing. She closed her eyes, listening to the catbird that was rustling about in the thicket, and wrapped her hand around the wooden pendant her daddy had carved. She dozed off.

Awakened with a start by a hand shaking her shoulder, Carolina heard a faraway voice.

"The poor thing," the faraway voice said.

Groggy from sleep, her mouth dry as a bone, Carolina was momentarily confused as to where she was. She looked up and saw three ladies standing on the porch, staring down at her. She sat up quickly. It made her dizzy. The words *poor thing* stuck in her head.

Carolina recognized the ladies as the three old maids from Auntie Shen's church. They always sat together in the fifth pew on the left. The lady who had called her *poor thing* was the small-boned one who had a long brown braid down her back. It was tied with a red ribbon. This old maid always sat closest to the aisle. She started to sit down but crinkled up her nose when she caught a whiff of the sofa. She pulled the rocking chair over and sat down.

"We heard the news about Ada," said the old maid, "and we've come to help."

"Who?" Carolina asked.

"Ada," the old maid repeated. "Ada McClaine, you silly girl, the one you've been living with."

"You mean Auntie Shen?" Carolina asked again.

"Left here all alone to fend for herself," said the stout one. She was wearing a green hat. Red curls bobbed against her cheeks as she shook her head, making a *t-t-t* sound that meant *awful, awful, awful.*

"You must be terribly lonely," said the one with the red ribbon in her braid. Her voice was filled with sympathy. Carolina looked at all the cats on the porch, some licking their paws, others sleeping in squares of sun, and a few nibbling at the plate of food she'd set out. They were keeping her company.

"Miss Abigail and Mr. Jim let the church know of your dire situation," said the third old maid. This one was as tall and thin as a number-two pencil and stood as stiff and straight as one too. She had short salt-and-pepper hair, and her black sweater was buttoned up to her neck even though it was hot out.

"We have discussed it with those concerned, and Cousin Clayton has gone ahead and made all the arrangements," she continued. "Get your things now. It's time to leave."

Carolina's senses came rushing back to her. "Leave? I can't do that. Auntie Shen will be expecting me to be here."

The old maids glanced at one another as if they were keeping a big secret.

"You are a lucky little girl," said the small old maid, pulling her long braid in front of her so she could fuss with the ribbon, "to be invited to such a lovely home."

"Down in the lowlands, over in Huntsville," said the old maid in the green hat. She was all excited, as if she'd handed Carolina a birthday present all wrapped up in pretty paper.

"It's a good Christian home," said the tall old maid in a matter-of-fact voice.

The old maid with the braid patted Carolina's hand. "Most orphans go to the Children's Home. It's a blessing you can live with a family," she said.

"I live with Auntie Shen," whispered Carolina. "She's my family."

The three old maids began to talk as if Carolina wasn't there listening.

"Seems Ada took on more than she could chew this time," said the number-two pencil maid.

The lady said it as if Auntie Shen had done something wrong. Maybe they didn't even like Auntie Shen. As far as Carolina knew, this was the first time they'd ever come visiting, and this wasn't much of a visit.

"She's not even related to the child," said the red ribbon maid.

"Not blood kin," said the green hat maid.

"Families around here have more than enough mouths to feed already," said the tall one. "Can't be taking in a stray."

A stray? Carolina thought if she bit her lip any harder it might bleed, but she wasn't about to let that mean old maid see her cry. Carolina crossed her arms in front of her chest and stared straight ahead at a pot of pansies. She refused to listen to another word.

A silent war ensued. It was full of mean looks. The old maids lost every battle.

In a huff, they set off down the path, clucking angry words like banshee hens. Carolina stood on the railing and watched them go. Satisfied they were gone, she climbed down and plopped back onto the sofa cushions. She pulled the kitten to her lap and stroked its fur with one hand while her other hand held on to her catbird pendant.

She thought about what the ladies had said about feeling lonely, and the silence around her didn't feel so peaceful anymore. Could they really make her go away? Fear and worry flew into Carolina's mind like an owl stealthily gliding through the night. It made her insides jumpy.

Carolina needed help. She knew just where to find it. Carolina set off for Miss Ruby's.

The very next morning, Carolina was sitting on the porch steps licking raspberry jelly off a spoon and staring at a bumblebee sipping nectar from a blossom. She was wondering where Miss Ruby might have gone to. Carolina had searched for her everywhere when she ran down into the holler yesterday, but Miss Ruby was nowhere about. Carolina scraped her spoon against the glass at the bottom of the jar.

When she looked up, the tall old maid was coming up the path. She had the sheriff with her. Carolina's instincts told her to run away, take to the hills, but she couldn't move. It was as if fear had turned her into a pillar of salt. Carolina didn't move from the top step of the porch. She held her spoon in midair, and it looked as if she was holding out the jelly jar to collect the sun. The taste of raspberries was still on her tongue when the old maid and the sheriff reached the patch of grass right in front of Carolina.

The sheriff—who, it turned out, was Cousin Clayton—stood by with his hands folded over his big belly. Carolina was forced to listen—again—to how there wasn't a single solitary family in these parts who could take her in.

"What about Miss Ruby?" Carolina asked. "Miss Ruby didn't say no, did she?"

The old maid suddenly pursed her lips together as if she'd bitten into a lemon.

"You'll be living with your own kind," said the sheriff. He put on a smile, but it was a sarcastic kind. It caused Carolina to feel bad inside.

Carolina thought about Johnny Tremain and how brave he was in that book she was reading. She lifted her chin and mustered her courage.

"I'll be staying right here. Thank you anyway," she said.

The sheriff leaned down and put his face right up next to Carolina's. He looked like a bear, the way his lips went up and showed his clenched teeth. His breath smelled like tobacco.

"You have exactly three minutes to get your things, young lady."

Carolina stomped across the bare wood floor of the kitchen and entered the bedroom that she and Auntie Shen had fixed up so special. She was mad at Mr. Jim and Miss Abigail for going behind her back. She was mad at the tall old maid who'd never once said hello when

Carolina and Auntie Shen had gone to service. *Auntie Shen will have a fit when she hears about this*, thought Carolina.

She took her mama's yellow sweater that was hanging over the chair, a pair of shorts that were lying at the foot of the bed, the button-up top with the white rickrack that Auntie Shen had stitched along the bottom, and her red Mary Janes. Auntie Shen had traded a jar of her best honey for those pretty shoes at the thrift shop, and Carolina had worn them practically every day of fifth grade. Lastly, she picked up her mama's pillow, held it a moment, and then buried her face in it, filled with a longing to cry on her mama's shoulder. *Be brave*, she thought.

She shoved her clothes and *Johnny Tremain* between the pillow and the pillowcase. Then Carolina scribbled a note to Auntie Shen. She put it in plain sight on her chest of drawers and put her wishing stone on top of it. In her haste she knocked down a carved figure of a giraffe. She stood it back up, looking over the set of animals her daddy had carved. He'd often brought home chunks of wood, scrap pieces that landed on the floor of the sawmill where he'd worked. He'd carved all these animals—two of each kind—and an ark just like Noah's in the Bible.

Carolina dragged her feet as she followed the old maid and the sheriff down to the road, where his cruiser was parked. He pulled out fast. A minute later, they were whizzing past Morning Glory Jelly Stand. Carolina had never seen it look so forlorn. It was still boarded up as if it was winter, and here it was a warm summer day when she and Auntie Shen should have been hanging out the sign and placing jellies on the shelves. The roof seemed to sag from heartbreak.

Hours went by. They'd left the mountains far behind and were now traveling along land as flat as a pancake. A long highway stretched out before them in a straight line. Finally they turned onto a winding road and then down a street that led to a fancy neighborhood, and then they were turning into a long driveway. At the end of the driveway was a big white house with black shutters at each window. It was the most elegant house Carolina had ever seen.

"You'll be staying with the reverend," the tall old maid said. A harsh look and a stern voice followed. "Watch your manners and follow the rules."

Carolina walked slowly up the blue painted steps of the wide porch.

"You are a very lucky girl," said the tall old maid.

Lucky? Lucky was winning at marbles.

Carolina continued up the steps as the front door was opening. She kept her eyes down. She saw shiny black shoes and black pants with a sharp crease. She saw blue high heels and a dress with blue forget-me-nots in the pattern. Carolina wondered why they were all dressed up on a Monday. Auntie Shen only put on her good dress for church.

"Carolina, I'd like you to meet Reverend and Mrs. Sanctem," said the old maid.

A queasy feeling began in the pit of Carolina's stomach. It worked its way up to her throat and positioned itself for a giant leap. If she threw up on their polished shoes, would she have a chance to escape? Would the sheriff take her to jail?

"Look up when you're spoken to, child," said the reverend.

Carolina raised her eyes. She gave the old maid a pleading look, but the woman turned away without even noticing, as her attention was on the sheriff. He was coming onto the porch.

"If she gives you any trouble, give a holler," said the sheriff.

"Thank you, Clayton," said the reverend. "I'm sure we'll make out fine."

The sheriff and the reverend shook hands like old friends.

Then they drove away, just left her there. She watched the police cruiser head down the street. Carolina felt a firm hand upon her shoulder. The reverend steered her through the front door and into a large sitting room.

"Won't you have a seat, Carolina?"

Reverend Sanctem motioned with a sweep of his hand toward a large cushioned sofa. The reverend and Mrs. Sanctem sat side by side in wing chairs. Carolina stared at the zigzag design in the fabric of their chairs until her sight got blurry. She caught a phrase here and there like *good Christian family* and *don't bring shame* and *follow the rules*.

It was as hard to sit through Reverend Sanctem's lecture as it was to sit through a Sunday sermon. Her fingers seemed to be moving all on their own. First they twined together as if she was praying; then her thumbs began to twiddle around and around themselves; then she began to play a finger game she'd learned when she was a little girl. *Here's the church, here's the steeple, open the doors and see all the people.*

Reverend Sanctem droned on.

"Would you like to see your room?"

Carolina looked up.

She *was* curious about this.

Carolina followed them up a carpeted flight of stairs, down a hallway, and then up another staircase that was narrow and had bare wood steps. It led to a room with a bed with a brown blanket pulled up tight over a flat pillow. There was a small chest of drawers and a small table with a lamp on it and a big black Bible.

"Go ahead and get settled," said Reverend Sanctem.

"Supper will be ready soon," said Mrs. Sanctem.

Carolina stood in the room and listened to Mrs. Sanctem's high heels click down the wooden stairs. Before he turned to leave, Reverend Sanctem did something Carolina wasn't expecting. He smiled at her. She couldn't understand why it made her feel scared inside. It was a worse feeling than when the sheriff had given her his sarcastic grin.

When Reverend Sanctem left the room, Carolina sat on the edge of the bed and held her lumpy pillowcase on her lap. Her stomach seemed to be trying to turn itself inside out.

She looked at the bare walls. She was already missing her bedroom at Auntie Shen's, with their homespun paintings decorating every wall. Leaves of a maple tree brushed against the screen. It was one of those adjustable screens that stretched to fit the window. It opened and closed like the baby gate her mama and daddy had put up when Caleb started walking and getting into things. Beyond the window was a wide green lawn and a long driveway, but there were no mountains.

Carolina held her pendant and rubbed her thumb over the carving. She reached into her pillowcase and pulled out her book. She looked down at the picture of Johnny Tremain, his face set in determination. *Be brave, Carolina.* She could hear him say it.

Footsteps echoed on the stairs and then two little girls appeared in the doorway. They were the same height. They both had blue eyes. They both had long blond braids. They wore matching pink blouses and matching blue skirts.

"Supper's ready," they said in unison.

"Are you twins?" Carolina asked.

"Yes," they said, and began to giggle. They scurried away, their shoes tapping down the narrow staircase.

On the way downstairs, Carolina peeked into the bedroom that the little girls shared. It looked like a picture out of the Sears, Roebuck catalog. There were two canopy beds with white ruffles overhead and matching pink bedspreads. There were two identical desks separated by a long window framed with white lace curtains. A whole row of dolls in clean white dresses sat neat and prim along a pink shelf. Carolina remembered having a favorite doll. She had dragged it everywhere until dirt was caked in its eyes. These dolls looked barely touched.

"We are not to be late for supper."

She jumped, startled at Reverend Sanctem's sudden appearance at her side.

"Yes, sir," she said.

He walked with her down the wide carpeted stairway and escorted her through a wide room with red carpet and long windows, the glass barely visible behind the heavy gold draperies. They entered the dining room. The smell of furniture polish reminded her of the shellac her daddy had used on his carvings. The girls were already sitting next to each other on one side of the long gleaming table. Mrs. Sanctem was sitting at the end closest to the kitchen. Reverend Sanctem stood at the head of the table. There was only one place setting left, so Carolina sat on that side of the table, all by herself, facing the girls. The reverend said a long grace. Carolina bowed her head and stared at her plate.

Bowls were passed. She spooned out a tiny portion of mashed potatoes and one spoonful of corn onto her plate. Suddenly she was hungrier than a bear. She pretended she wasn't. It seemed like a good time to show her best manners. She took one slice of roast beef, the end piece, because it was small. It seemed the polite thing to do.

The twins talked about seeing their best friends at summer Bible school. Carolina listened and took small bites, remembering to chew with her mouth closed. There was so much strangeness; people all dressed up for supper, a fancy tablecloth with a silver spoon stuck into the mashed potatoes. Even the stick of butter lay neatly on a silver tray with its own special knife. Carolina sat very still.

"Do you have a best friend, Carolina?" Mrs. Sanctem asked.

"Yes, ma'am," she said.

Everyone was staring at her. She swallowed the corn that she had chewed into mush and answered Mrs. Sanctem's many questions. What was her friend's name? *Mattie.* What did she look like? *She's pretty.* What color is her hair? *Black.* Does she come from a good family? *Yes, ma'am.*

The questions continued until Mrs. Sanctem said, "Why, from your description, I'd say she's a Negro."

A hush fell over the room.

The twins' mouths hung open. They spoke at the same time, saying, "You're best friends with a colored girl?"

They made identical expressions, as if they'd just seen something dead and run over on the road.

"No," said Carolina, "not *best* friends."

There it was. A lie, delivered clean and smooth. It was the first lie Carolina had ever told. It dropped to the bottom of her heart as heavy as a lead lure and stayed there, lodging itself like a fishing hook.

The next day, a brown grocery bag full of hand-me-down dresses arrived in the arms of a plump and cheery woman. Carolina overheard the words *charity* and *orphan girl* in the conversation between the woman and Mrs. Sanctem. It seemed news had spread fast.

In Carolina's opinion, the best thing about summer was running outside without wasting a minute looking for her shoes. The next best thing was wearing shorts. When Mrs. Sanctem handed her a starched and ironed dress, Carolina stared at her in disbelief.

Mrs. Sanctem announced it was time for Bible school.

Carolina sat between the twins in the backseat of the Buick, and Reverend and Mrs. Sanctem rode up front. *Not a cloud in the sky and I have to be stuck inside a building learning more lessons.* Her neck itched from the starchy dress. Her feet were cramped in the black-and-white saddle shoes that Mrs. Sanctem had insisted she wear.

Everybody knew everybody, except Carolina. Kids ran around the church hall, talking excitedly and breaking off into groups. Carolina stood against the wall, between a piano and a painting of Jesus, until Mrs. Sanctem spotted her and came over. She led Carolina to a classroom.

The teacher had blue-gray hair and soft round curves that hid the belt of her dress when she sat down. She read a story from the Bible about a disciple named Peter who denied Jesus three times before the rooster crowed, and then Peter wept. Carolina understood that Peter cried because he had betrayed his friend. Carolina thought about Mattie. By telling that lie, she'd betrayed her friend too.

Bible school took place every morning for the remainder of the week. Carolina silently rejoiced a bold Hallelujah every day at noon when it was time to leave. She couldn't say evenings were much better. Reverend Sanctem stayed in his office. Mrs. Sanctem disappeared into her bedroom. A housekeeper showed up to vacuum and dust. The twins followed Carolina like puppies. She really didn't mind. She pushed them high on their swing set. She taught them hide-and-seek in the yard and pretended she couldn't see them hiding in the shrubs alongside the house.

After all those days of Bible school, Carolina had to put on another dress for Sunday service. Reverend Sanctem preached a long sermon. Carolina counted the squares in the high ceiling of the church.

The car was sweltering hot on the ride back to the house. The car windows were open only an inch, as Mrs. Sanctem didn't want her hair to get mussed. Carolina was about to suffocate. She could think of nothing else but swimming in the cool creek behind Miss Ruby's cabin.

Reverend Sanctem pulled up to a gas station that was also a general store. He said he was going in to buy a newspaper, but everyone else had to sit in the hot car. Carolina saw a big sign above the store that said COLD BEER. She started thinking about how good a root beer soda would taste. She imagined the sweet cold liquid going down her throat. The more she imagined it, the more she wanted it, and the words popped out of her mouth.

"Boy, I could really go for a *cold* beer!"

"Carolina!" Mrs. Sanctem said with a gasp, turning her head quickly to the cars on either side of them.

The twins covered their mouths, grunting in spits and spurts, trying desperately to keep their giggles in. The moment Reverend Sanctem opened the car door and slid in, both girls hushed. Mrs. Sanctem heaved a great sigh. Many more followed until finally they reached the Sanctems' home.

Carolina was sent to her room. The reverend sat beside

her, instructing her to read Bible verses aloud. They were about temptation and sin. His breath smelled sweet and disgusting at the same time. His smile reminded her of a rotting corncob with brown-tipped kernels. He placed his hand on her back, and it made her insides quiver, as if a black snake had slithered over her shoes.

She was left alone in her room for the remainder of the long hot evening. She was supposed to be "thinking" about what she'd done. She was thinking that the last six days had been the longest days of her life. Carolina pulled the screen out of the window frame and leaned it against the wall. She reached out and rubbed the smooth leaves of the maple tree between her fingers. A catbird alighted on a thin branch above her head.

Carolina held her breath. She kept perfectly still. She barely whispered.

"What is it, catbird?"

The catbird chirped as if it was trying to talk human. It ended its song with a kitten-soft *mew*. Then it flapped its wings and flew away. Carolina watched it go. *Fly away.*

It was a sign. The catbird had delivered a message. She was sure of it. A plan began to form in Carolina's mind as hope rose up in her heart like water from a spring.

The following week was worse than the first. It seemed like even the act of her breathing sent Reverend Sanctem into tirades about sin. He said he was bound and determined to save her soul. Carolina couldn't figure out what she'd done to endanger it.

On Saturday night, Mrs. Sanctem rolled Carolina's hair

up in hard pink curlers. Carolina figured she was being tortured so she'd look nice when they showed off their *little orphan girl* at church the next morning. The curlers were tight. Their little spikes pricked her scalp when she tried to sleep. She lay facedown with her nose in her pillow. It made it awfully hard to breathe.

During the night a hard rain fell. It tapped on the roof. A solid sheet of black water cascaded before her window. A burst of lightning lit the sky, splitting it in two at the same time that a burst of wind sent the screen crashing to the floor. Thunder rumbled like an angry giant. Carolina huddled at the head of her bed, her knees pulled up, hugging her pillow. Lightning flashed again and shadowed images on her wall jumped out at her.

She wished for home. She wished she could run down the hall to her parents' room. She wished she could whisper *bad dream* to her daddy and hear him say *climb in*. She'd crawl over him and he would grunt when her knee jabbed him in the chest. She'd whisper *sorry* and slip under the blankets and feel her mama's kiss on her forehead. Then she'd snuggle close to her baby brother and feel his hand wrap around her finger. She'd sleep soundly in the comfort of their circle.

Wishing won't make it so. She scolded the thought away. She could no more stop the events of her life than she'd been able to stop Caleb's tears when he wanted their mama. She reached up and absent-mindedly rubbed her thumb along the wings of her carved catbird. Then she remembered the real catbird that had alighted on the maple branch. Its message rose from a place deep inside her.

Fly away. With hope renewed, her heart filled with glad

feelings, and she couldn't help smiling. Carolina squeezed
her catbird pendant, for luck, for strength, for courage. Her
decision was made.

Toward morning, the moon appeared in the break of fast-
moving clouds. The rain had finally stopped and the cover
of darkness would be gone soon. Carolina stepped over
the curlers scattered on the floor, dressed in her own
clothes, and stuffed her belongings into her pillowcase.
She tied a knot in the end. She held it as far out the window as she could and let it go. It hit the ground with a
muffled *pumph.*

She held tight to the window frame with both hands,
her left leg hanging out the window and her right foot on
the floor. She tapped the air with her left foot until it hit
solid on the wide branch. Leaves limp with rain brushed
against her leg. A mass of clouds glowed with yellow light,
and then a full moon appeared in the break, illuminating
the shadowed branches below. It was a long way down.
The smooth soles of her sneakers slipped on the wet
branch as if it was covered in grease.

She pulled her sneakers off and let them drop to the
ground below. She pressed one bare foot onto the rough
bark and got a solid footing. She grasped the branch above
her with both hands. She dragged her other leg out the
window. Sliding her feet along the branch and holding on
to the one above brought her safely to the trunk.

A light flashed in the window directly below, *his*
window.

Carolina eased down through the branches, using the

crooks in the tree trunk for footholds. She could see Reverend Sanctem pacing back and forth across his bedroom. Carolina quietly slipped beneath his window, her heart pounding wildly. Each thump was like a beat on a drum. She thought for sure he'd hear it too.

On the lowest branch she pushed off and landed softly on the soggy ground. She grabbed her pillowcase. She moved her hands through the grass under the tree. Where were her sneakers? An owl hooted. She heard the sash of the window opening above her.

Carolina ran.

Chapter 7

PIE

Water kicked up on the backs of Carolina's legs as she bolted across the rain-soaked grass. At the road, oncoming headlights blinded her. The car sped by, its tires whooshing on the wet surface of the blacktop. Water sprayed up onto her legs and arms. She ducked into the shadows. Certain that the car would not stop and turn around, she ran along the edge of the road, tiny stones pricking her feet. Feeling the jab of a pointed rock, she stumbled. Carolina took to the center of the road where the blacktop was smooth and began running as fast as her legs could carry her, as if the boogeyman himself was chasing her.

She left the neighborhood of fancy houses far behind. By the time the sun was peeking over the horizon,

Carolina was stepping swiftly along a road of farm fields and meadows in her pretty Mary Janes that luckily she had packed in her pillowcase. She stopped at an abandoned barn to watch swallows. They dove under the old boards and in and out of the open doors, flying fast on sure wings.

She meandered down a winding dirt road. Rain had washed the world clean. Morning light filtered through soft blue clouds smudged with pink hues. Leaves glistened. The scent of decaying leaves and black woodsy soil filled the air. Carolina sat down to rest her tired legs under a hickory tree. She undid the straps of her red Mary Janes and pulled them off. Her toes felt sore and had pink rub burns on them. How could her favorite pair of shoes be getting too small? Carolina sighed and massaged her toes.

The day was already warming up and getting humid. A breeze blew and shook the leaves above her. Rainwater pattered onto her arms.

It was Sunday morning. Carolina wondered what Reverend Sanctem would do when he realized she was gone. Would he go to church and pretend nothing was out of the ordinary? Would he explain how his little "charity case" had gone and run off? She shrugged, knowing for certain that no matter what he said, everyone would take his side. At least she wouldn't have to stand beside him after church service again, shaking hands with the parishioners as they filed by. At least she wouldn't have to smile politely when they pinched her cheeks and gushed over Reverend Sanctem. *Oh, is this the little orphan girl? Oh, isn't she adorable? Oh, what a generous soul you are.* It had been downright embarrassing. It had made her want to hang her head in shame.

A knock-knock-knocking sound came from deep within

the trees. It was a woodpecker hammering away. Two blue-birds alighted on the phone wires above her. Carolina grinned. She too was as free as a bird.

She moseyed along the road with renewed energy. She threw her pillowcase over her shoulder and began to skip barefoot, singing a song about a happy wanderer. It was a fine beginning to a new day.

Before long, Carolina's stomach was tight as a fist and she was losing steam. Visions of scrambled eggs and hash and Auntie Shen's buttered biscuits made her mouth water. Nagging thoughts tapped on her shoulder. *Nowhere to go. No one to ask for help.*

A distant sound, a sweet singing sound made Carolina stop shuffling her feet in the sand and dirt and listen. It *was* a singing voice, and it rose higher and became clearer. She'd heard that voice before. She was certain of it. Could it be? Then she saw.

Up ahead, strolling down the road right toward her was a large dark-skinned woman wearing a broad-brimmed purple hat. A swarm of children moved along with her like bees buzzing around their queen. They all were dressed in their Sunday best. Some of the children were laughing and chasing each other. Some of the children were singing along. At that moment, Carolina believed in miracles. The queen bee was Miss Ruby. Her voice was rising and falling in rhythm and harmony.

"Miss Ruby!"

Carolina ran down the road toward them, her pillow-case thumping against her shoulder as she cried out Miss Ruby's name.

"Carolina Campbell, is that you, child?"

Carolina stood in the middle of the road with a grin from ear to ear.

"Yes, ma'am, it's me."

"My . . . my . . . my," said Miss Ruby, speaking in a soft slow voice.

Carolina melted into big loving arms. Miss Ruby's hug felt like going home.

"What are you doing all by your lonesome in this neck of the woods?" asked Miss Ruby, eyeing the sack flung over Carolina's shoulder.

"It's a long story," said Carolina.

"Well, you've got all evening to tell it," said Miss Ruby. "Come on. The family is putting out Sunday supper. We're having a celebration."

"What are you celebrating?"

Miss Ruby told Carolina that the minister had announced that Martin Luther King Jr. was doing his very best in Washington, and they were all praying that President Johnson would sign the Civil Rights Act and make it law.

"Things are going to be different now," said Miss Ruby, and then she lifted her face to Heaven and practically sang the words. "Oh yes. You wait and see."

Carolina realized she'd been in this neighborhood before, with Mattie. Sure enough, Miss Ruby and Carolina and all the other children walked together down the road to a small brick house that belonged to Miss Ruby's eldest son. Several cars were parked out front, and Miss Ruby's family was taking up every bit of grass in the backyard.

"Hey, everybody!" Miss Ruby yelled. "Y'all remember Mattie's friend, Carolina?"

"Oh yes, I remember Carolina," said one of Mattie's aunts. "How are you? I bet you're missing Mattie. We sure do."

"Yes, ma'am, I do. I miss her something awful," said Carolina.

Mattie's aunts hummed gospel songs as they placed tablecloths on folding tables, continuing their rejoicing from the morning church service. Men gathered in groups, talking and smoking. Conversation was centered on one thing—civil rights.

Carolina helped Mattie's aunts set out platters of food while Mattie's uncles set out lawn chairs. It was a gathering much like Mattie's birthday party. There was a pig turning on the spit. There was corn roasting on the husk right in the fire. There was potato salad and cornmeal hush puppies and pie—lots of pie. Blackberry pie, strawberry pie, and sweet potato pie all made their way over Carolina's taste buds and into her happy bulging stomach. The only thing missing was Mattie, and her absence left a hole that neither food nor singing could fill.

The voices of the men got near to shouting as they talked about the violence breaking out all over the South and the need to stand up for their rights. The women had their own discussions going on about the right and wrong of fighting as they washed up dishes right in the yard in a big tub of soapy water. As Carolina rinsed dishes in a second bucket full of clear water, she listened to the conversations and heard stories of cruelty and prejudice. She was suddenly fearful, waiting for blame to be thrown at her because of her white skin. Her mind was quickly put back at ease. Mattie's aunts couldn't thank her enough for helping, and then Mattie's cousins begged her to come play hide-and-seek.

When the sun was still shining hot, Mattie's aunts started rounding up their children. The older ones complained, and the littlest ones reached up for Miss Ruby's hugs and kisses, then landed on their daddies' shoulders. Miss Ruby's suitcase was put in the trunk of her son's car, and when he drove her home, Miss Ruby made sure Carolina was sitting right beside her.

For a long while, they drove west on a two-lane highway while the glaring rays shone through the windshield. Carolina smiled when she saw the mountains come into view. They traveled north along the Blue Ridge Parkway, with the sun to their left, and finally they were headed down a familiar dirt road. The road was so rough it felt as if they were driving over an old washboard.

Miss Ruby lived at the far end of an abandoned cow pasture, down in the holler near the edge of a swift-moving stream. This was a familiar place, and Carolina's worries cleared away like the sun had cleared away last night's rain.

Miss Ruby's cabin had a low sloping roof, a stone chimney off to one side, and a solid front porch that spanned the entire front of the cabin. That was where they stood as they both waved good-bye to Miss Ruby's son as he drove away. Then Miss Ruby went inside to change out of her Sunday clothes.

Carolina hung her legs over the tire swing and leaned her head on the rope. She remembered a time when

Mattie's uncle had pushed Mattie and her so high on this swing they had kicked the leaves in the branch above. She swatted a mosquito. It left a blood mark on her arm.

Miss Ruby had changed into an old housedress. She fell into her rocking chair on the porch with a tired sigh, and Carolina slid off the swing. She sat beside her, leaning her back against the house.

"It's gettin' late," said Miss Ruby.

Carolina stretched her legs out straight across the floorboards.

"Yes, ma'am," she replied.

She avoided Miss Ruby's gaze by examining three new scabs on her legs and figured she must have gotten scraped on the maple branch this morning. Morning seemed like a hundred years ago.

"I received a letter from Mattie's daddy. He says they're doing fine, says his new job is hard but good, and says Mattie took a swim in the ocean."

"The ocean? Mattie?" Carolina had begged Mattie to swim in the deep part of the creek and she refused. Now she was swimming in the ocean.

"Lots of changes," said Miss Ruby.

"Yes, ma'am," replied Carolina.

Miss Ruby rocked back and forth.

"I expect your Auntie Shen is worrying about you," she said.

"Yes, ma'am," said Carolina. "I'm worrying about her too."

The floorboards creaked under Miss Ruby's chair.

Miss Ruby's face held an intent expression, as if she was trying to make a decision. Carolina tried not to stare.

Finally Miss Ruby said, "It seems you'll be spending the night. We can put those sheets on the bed. They've been hanging on the line since I left to visit my son two weeks ago. Guess they're good and dry." Miss Ruby laughed.

So that's why she wasn't home, thought Carolina.

"How about we get a bath going? Your feet are black with dirt, and I won't have you putting them between my clean sheets."

They grabbed two metal buckets and headed down to the stream. Carolina stood ankle deep and held her bucket with a firm grip as the current rushed in. Water sloshed over the side as she struggled to carry it back to the house.

They poured the water into a big claw-foot tub. After the third trip, Carolina's dirty feet had made muddy footprints all over the damp floor. Miss Ruby took the water she'd heated on the woodstove and poured it into the cold water. Steam rose up. She eased down onto her knees and leaned over the tub, stirring with a washcloth in a large figure eight. She leaned her hand against the tub as she struggled to rise, and then pulled a curtain across the doorway.

Carolina had her privacy. She peeled off her dirty clothes and stepped over the side of the tub. The water made her toes pink, and she gasped each time she sank a little lower, letting the hot water creep up her back. Finally she sank down until water covered her whole body like a warm blanket.

Carolina soaked until the water had cooled so much it made her shiver.

"There's a clean nightgown hanging over the chair. Just reach around the curtain and grab it," yelled Miss Ruby, "and for Heaven's sake, put something on your feet. You can wear Mattie's old sneakers that she left here. I've washed them up good."

Carolina pulled on Miss Ruby's nightgown and it fell over her body and landed in a heap on the floor. When she buttoned it up, it slid off only one shoulder. It was good enough. Carolina slipped her feet into Mattie's sneakers and wiggled her big toe that was sticking out of the hole. They fit nearly perfect.

Miss Ruby and Carolina gathered up the sheets from the clothesline. The moon was almost as full as the night before. Carolina had to wrap Miss Ruby's nightgown around herself three times, and with the wind picking up, it billowed out about as much as the sheets. Miss Ruby laughed and shook her head. Carolina laughed too. She knew she must look pretty funny. She opened her arms wide and let the nightgown fill like sails.

Carolina had never seen Miss Ruby climb up into the loft, but this night she made the effort. By the time they had finished making up the bed, beads of perspiration lined her curly hair like pearls. Carolina slid between the sheets, crisp from drying in the sun and filled with the sweet scent of river birch.

Under the spell of Miss Ruby's warm and gentle hand, Carolina felt the tensions of the last few weeks drain out of her. Miss Ruby brushed her hand over Carolina's temples and smoothed the hair back from her forehead. Carolina felt a fearsome tiredness taking hold.

Darkness settled down around the house as they talked

about Mattie and why her daddy had to move the family away. Miss Ruby said a man had to provide for his family. She said he had to go where the work was.

"Now it's time for you to tell me why you're roaming all over tarnation," said Miss Ruby in a gentle voice. "Did you and your Auntie Shen have a fight?"

"A fight? Lordy, no!" Carolina exclaimed with surprise. She told the story from the beginning.

Miss Ruby shook her head and said, "Times used to be we'd tend to our own here in these mountains. Land sakes, child, I have a bed right here you can sleep in."

Carolina thought about the sheriff's sarcastic smile. She didn't dare mention it, for it would have hurt Miss Ruby's feelings. She did tell her how Reverend Sanctem scared her and how it made her stomach hurt when he sat close. She told Miss Ruby that he preached about loving your neighbor, but he seemed to be aggravated with just about everyone.

"Some peoples got mean blood," Miss Ruby said, and then without missing a beat she filled Carolina's heart with glad feelings. "You're staying right here until your Auntie Shen gets on her feet again. She's got good reason to get better. She's got you."

Miss Ruby's body made a deep indention in the mattress. Carolina rolled into it, settling onto her soft comfortable lap. Miss Ruby smelled like sweet butter on warm bread.

"Miss Ruby?"

"Yes, child."

"Mattie is my *best* friend. She truly is."

Speaking this truth released the hook that had been pinching her heart.

"I know that she is," said Miss Ruby.

"I love you, Miss Ruby," said Carolina.

"My, my, you are a precious child," said Miss Ruby.

Carolina could hardly stay awake during evening prayers, what with her eyes closed and all, but she caught the last of Miss Ruby's words.

"Thank you, Lord, for every good blessing on this day. In times of poverty, in times of weakness, thank you, Lord, for watching over us. I thank you, Lord, for taking the bad into your mighty hands and creating a miracle."

Carolina was thankful for the miracle too. She drifted off to sleep, listening to Miss Ruby's soft prayerful conversation with God.

Yeast bread rising in the oven brought joy to the morning. The aroma stirred Carolina from sleep, and she nearly floated on it down from the loft. Flour covered the kitchen table. Miss Ruby poured Carolina a tall glass of milk and buttered a thick slice of warm bread.

"Mmmm," said Carolina.

"Wait until you taste the pie," said Miss Ruby with a wide smile.

"I love pie," Carolina said. Her eyes fell on a bowl full of wild raspberries.

"Would you like to try your hand at rolling out this crust?" asked Miss Ruby.

"Yes, ma'am."

Miss Ruby laid her large hardworking hands on top of Carolina's. Together they pushed the rolling pin back and forth, lifting up at the edges.

"Uh-huh. Yes. That's the way. Oh, you're getting it now," said Miss Ruby.

"Is this big enough?" asked Carolina.

"Oh yes! It'll make a fine crust," said Miss Ruby.

Miss Ruby lifted the dough and placed it into a pie plate. She held the bowl of raspberries, and Carolina guided them as they tumbled onto the dough.

"That's enough," said Miss Ruby. "We'll eat the rest while we wait."

She opened a window to let some of the oven heat escape.

"Oh my." Miss Ruby's words were drawn out like a low whistle.

Carolina squeezed into the space under Miss Ruby's arm to get a look at what was outside. The sheriff's police cruiser was slowly making its way up the dirt road. She saw the red light on the roof, set there like a plump cherry. Miss Ruby and Carolina sprang into action.

Carolina hid in an old wooden icebox that had been taking up space on the porch. Squeezed into a space no larger than a cupboard, she wished she had taken off into the woods instead. She held her knees tight to her chest and listened.

Carolina heard meanness in the sheriff's voice as he spoke to Miss Ruby.

"I'm here to fetch the Campbell girl."

"Campbell girl? I don't know nothin' about a Campbell girl."

"Ruby, I know she's here," he said, practically growling, and then his voice got all casual-like. "Hear tell your son Cletus was by this way yesterday. Heard he had an extra passenger."

Carolina imagined he was putting on his sarcastic smile again.

"Sheriff, I'm baking a raspberry pie," said Miss Ruby in an easy voice, changing the subject. "I'd be happy to dish out a nice fat slice for you."

Carolina couldn't believe her ears. How long did Miss Ruby think she could stay squished up like this?

"Thank you kindly. Don't mind if I do," said the sheriff. "I'll just have a look around while I wait for that pie."

Carolina pressed her ear against the wood. It was quiet. Her legs were starting to ache from being squeezed up like a bundle of sticks. She shifted her body.

"Sounds like you got a raccoon in that old icebox," said the sheriff.

She felt the vibration of his heavy footsteps as he crossed the porch.

"Oh yes, I have been having a terrible problem with raccoons—skunks too," said Miss Ruby. "Oh yes, especially skunks. Don't go poking about, Sheriff. You better be careful. That skunk will spray you good. I'm telling you, you don't want to open that door."

The icebox door flung open and Carolina tumbled out with Miss Ruby's white nightgown heaped around her.

"Yep, looks like a skunk all right," said the sheriff.

The sheriff stood over her, his hands folded on his belly, and he was smiling as if he'd been declared the big winner at hide-and-seek.

"Go ahead. Git in the car," he said.

Carolina scrambled up and ran to Miss Ruby's side.

"No, I won't go."

The sheriff looked at Carolina as if she'd gone crazy. He shook his head.

"Little girl, this ain't nothin' but a Nigra shack. Go ahead now. Git in the car."

"No, I'm not going."

She put her arms as far around Miss Ruby's waist as she could and held fast.

The sheriff lost his patience as fast as a blue tick hound dog catches the scent, and Carolina and Miss Ruby were like a couple of coons caught up in a tree. They fought as best they could, but in the end, Carolina was stuck in the backseat of the cruiser.

Carolina turned around and waved to Miss Ruby out the rear window. She waved and waved until the cruiser rounded a bend and Miss Ruby disappeared from sight.

So much for my miracle, Carolina thought.

Chapter 8

YELLOW MUSTANG

"That was a foolhardy stunt you pulled, little girl," the sheriff said, eyeing Carolina in the rearview mirror. Carolina saw his eyes in the reflection. She pulled at her shorts. They were sticking to her. Miss Ruby had had to pull them off the clothesline still wet.

"I've known Reverend Sanctem for years," continued the sheriff, "and it was a decent thing he did, taking you in." He shook his head, "Running away to repay him. Shameful. Just shameful."

Carolina figured Reverend Sanctem would have her reciting so many Bible verses she'd have the whole New Testament memorized by next week.

"I don't want to go back there," said Carolina.

"Well, today's your lucky day," the sheriff said sarcastically. "They don't want you back."

"Am I going to jail?" Carolina asked.

"No, you're not going to jail," said the sheriff, "but I got to take you to the police station down near Hucklebee. They're the ones to figure this out—got one of them social service agencies down there—new laws concerning these things . . . darn if I know what it's about."

At the police station, Carolina sat in a folding wooden chair against the wall and waited. She listened to the whirr of a big circular fan. She was thinking about how the sheriff had said today was her *lucky* day. She watched the clock tick away the seconds and the minutes and the hours. Her stomach growled.

Finally a police officer tapped her on the knee.

"Hey there, Carolina," he said. "My name's Bobby. How y'all doing today?"

He stood there grinning, as if she'd been waiting there all day just for him. His uniform had been ironed so well that creases ran in straight vertical lines down his arms and down his legs. He didn't look at all like the sheriff. He had blond hair cut short and a big white smile.

"It's time to head out," Bobby said.

Carolina figured she didn't have a choice. She was bored to death anyway. She picked up her lumpy pillowcase. Bobby held the door open for her. She plodded past him.

Out on the sidewalk, heat rose up in ripples. The sun

was at high noon and beating down on the buildings and the street and the cars. Every person who walked by had a washed-out look, as if they wouldn't mind being wrung out like a wet rag. Carolina stood next to the back door of the police cruiser.

"Aw, you don't have to ride in the back. You ain't no criminal," he said.

He opened the passenger-side door and Carolina plopped down on the seat. He put her pillowcase in the back and slammed both doors shut. As he pulled the cruiser away from the curb, she leaned her head against the window.

"Is that your stomach I hear?" he said.

He opened the glove compartment and pulled out a bag of potato chips.

"It ain't much, but it might hold you over till we get there," he said.

Carolina munched one chip after another with barely a breath in between.

"There's a big carnival going on this weekend," he said. "You like carnivals?"

Carolina stared straight ahead. Bobby talked a blue streak.

"I plan to win a big stuffed animal for my girlfriend. Let me tell you, she is something special. She's going to school right now in Knoxville. Vivi's Beauty School."

Carolina tore the bag down the side. She wet her finger with spit to make it sticky and stuck it in the salty crumbs.

Bobby kept talking. "She's studying to be a beautician.

One day she's going to open her own *salon*. That's what she calls a beauty shop. She will too. She's *ambitious*."

Carolina licked the crumbs that were stuck to her finger.

"I tell you what," said Bobby, "we can listen to the radio." He turned the round silver knob. "Here's the station I like. WCHQ plays all the good songs."

"Chapel of Love" was playing. To her surprise, Bobby started to sing in a soft voice.

> "Goin' to the chapel
> and we're . . . gonna get maaarried."

He had a pretty good singing voice. When the DJ played the Beatles hit "Can't Buy Me Love," Carolina joined in. It was the first time she'd heard it, but it didn't matter. She had a knack for picking up lyrics.

When the song ended, an advertisement for shampoo came on. Carolina leaned back in the seat and propped her feet up on the dashboard.

"You don't look anything like a police officer," she said.

Bobby tapped her legs, and she put them back on the floor.

"What's a police officer look like, then?" he asked.

"Well, I never saw one as skinny as you," she said. "Plus you got nice teeth. I've never seen that either."

Bobby laughed hard.

It had been a long time since Carolina listened to Top 40 radio. There were so many new hits. She loved every one. Bobby and Carolina sang at the top of their lungs. They belted out "Surfer Girl" and "Leader of the Pack."

Sometimes Bobby didn't know the lyrics, so he made up his own. He got downright silly. Carolina started making up silly lyrics too, and before long they were both laughing and having a good time.

Her singing faded out midchorus when Bobby pulled onto a neighborhood street, slowed the cruiser, and started counting house numbers. Carolina felt a stomachache coming on.

"One forty-four, one forty-six, one forty-eight Maple Avenue," he said, pulling the cruiser to the curb. "We're here," he said.

The house at 148 Maple Avenue was tall, thin, and green, with long windows. It was what Auntie Shen would call a snugger house. Carolina figured a kid could throw a ball through the window of one house and have it land on the floor of the one next door.

Bobby pushed open the metal gate. The broken latch fell onto the sidewalk with a clink. He picked it up and tried to reattach it, then gave up and hooked it on the chain-link fence. Carolina took back all her good thoughts about him and walked right past, refusing to look in his direction.

She'd once read a story about a black knight forcing a peasant girl to the guillotine. The sad and pitiful story played out in her head as she dragged her feet up the cement steps, as if she was about to have her head chopped off. After pretending to be her friend, Bobby was leading her to her doom.

He leaned way down to talk to her. Bobby sure was a tall man.

"Miss Lily Jean takes care of lots of kids. You'll have a good time here."

He put his hand gently on Carolina's shoulder. She shrugged it off.

A yellow Mustang cruised down the street, its radio blaring. The group Peter & Gordon was singing.

I don't care what they say, I won't stay
In a world without love.

The words to the song played over and over in her head as the butterflies in her chest bumped into each other.

Miss Lily Jean started gushing the moment she opened the door. She had bleached-blond hair teased up like a bird's nest.

"Well, look at you," Miss Lily Jean practically squealed. "I love these long braids you have. I love your red hair too. Well, actually that color would be called auburn, wouldn't it? I dyed my hair red once, but it didn't suit me. Oh, and don't you have the greenest eyes. Look at those cute little freckles."

The woman had on a tight dress that showed off her bosoms. She spoke to Bobby in the same sickening way the girls in her class talked to the boys they liked. When Bobby and Miss Lily Jean got to the part about her being an orphan, Carolina turned up the volume in her head and tried to get the song to drown out their words.

Bobby leaned down and spoke into Carolina's ear. "Y'all take care of yourself."

Carolina turned away from him and walked into the house.

Miss Lily Jean gushed her good-byes and waved to Bobby, wiggling her fingers in the air. When she stepped inside and tugged on Carolina's arm, moving her out of the way, Carolina knew that all this woman's niceties were just pretend. She figured Miss Lily Jean had been last in line when God had handed out manners.

"Every kid is shy when they first get here. You'll get used to things quick enough. Come on. You'll want to know where you're sleeping."

Miss Lily Jean's rear end swayed back and forth like a clock pendulum as she headed up the stairs. Carolina plodded up behind her, stepping over a stack of magazines, a sock, and a naked Barbie doll with no head. Miss Lily Jean entered the room directly at the top of the stairs.

There were three beds. On two of the beds, blankets were jumbled up with the sheets. Pajamas were thrown into the mix. The third bed had no sheets or covers. The bare mattress was piled with toys and coloring books. With one quick swipe of her arm, Miss Lily Jean brushed everything off onto the floor. She fished around in a closet, brought out a sheet, and handed it to Carolina.

"This bed is yours. Toys are for everybody. I don't want to hear no fighting," she said. "The other kids are out playing, but they'll be back."

She grabbed Carolina's pillowcase, took a quick peek inside, and tossed it on the bed. When she left the room, Carolina sat down at the edge of the bed and stared at the mess of toys and papers strewn across the floor. A T-shirt hung off an opened bureau drawer. A calendar had been drawn on the wall with crayon. It seemed February would be displayed in bright purple crayon all year long. Beyond the long narrow window she saw rooftop after rooftop with only a thin slice of sky above it all.

She got down on her belly and pushed her pillowcase all the way to the wall under the bed. Leaving the sheet lying on the bed, she quietly stepped downstairs and followed the sound of laughter. It was coming from the living room. It was coming from a television set. The sound blared and a picture played, even though no one was watching.

The only time Carolina had seen a television show was when her mama had taken her shopping down in Boone. The latest models of RCA television sets were all lined up in the appliance store window. Each one had played the same moving picture, and she'd been captivated by them.

Carolina sat cross-legged on a braided rug in front of the television set and watched the picture show. There was a horse standing at a stable door. The horse was talking. His owner talked with him. The story was about the horse and man keeping it secret that the horse could talk. The black-and-white picture show changed and a commercial came on showing a woman all dressed up, as if she was going to a party, only she was washing clothes and smiling real big, as if that box of laundry detergent was something she'd always wanted. Then the horse was back.

At school, the kids had talked about their favorite television shows. Carolina figured the horse was Mr. Ed. After *Mister Ed* a cartoon came on. It was called *The Flintstones*. Then a commercial came on with a funny bird wanting a cereal called Cocoa Puffs. A loud commotion in the kitchen grabbed Carolina's attention.

A group of kids, hot and sweaty from playing outside, were taking turns at the sink filling a glass from the faucet and guzzling down the water. Carolina peeked at them from the doorway. All eyes turned toward her.

The tall boy wearing dungarees and a plaid shirt eyed Carolina up and down.

"Who are you?" he asked.

"Who are you?" Carolina repeated in the same rude tone of voice.

"I'm Pammy." A skinny girl with stringy brown hair looked up at Carolina with her eyes big and full of playful delight. She had on bright yellow shorts with grass stains all over them. "I'm in fourth grade. What grade are you in?" She gave Carolina a sweet smile.

Before Carolina could answer, the tall boy knocked Pammy in the back of the head with the palm of his hand. "You're not going into fourth grade," he said with a sneer. "You stayed back, remember?"

"Oh, I forgot." Pammy stared down at her hands and started picking at tiny patches of pink polish on her nails.

"I'm Joey," piped up the other boy. "I'm a foster kid like them, but Russell is Miss Lily Jean's nephew. He gets away with murder."

Carolina looked over at the tall boy.

"Don't look at me," he said, "my name's Buck."

Long after dark, after the last time Miss Lily Jean had yelled at everyone to be quiet, Carolina pulled a blanket up around her neck. She still had all her clothes on. She wondered when the girl who slept in the bed next to Pammy was coming back. Carolina had learned that some kids actually got to leave to visit their parents. It didn't make sense. Why had they left home in the first place?

With her eyes shut, she listened to Pammy. She was whimpering. It reminded Carolina of a little kitten mewing. Pammy sniffled in between tears.

Carolina slipped out from under the blanket and sat on the edge of Pammy's bed.

"It'll be all right," Carolina said. As she patted Pammy's back, she hoped it was true.

All night long springs poked up through Carolina's mattress and jabbed her in the ribs. She'd finally fallen asleep when an argument broke out in the house next door, and it woke her up as bad as a nightmare. She lay there staring at the ceiling, listening to their voices rise and fall as they pitched into each other. She hugged her mama's pillow and breathed in the scent. She couldn't smell her mama anymore, not even if she closed her eyes and thought hard. It smelled like road dirt.

At early dawn Carolina was up for good. She wanted to see the stars. She tiptoed out of the room, crept down the dark stairs, and slipped out the back door. She leaned her head way back. The skies were all clouded up.

Carolina sat on the cement stoop with her head in her hands. A building down the street had a neon sign that was blinking on and off. A palm tree and the words BLUE MOON lit up in bright green and blue light. Then the sign went dark. Then it blinked on again. Buck said that building was a bar. He'd bragged that he'd walked right in once. *Nobody said nothin'*, he'd said.

"Hey," a voice whispered.

Carolina jumped. A boy stepped out of the shadows.

"What are you doing up so early?" he asked.

"Nothing," said Carolina.

"Well, come on, then," he said.

The boy wasn't much older than Carolina. He had dark curly hair and his cheeks dimpled up when he smiled at her. He had showed up long after supper, long after the fight broke out over the last hot dog and the last spoonful of potato salad, long after Miss Lily Jean picked up the paper plates and shoved them into the garbage. The boy held out his hand.

"C'mon," he said. "There's a pretty place down by the river I want to show you."

Carolina put her hands in her pockets.

"C'mon, please," he said, and he smiled. "You'll like it. I promise."

He climbed up the chain-link fence and hopped to the other side.

Desire comes in all shapes and sizes, and right at that moment, climbing over that fence was Carolina's heart's desire—just the right shape and just the right size. As she dropped down to the other side, she felt different, felt as if she was taking charge.

"Hi, I'm Russell," he said, and extended his hand.

It seemed he had no intention of putting his hand back down until she shook it, so she did. "I'm Carolina."

He gave her hand a hearty shake.

"Let's go," he said.

He cut through several backyards and across many streets until they were on the edge of town. Broken pieces of equipment from an old factory were scattered along an embankment that led down to a swift-moving river. They made their way along a pathway bordered by birch saplings. Patches of yellow buttercups bloomed amid beer bottles, candy wrappers, and rusty cans. White water rushed over a concrete dam.

"So, what do you think?" Russell asked.

"It's nice," she said. She was being polite. Nothing could compare to the streams of her mountain home.

Russell picked a tiny buttercup. "If you put a buttercup under your chin and it shines, it means you like butter," he said.

"I know," said Carolina.

"Let me see for sure," he said.

Carolina looked up and saw the sun coming up over the horizon. Russell held the buttercup beneath her chin. "I can't tell," he said.

"It works better when the sun is shining," said Carolina.

"Okay, we'll come back later on today," said Russell.

Carolina smiled.

The promise of friendship was as welcome as the first rays of light. Carolina loved the curls in Russell's hair and the way he sauntered along, whistling a tune, like he didn't have a care in the world.

"So you're the new kid," said Russell.

She nodded her head.

"It stinks living there," he said. "My aunt is a nutcase. But don't pay her no mind. I've got her in the palm of my hand."

They came to a hill formed by chunks of cement, and Russell scrambled to the top.

He put his hands on his waist and began to imitate his aunt.

"Now, you kids be quiet. Go out and play." He began to sway his hips back and forth. "I'm trying to watch my soap opera."

Carolina could not stop the grin that crept up her cheeks. Russell seemed inspired by it. He continued to imitate every kid in the house until Carolina was laughing out loud.

Feeling hungry, they decided to head back to the sticky-up house. Everyone else was still asleep when they got there. Russell poured cornflakes into two huge bowls. He opened the drawer without making it squeak and grabbed two spoons. Then he took the container of milk out of the icebox. He motioned for her to follow with a nod of his head.

Sitting on the grass in the backyard, Carolina shoveled the cereal into her mouth. At last night's supper table, she hadn't grabbed food fast enough, and now she was starving. She put the cereal bowl to her chin and drank the sweetened milk.

"Want to play a game?" Russell asked.

He stood up and casually pulled a knife out of his pocket. He flipped it into the air with a twist of his wrist and caught it by the handle.

"What kind of game?" Carolina asked. She'd had plenty of tricks played on her by the boys at school, and she was already feeling suspicious.

"It's called Dare," he said. "Stand here, with your feet together, like this."

Carolina faced him and placed her feet the same as Russell. He threw the knife down. It stuck into the ground only two inches away from her big toe that was sticking out of Mattie's sneaker.

"Okay, now you try," Russell said.

Carolina picked up the knife. The blade came up to a silver point. She ran her finger over it and gasped as a tiny dot of blood grew on her finger. She looked at his feet. If she accidentally hit him, she wondered if the knife would bounce off the rubber tips of his sneakers or stick right through. She sure didn't want to be called a baby, so she held the handle with a tight grip, aimed, and threw it down. The point of the knife hit the ground three feet away from his sneakers and then fell on its side in the grass.

"Aw, let me try again," she said.

"No, you had your turn. You missed, so you have to take a step out," he said.

She placed her feet a little farther apart. With a flick of his wrist, Russell threw the knife. Whish! The blade stuck solid so that only the handle was visible in the grass.

Carolina picked up the knife. She put her fist around the handle with the blade down and aimed. Again, it landed in the grass on its side.

She stepped out again.

Russell threw. His aim was perfect.

"I bet if I ran away with a circus, I could be the knife thrower," he said.

Carolina nodded. She was reminded of another story she'd read about a circus lady who stood as relaxed as could be before a round target while a knife thrower threw knives, hitting the target between her arms and her legs and all around her head.

It was Carolina's turn. She concentrated. She threw. The knife stuck smooth and solid into the ground right beside Russell's sneaker. She smiled. Now the game was getting to be fun.

"What are you kids doing out there?" Miss Lily Jean was standing at the back door in her bathrobe and with a mess of curlers in her hair. "Get in here."

Russell gave Carolina the go-ahead with a nod. She glanced down, but the knife was no longer in the grass. She hadn't even seen Russell stoop to pick it up, but she knew he had.

A loud commotion was breaking out in the kitchen. Pammy was crying because Joey had pulled her hair. Buck was accusing Joey of eating all the cornflakes. Miss Lily Jean was at the stove, scrambling eggs in a skillet. She didn't even turn around. Carolina and Russell rushed through.

In the living room, Russell turned the knob of the television set from channel to channel. One station was showing pictures of soldiers running through jungles, and then the picture changed and a general was talking to some of the soldiers who'd been hurt. Russell sat close, listening intently to every word.

Miss Lily Jean waltzed right in and turned the channel.

"I already told you not to watch this stuff, Russell," she said. "It'll make you feel bad."

She turned the station to a cartoon. Deputy Dawg was

laughing at Muskie Muskrat, saying, "Don't go away mad, Muskrat, just go away."

A few days later when they were down by the river skipping rocks, Russell told Carolina that his older brother, Randy, had joined up with the Marine Corps and was serving in Vietnam.

"Vietnam is what we were watching on the news," said Russell.

He told her how he and his brother had been shuffled between their aunts and uncles since he was five years old. He said his brother got smart and joined the service the day he turned seventeen.

"I'm not holding it against him. I'd have joined up too if I was old enough. Besides, Randy promised that as soon as he gets home, he'll be coming for me. We're going to live on our own. Nobody will tell us we can't," said Russell. "Nobody messes with a soldier."

"Where's your mother and father?" Carolina asked.

Russell's eyes flashed a dark look.

"They run off," he said.

Carolina couldn't even imagine such a thing.

Russell reached in his pocket and pulled out a pack of cigarettes. He tapped the bottom of the pack on the heel of his hand and peeled the cellophane wrapper. He pulled one of the sticks out as casually as if he'd done it every day of his life and stuck it between his lips.

"Where did you get those?" asked Carolina.

"Uncle Freddie has cartons of them," said Russell. "He won't miss one pack."

"Who's Uncle Freddie?" asked Carolina.

"Aunt Lily Jean's husband. All the kids call him Uncle, but I'm the only one actually related to him since he went and married Aunt Lily Jean. He's a traveling salesman. I expect you'll be meeting him one of these days."

Carolina caught the strong scent of tobacco the moment Russell lit the cigarette. It made her nose hairs burn. She coughed.

"All the soldiers smoke Camels," Russell said. "The filtered ones are for sissies."

Chapter 9

FOURTH OF JULY, 1964

On the Fourth of July, families in the neighborhood were having picnics. Posters were plastered on the sides of buildings all over town, announcing fireworks. To Carolina and the other kids it looked like one more hot sticky day. The red line on the thermometer rose to 100 degrees. Even the shade trees drooped.

The only fireworks they'd get to see had already happened. Miss Lily Jean had caught Russell stealing another pack of Uncle Freddie's cigarettes. She chased him around the kitchen table, holding a cast-iron frying pan over her head. Carolina thought Miss Lily Jean was mad enough to kill Russell.

Not more than an hour later, Russell surprised her with

a bouquet of garden flowers and went on and on about how they weren't nearly as pretty as she was. Miss Lily Jean gushed. Carolina and Pammy exchanged glances and rolled their eyes. Didn't Miss Lily Jean have sense enough to know that Russell had stolen those flowers from the neighbor's garden? As soon as Miss Lily Jean turned her back to get a vase, Russell whispered in Carolina's ear.

"Got her in the palm of my hand," he said.

The day dragged on. Carolina got bored watching television and went to find Pammy. She found her in Miss Lily Jean's bedroom. Pammy was leaning her elbows on the dressing table, her chin in her hands, looking on in genuine fascination. Miss Lily Jean had bleached her hair again. This time it was so blond, it was almost white. She was primping it all up into a fancy beehive style. She sent out such a mist of hair spray over it that not a single hair moved, even when the fan blew right on her. Now she was taking an eyebrow pencil and making a mark on her cheek near her nose.

"This is what the fashion magazines call a beauty mark," she said.

Carolina thought the mark should be called what it was, a brown dot that needed a washcloth. She couldn't figure why Miss Lily Jean was getting all gussied up to sit around and sweat. Then she heard a man's voice booming in the living room.

"Hello, scamps and ragamuffins!"

"Uncle Freddie!"

Carolina poked her head out of Miss Lily Jean's bedroom door. The boys were clamoring around a giant of a man, leaping into his arms like hungry puppies. *So, this is Miss Lily Jean's husband.*

Uncle Freddie's head nearly touched the ceiling. He was practically as wide as a doorway. He looked as if he could break someone with a tap of his finger, but he was acting downright silly. He laughed as the boys leaped up, grabbing candy bars out of the pocket of his shirt. Pammy shyly approached him and he reached down and tickled her.

Carolina wasn't about to climb on this giant, but she couldn't stop herself from staring. She noticed Russell didn't budge either. He stayed in the green chair in front of the television, one leg draped over the side, casually picking at the foam poking through the threadbare arms on the chair.

Miss Lily Jean strolled out of her bedroom in a tight sundress that showed off her bosoms. Uncle Freddie let out a long slow whistle.

"Well, if it isn't the gorgeous and effervescent Miss Bombshell."

Miss Lily Jean's transformation didn't end with her outfit. She had taken on a whole new personality. It was as if she was pretending to be a movie star. Carolina gawked along with the rest of the kids.

Uncle Freddie's voice boomed. "Are y'all ready to go swimming?"

The kids scrambled around so fast you'd think somebody had yelled "Fire!" In no time flat they were ready and waiting, bathing suits on, thin and ragged towels slung over their shoulders. Carolina was amazed. In this house, no one picked up after themselves. Not a single kid could bother throwing a paper plate into the garbage can, but somehow they'd all found bathing suits in the mess heaps.

Carolina stayed put. There was no reason to run around. She didn't have a bathing suit. She refused to wear the hand-me-down rags that were left from the last foster kid to come through this place. She was wearing the same shorts and the same top as the day she'd arrived.

"Here," said Miss Lily Jean as she forced a pink bundle into Carolina's hands. "This will most likely fit your skinny body."

Uncle Freddie tapped his hand to Miss Lily Jean's backside as she headed out the door. Miss Lily Jean wiggled and laughed. She turned around and blew him a kiss. It was downright pitiful.

Carolina held up the bathing suit. It was pale pink, all stretched out and faded, with little white ruffles stained yellow. Round nobbies covered the bottom. The fabric was nearly worn through in spots.

Uncle Freddie was standing by his car, a big black Cadillac. Carolina remembered Auntie Shen speaking badly about a man who once tried to cheat her. *"Nothing but a traveling salesman,"* she'd said. Auntie Shen had said that man was a *fast-talker*. Carolina had a feeling that Uncle Freddie must be one of those fast-talkers. He stood beside his big car, laughing deep from his big belly, and waved them all over as if he was transporting them to the Island of Fun.

"C'mon, y'all. Get in."

Carolina had to squeeze into the middle with Pammy because Buck and Joey had grabbed the window seats and wouldn't budge. Miss Lily Jean yelled out to Russell, who was headed down the sidewalk.

"You coming?"

Russell turned halfway around and shook his head. Miss Lily Jean looked at Uncle Freddie and shrugged her shoulders.

"It don't bother me none if he don't come," said Uncle Freddie. "He's more trouble than he's worth."

"Suit yourself!" yelled Miss Lily Jean, and then she slid over in the seat so she was squeezed up tight against Uncle Freddie.

She positioned the rearview mirror so she could see herself and then pushed her lips together as if she was about to kiss herself. She smeared bright red lipstick all over her lips, and then she smacked them together. Carolina saw Freddie touch a silver button on his door. The windows went up. The kids looked at him as if he was a magician.

"Electric windows," said Buck with genuine awe.

As the car windows went up, the cold air poured in. A hush fell over all, and for a few precious seconds there was peace. Carolina had no idea there was such a thing as an air-conditioned car. She was as grateful as the rest of them.

As the Cadillac pulled away from the curb, Carolina watched Russell heading off in the direction of the ravine, where they'd made a fort down near the cement waterfall. She was wishing she'd stayed behind too. The last thing she wanted was to be squished in the backseat of this car, no matter how cool the air felt.

They drove down a yellow-lined main road and then headed down a back road. The sign said County Road 987.

Carolina saw horses grazing in fenced pastures. She saw grandmas bent over, tending their flower gardens. Farm fields opened the view. Miss Lily Jean started tapping Uncle Freddie's arm.

"Freddie, stop. Let's get sweet corn," she said.

A large sign hung from a tree limb next to a farm stand.

Sweet Corn

Tomatoes

Peppers

The moment the car rolled to a stop, Uncle Freddie made the windows go down. Carolina reached over Joey and grabbed the door handle at the same time as Miss Lily Jean leaned in the window, giving them all the evil eye.

"Y'all wait here."

She hooked her arm into Uncle Freddie's. She hung all over him. They strolled around the farm market together, taking their sweet time.

Inside the hot Cadillac, the black seat was starting to stick to the backs of Carolina's legs.

"I need more room," Pammy whined.

"You have room," said Buck.

"I do not! You have your legs spread wide open, and we're squished," she said.

"I have to keep my legs open," Buck said. "Boys need room."

"Room for what?" asked Pammy.

It took Carolina half a second to realize he was talking about his body parts.

"That's the dumbest thing I ever heard," Carolina said.

"Who you calling dumb?" said Buck. He hauled off and socked her in the arm. Carolina socked him back in the leg.

It was as if the backseat exploded. Carolina was caught in a tangle of fists and arms. She felt the stings as she was punched and pinched. She felt a yank on her hair and thought they'd pull it right out of her head.

"Ow!" she screamed.

Carolina's fist was connecting with Buck's chin at the moment when Uncle Freddie and Miss Lily Jean reached the car. Buck pretended he was hurt bad. It was a real show. Joey sat still and quiet, as if he'd been doing nothing but polishing his halo. Miss Lily Jean glared at Carolina with a look of disgust on her face. That look was something Carolina had gotten used to, but Uncle Freddie's staring her down struck fear inside. He would have liked to kill her with that look.

Luckily, Uncle Freddie let the incident go, and they were off on the road again. Pammy was sniffling. Carolina put her arm around Pammy's shoulders and patted her knee. She could see the mountains coming into view. Her spirits lifted the more the landscape changed. As they headed down mountain roads, Freddie lowered the windows and cool breezes blew in.

Blue water glistened in the sunlight, and Carolina caught glimpses of it through the openings between branches and leaves. That lake was sparkling like diamonds and glimmering like lightning bugs. She was going swimming! Carolina could hardly wait.

The moment Freddie stopped the car, the kids fell over

one another getting out the doors. They raced down to the water. Carolina was in the lead.

"Carolina!" yelled Miss Lily Jean.

Carolina stopped dead in her tracks. She turned around. Miss Lily Jean was holding her arm out straight, that awful pink bathing suit dangling from her hand.

"Get your scrawny butt over to the ladies' room and put on this bathing suit. You want to make us all look like fools, swimming in your clothes?"

Carolina took the bathing suit, pretending she couldn't see the way Uncle Freddie was looking at her.

"Yes, ma'am."

Carolina walked to a little pavilion on the edge of the beach. The smell of charcoal and hamburgers cooking on barbecue grills mingled with the scent of clear mountain air. She walked by families seated at picnic tables. Moms and dads reached into big red ice chests and handed sandwiches to wet-haired children wrapped in towels. She saw a baby reach up to be held. She watched a father put his arm around his daughter and stroll with her down to the water.

Carolina stood in a toilet stall in the ladies' room. She looked down at the yellowed ruffles on the old bathing suit. It looked like pee. She could hardly bear to touch it. She started at the top and worked her way down to the bottom, rolling up that bathing suit tight. She tied it together with the arm straps. It made a nice firm bundle. She walked behind the building and threw the bundle as high as she could. It stuck tight between two branches and stayed there, perched like a little pink nest.

Carolina peeked around the side of the pavilion. Uncle

131

Freddie was putting an umbrella into the sand at the edge of the lake. Miss Lily Jean was putting on suntan lotion. Carolina made her way down to the strip of sandy beach. She heard Miss Lily Jean yell. *She has the eyes of a hawk,* thought Carolina.

"Carolina, don't you dare take another step!"

Miss Lily Jean was yelling so loud that folks sat up on their blankets and turned to stare. Carolina could feel their eyes glued to her back. Her first thought was to obey. Then a new thought took shape in her head. It began and ended with Russell. He never did as he was told and he was never punished. Miss Lily Jean would never take out the belt on a crowded beach. *If Russell was here, he wouldn't listen. He'd run to the water and Miss Lily Jean wouldn't do a thing.*

Carolina looked straight ahead, her heart beating faster. Her feet took off, as if they were trying to catch up. Carolina ran across the sand. Her feet kicked up sand and then her toes hit water. She ran until water splashed up onto her shorts, and then she dove under.

Aaahhh!

Beneath the water she was free. Carolina kicked her legs out and back like a frog, propelling her body forward. She broke through the surface with a happy grin on her face. She began to wake up her swimming muscles. First the crawl, then the backstroke. She swam out until she couldn't touch bottom and then casually moved her arms and legs, treading water, looking across the wide blue lake at the trees and rocks rising up the mountainside. She looked back at the families and blankets stretched along the beach.

Uncle Freddie was standing at the edge of the water. He had on a pair of bright red swimming trunks. His face was flushed to match. He was looking out over that great expanse of water, and his eyes were locked on Carolina. Miss Lily Jean was standing beside him, waving her hands and arms like a wild puppet. Whatever she was saying did the trick. Uncle Freddie entered the water like a mighty giant.

"Oooh, you're in trouble!" Buck and Joey yelled.

They swam closer. They wanted a good look. Carolina felt her arms and legs turning to rubber. Uncle Freddie's big legs splashed water high into the air as he stomped through. Carolina got her arms moving and headed into deeper water. There was no way she'd let Buck and Joey see her get dragged out and beaten. Between strokes, she glanced back. Uncle Freddie's arms were slapping at the water.

Carolina switched to the breaststroke. Her arms pumped. She could feel the energy moving through her like tadpoles darting through her veins.

Stroke, stroke, stroke—breath. Stroke, stroke, stroke—breath. She was more than halfway across the lake, and Uncle Freddie was still on the chase. Breathless, she switched to the crawl, pushing through the water, fear driving her on. She dove under and swam until her lungs felt as if they'd burst. She rose up, gasping for air.

Uncle Freddie had turned around and was swimming back to shore. She could see he was struggling, slowly making his way. Carolina stayed on course, swimming to the opposite shore until she could touch bottom.

Tall spikes of grass grew up through the shallow water. She scrambled up onto a beach full of pebbles. She made her way over sticks and stones and hid in the cover of trees. She crouched down low and looked out over the lake, her chest rising and falling as she caught her breath.

She looked over her shoulder at what was behind her. It was a rough terrain of tall trees and steep mountainside chunked with ledge and boulder croppings. The only human sound was her own breathing.

Chapter 10

LOST IN THE WILDERNESS

As the day wore on and shadows lengthened, the fear of being punished was replaced with the fear of being left alone. *Is Miss Lily Jean just going to leave me here?* Carolina sat on a log and buried her feet in the sand. Water gently lapped at her ankles.

Two snapping turtles were doing a mating dance out in the lake water. Their wrinkled necks stretched out long, snapping at each other. Carolina tossed a handful of pebbles and sand into the water just beyond her toes and watched the surface prick up and move out in ever-widening circles.

Mosquitoes buzzed in her ears. She slapped at her arms and legs.

"Law, can't you skeeters leave a little meat on my bones?"

Carolina imagined hamburgers cooking on fire pits across the lake. It made her mouth water. Should she swim back? The lake seemed so much wider than it did before. Did she dare swim past the snapping turtles?

As nighttime approached the sun perched itself on the mountaintop. Carolina stood on the pebble-strewn shoreline and looked out over water smooth as a black mirror. It reflected light from an orange sun in a wide band that stretched across the water. Amber glows, campfires, began to dot the beach on the opposite shore. She imagined families spreading out blankets and opening bags of potato chips and bottles of Coke as they waited for fireworks. She scratched at red welts on the back of her neck and swatted another mosquito. *Nobody is coming for me!*

One by one the stars came out, reflected in the water like tiny sparks. Darkness closed in around her. *She isn't coming.* A sudden chill made her shiver.

Suddenly there was a loud pop and whoosh, and a burst of light shot straight up into the starry heavens. Gold light glittered and cascaded down in a waterfall of sparkles.

Fireworks!

Whoosh. Up it went. Red and green sparkles fell in a celestial umbrella. Kaboom. It was loud as a gunshot. The sound rumbled against the mountains like thunder.

Oohs and aahs from the crowd echoed across the water. Carolina felt surrounded by a strange and empty silence. The spaces beside her where her mama and daddy should have been were barren. Instead of hearing her daddy's exuberant whoops and hollers, she heard tree frogs croak.

Instead of eating hot dogs and Good & Plenty candy, she felt hunger like a tight fist squeeze her belly. Instead of swirling a lit sparkler round and round, pretending to write her name, she swatted mosquitoes.

Grand finale! Streams of red, green, gold, and silver sparkles filled the sky, followed by explosions loud as cannonballs—boom, boom, boom, boom, boom, boom, boom. Smoke heavy with the scent of gunpowder drifted thick as fog over the water.

Across the lake, the taillights of cars were quickly disappearing. Carolina willed the last to stay and then watched as it too slipped into darkness. She was alone.

The lake before her was black and cold. The forest behind her was dark and deep.

A horde of mosquitoes descended upon her as if she was fresh meat. Carolina swatted and waved her arms. In desperation, she escaped into the trees. A pointed twig stabbed the arch of her foot. She stumbled. Reaching forward to stop her fall, she felt sharp thorns cut into her hand.

A loud screech pierced the night. *Painter cat.* Carolina's body went stiff. Her imagination conjured up Auntie Shen's stories: black panther cats seeking prey within the forest.

She heard the screech again, louder this time. A tremor raced down her spine.

She nestled up close to the trunk of a tree and wrapped her arms around her knees.

She wished for the safe covering of a tent that separated her from raccoons and bears. She wanted her flashlight.

She'd always kept it under her pillow when she'd camped with her mama and daddy, her sleeping bag tucked close to theirs.

Carolina curled up like a baby and barely breathed. Katydids, crickets, frogs, and other critters filled the night with their sounds. The moon was a silver crescent nestled into the stars.

She was awakened by something brushing her arm. She jerked her head up.

"Get away!" she called out.

Light was dawning in a gray haze. She could barely make out forms and shapes. Rubbing the crick in her neck, she tried to remember when she had fallen asleep. A shiver brought goose bumps to her arms.

She walked to the edge of the lake and peered through the mist. There wasn't a soul in sight, not even a fisherman. She looked up. Not a star was visible through the fog.

In the woodland, soft vapors were illuminated with a mystical light. She climbed the steep rise and entered a forest of giant rhododendrons with branches thicker than her arms. She was reminded of another time when she and Auntie Shen had strolled through a magical forest like this, a day when flowers were plump as purple balls. They'd sat beneath the arching branches, pretending to be fairies.

Carolina walked through their fallen leaves, soft and decomposing, covering the ground with soft duff. Her feet sank into the layers. She hiked farther, up steep rises full of lush green plants and towering trees. As the haze burned off, sunlight weaved in and out of the trees. Carolina jumped. Down the hill, on the trunk of a redbud tree, was a shadow.

She saw the dark outline of a head and shoulders. The light drifted and the shadow disappeared. The light floated back again, and again the shadow appeared. Carolina laughed. It was *her* shadow. She jumped up and down. Her shadow jumped up and down with her. Her catbird pendant flew up and bopped her on the nose. "Ouch!" she cried out. Then she spotted a real catbird. It was jumping along the ground too, its grayish feathers blending with the sticks and brambles.

A ledge of gray rock covered with lichen and moss jutted out of a steep embankment. It was begging her to climb it. She scrambled up and over and around, exploring, then crawled beneath the rock where the soil had turned rich and black and stretched out her legs to rest.

The sound of running water coaxed her up. She scooted out from under the ledge and made her way down to where stream water flowed gently over and around pebbles and rocks. A moss-covered boulder offered a comfortable seat. She slid her feet into the shallow water. It took away the sting of cuts and scrapes, but the icy mountain water was too cool for her to linger long. She reached in with her hands and splashed water up onto her face. She remembered her daddy's warnings about safe water. She let it drain through her fingers. Thirst defied all warning. She cupped her hands and drank until she was satisfied.

Renewed energy and a bright spirit led her on. She figured she was bound to come upon a cabin tucked into a holler. She imagined coming upon a friendly farmer woman working in her orchard or garden who'd be tickled to invite her in. She would even set out a nice breakfast for Carolina.

Cheerful imaginings began to pale as the sun rose to its peak. It was already noon. Carolina continued on, trying to get her bearings. Hours passed. As the sun began its descent to the west, she feared she would be spending another night alone. *I've walked a million miles*, she thought. She hadn't seen hide nor hair of another soul. The berries she'd eaten and the Indian cucumbers she'd dug up on the forest floor did little to ease the hunger in her belly.

Carolina began searching for a piece of flint rock. *Spark to fuel equals fire.* Her daddy had taught her how to create a spark and keep it alive with a tinder ball. More than anything, Carolina wanted the warm light of a campfire.

As she was searching the ground, she caught a glimpse of something glittering on a skinny twig branch above her, and she looked closer. It was human hair. *Someone ducked beneath this branch. It pulled their hair.* She searched farther and sure enough, she found a narrow path.

It was hardly wider than a deer trail. Still, it was a path. All paths lead somewhere, she figured. Carolina forged ahead. The path did lead somewhere. It led right to a furnace. Carolina wondered if it was for boiling molasses down and imagined the taste of warm sweet brown syrup.

Sapling branches were covering most of the rock and clay furnace, as if someone was trying to hide it. It was quite a contraption. Making molasses in the middle of the woods didn't make much sense, yet Carolina's mind was focused on food. She opened one of the glass jugs filled with amber liquid and leaned her head way back, expecting a slow drizzle of syrup to coat her tongue. What hit instead burned her mouth like fire. Carolina coughed a horrible cough, as if she was about to heave her innards. She spit.

This is a still! Someone is making moonshine whiskey! Carolina figured whoever it was had been here today. The smell of fire clung to the gray ashes. Carolina poked about with a stick and saw there was still a spark of fire in that ash.

There was a mess of trash scattered about, and a ratty blanket. Carolina found an old can and then she found a shovel, not much bigger than a spade. She carefully pulled hot embers out of the fire and placed them in the can. As she was hurrying away from the site, she spotted a cooler half-buried in the leaves. Inside was a Mason jar full of water. Carolina drank it down in one long gulp. There was a wrinkled apple in the cooler, too. It was mostly rotted. She put it in her pocket, saving it for supper.

By the time she'd found a little clearing far away from the still, it was getting dark. Carolina set about making her fire. She peeled the layers off a piece of birch bark one at a time. They were thin as paper. Then she kneaded each piece in her hand until it crumpled up. After a while she had a good tinder ball.

She peered into the can at the ember. It looked cold and dry. Her heart sank.

Breathing down into the can as softly as she could, she saw the ember glow. It was still alive. Smoke came up into her face and made her cough. She blew again, and this time, quick as could be, she dropped in her tinder ball. She blew a bit more and it burst into flames.

Carolina turned the can over and dropped the tinder ball onto the tiny twigs she had set up like a tepee. She added kindling, being careful not to smother the flame. Slowly and patiently, she added more and more sticks until she had a roaring campfire.

She could practically feel her daddy's hand patting her back, praising her. Oh, how she wished he was here to see it. Carolina sat back and smiled. She'd done it.

Come morning, black clouds were gathering above the treetops. Leaves twisted on their stems in a sudden wind. She'd seen storms come up in a hurry many times before. Carolina searched the spaces between trees, looking for shelter.

A wild jagged bolt of lightning was followed by a loud crack of thunder. Carolina darted through the trees. Her feet skipped over roots and rocks as the sky broke open and rain poured down. Pelted by raindrops as big as tadpoles, she was soaked in less than a minute. Tiny streams rose out of the ground, flowing down every hill. Hard clay soil was quickly turned to red mud, slippery as oil. Water rushed and crashed in white crests down through a gorge, carving a path through rocks and dirt. Carolina spotted shelter in a hollow tree on the other side of the surging waters. If she could jump to the boulders on the other side, she'd make it.

Her eyes took aim and she leaped. Green lacy lichen covering the boulder had turned slimy, and the instant she touched down, her feet flew out from under her. She was carried by the force of the white water, sliding down on her backside past saplings and over roots. Her hands slapped against leaves and brush as she tried to grab hold. A tall straight sapling stood in the path of the water. She hit it with a thud so hard it made her teeth chatter.

Gasping at the chill of freezing mountain water surging against her back, she held tight. White-water rushes flowed over and around her legs and arms. She weathered the storm like the roots of the tree, and then the rain ended as quickly as it had started.

Carolina forced strength into her aching joints and muscles and climbed to solid ground. An underground world of thirsty roots drank the puddles, and they seeped away, drawn down into the soil. The last pitter-patters of rain fell down through the leaves. An eerie stillness was draped in soft mist.

Carolina stared into the trees. Her eyes made out a figure. It began faint as a shadow, brown and black, tall and straight. She made out shoulders and the movement of legs, a hat, arms, and then she saw the old man's face. It was a wrinkled, serious face. It was another human being. Carolina stared at the old man, who was staring back at her. He disappeared into the mist the same way he had come.

"Hey!" Carolina cried out.

"Hey!" she yelled again.

A person imagined haints, could see them as clear as

could be, but they weren't real. Ghosts, on the other hand, were very real indeed. *It's a haint,* Carolina thought, but the spooked feeling wouldn't leave.

Her throat felt scratchy. Her skin was itchy from insect bites. She figured they must have been hidden in the filthy blanket she had taken from the moonshiners. Fleas must have nibbled away at her all night.

She entered a cove, a canopy of ancient trees that reached to the sky. She leaned her head way back and looked up to the very tops of the trees. *Why, even Jack's beanstalk couldn't have been this high,* she thought. The songs of birds floated down from heavenly spheres as if they were angels. Rays of light were like tall celestial beams. Water gently trickled over rocks and leaves.

She heard men's voices. There was a loud rustling of leaves from heavy footsteps. Carolina scrambled up the hill and hid behind a wide tulip tree. She figured it must be the men coming back to check their still. She figured if they knew the way *in,* they'd know the way *out,* and she was planning to follow.

At first the men were intent on their work. They got the fire under the furnace to flame again. They were paying particular attention to a pipe that stretched out like a snake and was connected to a barrel so big that Carolina could have climbed into it.

Carolina recalled a story Auntie Shen had told about her father making whiskey in a still. She said he had a real talent for it. Back then one could make a good living by selling moonshine. Then things changed. Her father had to stop when lawmakers started putting men in jail for it.

Carolina figured that was why these men had their furnace hidden so well. They didn't want to get caught.

The contrivance they worked at was a big jumble of wood and copper and plugs. She couldn't figure why anyone would go to so much trouble to make a drink that put fire in your throat. Crouched down in her hiding spot, she watched as they worked slow and with meticulous effort filling jugs and bottles. She was growing more bored and impatient at each passing moment.

Then the "tasting" started. It got to taking up more time than it takes for bread to rise. Carolina forgot where she was and heaved a loud sigh.

"Did you hear that?" asked one man.

"Naw, I didn't hear nothin'," said the other.

"I sure don't want any trouble," said the one man.

"If it's a revenuer, he'll be the one in trouble," said the other with a chuckle.

Carolina saw him draw back his work shirt and pat a pistol.

She quickly ducked back behind the tree, and, in her rush, knocked loose a fist-sized rock. She watched in horror as it tumbled down the hill, bouncing and jumping and finally landing square on the toe of the man's work boot. The man shot up from his seat. All his "tasting" had apparently made him dizzy. Swaggering, he pulled the pistol out from his belt and fired. Carolina screamed.

Their footsteps were louder than thunder. Carolina ran as fast as her legs could carry her. Gunshot blasts echoed all around as she pelted through the trees.

A man materialized so fast she landed on his chest with

a thump. His hand covered her mouth. Her feet left the ground. She was whisked into a hollowed tree trunk. The moonshiners ran past, so close she could have reached her leg out and tripped them. Their sounds became distant, and the man let his hand off her mouth. She looked up at him.

"You're the haint," she whispered.

Hunger, thirst, and fright made her legs give way. Somewhere between awake and dreaming, she felt herself being lifted into his arms, felt leaves brushing against her, and then everything went dark. When she opened her eyes again, the old man was kneeling beside her.

"Can ya walk now?" he asked gently.

"I think so," she said.

He helped her up onto wobbly legs. Carolina cried out. Her feet were swollen and bloody. She could hardly put her weight on them.

The old man bent down and Carolina hopped on his back, and that was how they went—piggyback style.

They'd gone a long ways—miles, maybe—when the man suddenly stopped. The old man stood still as the elder trees. He tilted his head. He was listening.

"Tanager," the man said with a smile. Carolina listened. She heard the sweet song of the red bird too.

He let go of Carolina's legs, which were wrapped around his waist, and as he put his hands to his mouth Carolina clung tight to his shoulders. The man sounded out a bird call. They heard the bird call back. The old man chuckled.

They continued on until they reached a tiny cabin. It was only one room. It had a narrow bed on one side, a small table, and a chair. There was a woodstove and a metal box where he kept his food. Carolina figured it was metal to keep the mice out.

The man started mixing up something, as if he was making a potion, and then he had her hold her feet out straight. He smeared it on.

"This smells like a baby's diaper," Carolina said, holding her nose.

The man didn't say anything. After he finished smearing the goop all over her feet, he wrapped them up in strips of cloth and deerskin. When he was done, she had on something like a moccasin.

"Who are you?" she asked. "Have you been following me?"

His eyes were sunk deep into withered skin. They were blue as robin's eggs.

After a long pause, he said, "I been keepin' an eye on ya."

The man checked her feet and then tapped them with his fingers, and Carolina knew he was satisfied with his work. Then he set about putting out a simple meal of beans and corn and a cup of fresh springwater. To Carolina it was a feast. With her belly full, a fearsome tiredness came over her, making her eyelids heavy and her head start to nod. Then her head clunked down on the table next to her empty bowl, and Carolina was startled awake.

She looked out the open front door and saw the man. He was sitting on a stump with his back turned to her, just gazing out upon the forest. Carolina thought about how kind he'd been to her. She figured that referring to him as a haint was downright disrespectful. He was a gentleman.

Carolina walked around the stump and stood in front of him.

"Thank you for the meal," she said. "And thank you for these foot coverings. They fit just fine."

The old man's lips barely lifted into a smile but his eyes had a sparkle in them.

"What's a young'un doing in this wilderness?" he asked.

Carolina shrugged her shoulders. "I'm lost," she said.

"I'll help yer find your way," he said.

The old man stood up and started walking without another word. His legs were sturdy and sure as he climbed up steep and rocky slopes. Carolina followed, stepping off boulders and holding on to the thin trunks of saplings as she scrambled to keep up.

They reached a creek where tall weeds grew alongside in sandy soil. The late-day sun warmed her shoulders.

"Follow this crick," the man said. "Yer'll see a meadow. Go into it. I 'spect someone will be along directly."

Carolina looked up along the creek bed. She didn't see any path at all.

"Who will be along?"

She turned to face him, but the old man was already gone. Not even a twig had snapped. Auntie Shen had talked about mountain people who considered the wilderness their home. It was people and towns, cars and machines, that made them nervous, even scared.

Carolina made her way up along the creek. She walked along a narrow path through ferns as high as her knees and came upon another short path that ended with a crooked farm gate slumped against a tree. She stepped over it and into an open meadow.

A wild apple tree grew here and there, but otherwise it was grass and weeds. Blackberry bushes, hundreds of them, grew along a gentle slope. Carolina picked a handful of berries and gobbled them up. The first swallows of sweet juice nearly choked her. Soon her parched mouth was moistened as she picked fistfuls of berries and practically swallowed them whole. She shoved them into her mouth as fast as a country boy at a pie-eating contest. She was sure she had never tasted anything so delicious in her whole life. It seemed the last meal she'd eaten had woken up her stomach. By the time she felt full, she had dyed her fingers purple and the front of her blouse was streaked with juice.

She walked through waist-high grasses until her legs would carry her no more. Grass was matted down from deer that had slept here. Carolina settled down in the same space. In less time than it takes to sing a lullaby, she fell asleep.

In her dream she heard a choir of angels. She saw golden light streaming from the heavens to the grasses in the field. The angel voices sang clear and strong. The angels were singing her name.

> *Carolina moon, keep shining,*
> *Shining on the one who waits for me.*

The angels were laughing.

Carolina sat up and rubbed her eyes. She peered over the feathery tops of the tall grass and there they were. One angel had long black hair and she was holding a basket. She was dancing. With her other hand she held her full skirt and swayed it this way and that as she stepped and twirled. The other angel had just thrown a berry into the air and was catching it in his mouth. The third angel had wild straw-colored hair and wore farmer's overalls. He was playing a fiddle like a spirit had hold of his hand.

I am most surely dreaming or I have died and gone to Heaven, Carolina thought as the three joyful angels danced toward her.

Chapter 11

SUNSET—JULY 14, 1964

Carolina's attention snapped back to the present by a high-pitched *keeeeeeer*. Its shrill call died out as the hawk soared below the rocks. It had suddenly taken flight, as if something had frightened it, or maybe it had seen prey.

She'd been lost in her memories and hadn't noticed that the sun was setting against the western slopes. Clouds glowed with pink and orange hues, making them appear to be on fire. She gazed to the north. Somwhere in those distant peaks was Blue Star Mountain, and Auntie Shen. *Will we ever find our way back to each other?* She looked to the heavens. *Mama, Daddy, are you flying on angel wings now? Is Caleb? Daddy, are you really with Orion?*

The hard surface of the stone was getting cold, and her

stomach was calling out for supper. When she'd set off to climb this mountain, she'd planned to wait for the stars. Now all she wanted was to be in Miss Latah's warm kitchen.

Miss Latah!

She and Mr. Ray would be home by now. Carolina figured she should have told Lucas where she was going. She had to get back. She scooted across the rock and headed down the mountain. It wasn't long before she realized she'd forgotten to mark her trail.

The trees and bushes didn't look the same as she remembered. When she'd climbed up the mountain, she'd bushwhacked part of the way, under arching branches and over boulders where there was no path. Now she couldn't remember what ridge she'd scrambled up or where she'd passed the giant tulip tree or where she'd crossed the stream.

Fear grabbed hold. It taunted her with its whispered *You're lost.*

Carolina stood very still. She reached up and held her pendant, pressing the catbird against the center of her hand. She closed her eyes and a wordless prayer took flight.

When she opened her eyes, she saw the honey locust. She remembered having been pricked by its thorns. Carolina smiled.

She looked to the west. The sun was grazing the tops of the trees. It wouldn't be long before it slipped below. Already, a sliver of moon and three bright stars were shining in the rust-colored sky.

Pebbles and loose rocks tumbled as she half climbed, half slid down the clay ravine. She came upon the old gnarled birch tree and the white boulder as the sun set for the night. The stream called to her with its gentle trickling waters. She followed its sound, guided by its music. It was flowing across the path she'd taken and was now lit with a magical shimmering light, as if the Milky Way had come down from the sky and was flowing at her feet.

She looked into the sky that was now lit with stars. The Milky Way was still there, wide as a river, with so many stars and so many tiny specks of light that it did look like a trail of cornmeal left by a spirit dog. She wondered about the Cherokee legend. Could a spirit dog *really* have flown across the sky, leaving a trail of cornmeal that he'd stolen from the old Indian man and his wife? Did the Indians in the village *really* scare the giant spirit dog away with their whoops and hollers? Was that *really* how the Milky Way had come to be?

There was a time when she believed such stories with all her heart. Now a new voice was speaking inside her, one that questioned fanciful notions. The stories were beginning to sound a little far-fetched. She didn't like these questions that rose up, creeping into her mind and spoiling all the fun.

Loud chirping, croaking, scratching sounds of the night forest surrounded her. In the distance she heard a dog bark. She heard lambs bleating. They were sounds of home. Carolina found the trail that led down to the meadow. The moment she emerged from the trees, she began to run through the tall grass. She ran down along the fencing that bordered the sheep pasture, and then she was sprinting across the farmyard.

Carolina took the porch steps two at a time. As she reached to throw open the screen door, she nearly collided with Miss Latah. Her strong hands grabbed Carolina's shoulders as if she was about to shake her, but instead Miss Latah pulled her close.

Carolina stayed in Miss Latah's embrace for a long moment. She felt Miss Latah's chest rising and falling.

Miss Latah released her. Her eyes were shining.

Carolina couldn't find the words to say what was in her heart. How could she say she wanted so much to belong here? How could she say how wonderful it felt to be held like that? How could she say these things when all the while she'd been holding so many secrets and telling so many lies?

"I forgot to tell Lucas where I was going," said Carolina. It was the best she could do.

Mr. Ray was sauntering across the grass from the direction of the barn. Lucas walked beside him. He was a head shorter, with black hair like Miss Latah's and the same long-legged gait as Mr. Ray's.

"Where did you run off to?" said Lucas. There wasn't a speck of worry in his voice. "I've been looking for you since supper."

Before Carolina could answer, her eyes fell on the sling Mr. Ray was wearing.

"Where's your cast?" she asked.

"Didn't need one," said Mr. Ray. "The arm's not broke after all. The doc said Miss Latah put my shoulder back in its socket better than he could. Looks like I'll be healed up quick enough."

"Are you hungry, Carolina?" asked Miss Latah. "There's a fat slice of sweet potato pie waiting for you."

Everyone sat down at the kitchen table. Miss Latah set out a pitcher of sweet tea and plunked down a full glass of milk in front of Carolina, as well as a fat slice of pie, a chicken leg left over from last night's supper, and some fresh green beans. Lucas was asking his father questions about tractor repair and Miss Latah was talking excitedly about the number of zucchini that were ripening in the garden. Carolina kept her eye on Mr. Ray the whole time she was chewing and swallowing, wondering when the conversation was going to come around to how it was her fault that the tractor accident occurred. But it never did.

It wasn't long before Mr. Ray leaned his head back and yawned wide and loud. Everyone else caught it and yawns went around the table.

"It's been a long day," said Miss Latah. "It's time for bed."

Carolina dragged herself up the back stairs of the kitchen to the room directly above. She hadn't been on the farm but a few days when she and Miss Latah moved the sewing table and fabric to one side of the room and Mr. Ray hauled in a mattress and bed frame that had been stored in the barn.

Carolina buttoned up pajamas that used to belong to Lucas and slipped between the covers. "All set?" asked Miss Latah. Carolina nodded. Miss Latah held the edges of a patchwork quilt and playfully shook it into the air while Carolina lay waiting, her arms outstretched. The soft comforting quilt floated down over her, covering her up, face and all, and Carolina couldn't help giggling.

Miss Latah sat at the edge of Carolina's bed and pulled the quilt away from Carolina's face.

"Miss Latah?" Carolina asked. "Is Mr. Ray going to be okay?"

"He should be healed up by the time the apples are ripe," she said.

Carolina thought for a moment. Apples got picked in the fall. That was over a month from now.

Miss Latah kissed Carolina on the forehead, blessed her dreams, and turned out the light.

Carolina gazed out the window. She had a perfect view of the barn and fields, the moon and stars. Her head lay on a soft pillow and she was snuggled under a warm quilt. A dreamcatcher that Miss Latah had woven hung on the wall near the head of her bed. If Carolina hadn't known better, she'd have thought the Harmony family had been expecting her.

Carolina yawned. As she was drifting off, her friend Russell wandered into her dreams. She dreamt she was back at Miss Lily Jean's. Pammy was wearing Carolina's red Mary Janes and Russell had found *Johnny Tremain*. Johnny was being brave and Russell was scared of the world.

Chapter 12

LEARNING NEW WAYS

Carolina was awake before the rooster crowed. She knelt beside the long window, chin resting in hands, elbows propped on the sill. Harmony Farm lay in a stillness of gray and black shadows. The sky still held stars.

She conjured up Orion in her mind until she could see his silver belt sparkling and his club raised high. Her daddy had told her many myths and legends of Orion. It was his favorite constellation. She remembered his words. *There he goes, the adventurer, running free, over deserts and oceans and mountains.*

"Run back," Carolina whispered.

The stars withdrew, giving way to the pale light of dawn. Then a thin orange light blazed out across the edge of the horizon. A moment later the sun rose like a red-hot fireball. Rays of yellow light radiated to the east and west, and the rooster called out a loud praise.

On many a morning, Carolina and Auntie Shen had stood side by side, greeting the dawn. Auntie Shen would speak in a soft voice and a solemn tone as if she were uttering a sacred prayer. "The sun rising up is our daily reminder that God keeps his promises."

Then Auntie Shen's voice would rise in a cheerful exclamation. "I love to get up early! I like to hear the birds talking to the world."

Carolina liked to get up early too. She wondered if Auntie Shen was watching the sunrise right now. She sure hoped so.

Bobolinks and field sparrows were flying over the alfalfa meadow that lay beyond her window. Swallows swooped and dived, looking as if they were playing a game of tag as they filled their stomachs with flying insects. Birds in the treetops sang out a chorus of trills and whistles in a joyous celebration of the new day.

Carolina wished she could sprout feathers of her own. She'd fly out this window and be one of them. She'd fly so high. She'd fly as high as Heaven.

Lucas's knuckles rolled across the door—his way of knocking.

"Coming," she answered in a low voice.

She pulled on blue jeans that she'd cut off into shorts and a cowboy shirt with white swirling threads on the front pockets—clothing that Lucas had outgrown years ago. Carolina was thrilled with them. She had lots of clothes to wear since she and Miss Latah had dug through a black trunk in the attic, and Carolina had picked out what she liked.

Carolina's bare feet made slapping sounds on the wooden steps as she pattered down the back stairs to the kitchen. Last night, it had been decided that she was to help Lucas with additional chores while Mr. Ray's shoulder healed up. She flew out onto the porch and then spun around and caught the screen door just before it slammed. Lucas was already halfway to the barn by the time she had pulled on his old pointy-toed cowboy boots and caught up with him.

"I'll race you from the henhouse to the barn, Lucas," she said.

"Okay, but if I win, you collect the eggs today."

"You're on," she said. She stuck her arm out straight, extending her hand. Lucas took it and they did three quick shakes, sealing the promise.

They crouched like runners on an imaginary starting line, and Carolina counted out loud, "One . . . two . . . three . . . GO!"

She sprinted like a rabbit. Damp morning air filled her lungs. Her shoulders barely reached his chest, but still she kept pace with him. She felt the heat in her muscles, the surge of energy moving through her veins, pushing forward.

Lucas's hands slapped against the barn. Carolina's hands hit a moment after.

She bent over, leaning her hands on her knees. "Next time," she said, breathing hard, "I'll be fastest."

"You might be," said Lucas, even though he was barely winded.

Their first chore of the day was to check on the sheep. They hiked to the upper pasture, a grassy slope bordered by wire fencing. Sparkles of light shimmered on the dew of the grass as if tiny stars had fallen to Earth and decided to stay.

Carolina had to run every third step to keep up with Lucas's long-legged pace. Then he stopped all of a sudden. He looked up and tilted his head, as if he was about to pose a question to the sky. She knew he was thinking up a joke.

"Hey, Carolina," he said. "Do you know why sheep grow wool?"

Carolina stared at him, then placed her hands on her hips and said, "Why?"

"They don't want to pick cotton."

Carolina rolled her eyes. "That's the dumbest joke I ever heard."

Even so, a chuckle rose up in her and came out in a hiccup. That was all it took. Lucas reached for her tickle spot and got her good. Weak with laughter, she pulled at his hands, struggling to break free. When she did, she ran ahead of him, cackling with laughter. She glanced back, but he wasn't chasing her. He was standing there laughing. Lucas was full of good-natured teasing. It made her feel as if having her around was something he'd always wanted.

Carolina walked among the sheep.

"Good morning, Mathilda," she said. "Did you have a good sleep, Josephine? How is Naomi this morning?"

"Have you named every ewe and lamb in this pasture?" Lucas asked.

"Course I have," she said.

Carolina counted the lambs and was relieved all were accounted for. A break in the fencing would make them easy prey for coyotes. She walked with Lucas along the fence line as curious sheep wandered behind. He casually reached over and scratched a lamb behind its ears.

After checking on the sheep, they headed to the barn. Lucas let Carolina try her hand at milking the cow. She sat on a three-legged stool practically eye-level with Elsie's bulging udders. The cow's teats were long and pink and squishy to the touch. Lucas placed his hands on top of Carolina's so she could get the feel of the pull and squeeze.

She could feel the heat rising to her cheeks. She knew she was wearing the blush of embarrassment. She wished Lucas would move away and hoped he would stay all at the same time. When she managed the first real squirt and heard the squish and ping in the milk bucket, Lucas thumped her lightly on the back. She smiled then, hoping he wouldn't notice her red cheeks. He didn't seem to notice anything at all. All he cared about was the milk in the bucket.

"Okay, you know what you're doing," he said, and then he left. She was alone with her disappointment.

Sometimes Lucas seemed like a big brother to Carolina. Other times she found herself gawking at him. If he caught her eye, she pretended to be admiring the view beyond. Her mixed-up feelings came again later that same morning when she helped him split and chop wood.

It was hard to imagine frosty winter snow on a steamy summer day, but Mr. Ray had said it was time to gather up the firewood, so right after breakfast Carolina and Lucas set out across the field. Months back, a tree had been knocked down by a fierce wind. Mr. Ray had taken his chain saw to it and sliced the trunk into pieces. He said it must have been a weak tree.

The stump of that tree told its own side of the story. Its roots still held a firm footing in the ground. Where its trunk had ripped off, its yellow insides were exposed. Hundreds of fine splinters stood straight up, like tooth-picks, and she imagined the tree fighting the fierce wind to the bitter end.

Now its trunk lay in thick chunks, half-buried in leaves and ferns. Lucas lifted one. Moist dark ground beneath revealed a haven for grubs. A salamander crawled on its belly and disappeared into the grass. Lucas set the chunk of wood upright on a flat stump lined with ax cuts.

"Looks like you've axed a lot of trees here," she said.

"Yep, I reckon I've axed a lot of trees," said Lucas with a laugh.

Carolina rolled her eyes. She knew he was teasing her.

"I'll do the splitting and you pile the pieces over there. Later we'll come up with the tractor and carry it all down to the woodshed," said Lucas.

The broad blade of the ax gave her the willies. She thought for sure that that sharp ax could cut a person in two. She stepped back a few paces as he lifted it. He brought the ax down. A loud crack echoed through the hills.

In no time at all, beads of sweat dripped down Lucas's forehead. He peeled off his T-shirt and tossed it aside. As he raised the ax, cords of muscle tightened in his arms and back. Carolina barely breathed as he brought that ax down. He split the wood in a single fluid movement, again and again and again.

When it was her turn to pick up the logs, she made Lucas lay the ax on the ground and take three steps back. He didn't tease her about it. She even saw him trying hard not to smile.

Lucas began to whistle. The tune was familiar to Carolina.

"My home's across the Blue Ridge Mountains," she sang, her voice rising and falling on the last word. She'd learned the song from Auntie Shen. They'd heard it sung by Doc Watson too, a musician whose singing Auntie Shen dearly loved.

Lucas joined in. Sometimes his voice sounded like a man's and sometimes his words got stuck in his throat and nothing but a squeak came out. That was what happened in the middle of the tune. Carolina covered her mouth to keep from laughing. Lucas stopped singing and furrowed his brow, pretending to be intent on his work.

"Oh, Lucas," she said.

She wasn't teasing or trying to be mean. Why, even Miss Latah and Mr. Ray had to stifle their grins when Lucas made those squeaks. Lucas ignored her. Carolina shrugged as if she didn't care.

As Carolina stepped into the noisy henhouse, she sorely regretted having made the deal with Lucas about collecting the eggs. So far she'd been able to avoid it. Now there seemed no way of escaping.

"Don't worry about the hens peckin' you," Lucas said. "See—we've clipped their beaks. They can't hurt you."

"Law," said Carolina, rolling her eyes.

She reached her hand toward a hen, then snapped it back, darted it forward, and then snapped it back again.

Lucas was beside himself, laughing so hard he had to wipe away tears.

"What are you doing? Imitating a turkey?" he said.

Carolina stuck her tongue out at him.

She reached her hand to the nest again and started to slide it under the hen when its beak hit the top of her hand.

"Ow!" she said, rubbing her hand. "I knew you were lying."

"C'mon, Carolina," Lucas said with a chuckle. "Who's the chicken here? You or her?"

"I'm not a chicken," Carolina said, "but you must be, or else you'd be doing this yourself."

"Okay, watch," Lucas said.

His hand reached under the hen as easily as if he was reaching for butter at the table. He held up a brown egg between his thumb and forefinger. With a satisfied look on his face, he placed it ever so gently in the wire basket that Carolina was carrying.

Carolina let out a quick breath of exasperation. She detested being called a chicken. She especially detested being teased when she truly felt chicken. Lucas finally grew impatient and left her to do the job as best she could. Her chance of getting a reprieve out of pity was gone.

She stared at the hen. It dared her with its beady eyes,

as if it was waiting for her hand to come close enough to peck. *Okay, that's it,* she thought.

One . . . two . . . three.

She thrust her hand under the hen and pulled back. She opened her hand. Two warm brown eggs filled her palm. She wished Lucas was here to see. She continued down the row of nests, making a game of it. It was a test of skill and daring as she proved her hand was faster than the hens' beaks.

The wire basket was full when she stepped out of the henhouse and into the sun. Carolina stood tall, victorious. She had to admit that she genuinely enjoyed farm work.

In less than two weeks, Carolina had learned how to do all kinds of chores, with plenty of time left over to run and play. When she got tired, she took a nap beside Homer, the old hound dog, or she played with the cats that lived in the barn. Carolina had followed Mr. Ray and Lucas around, happy to be a helper, eager to learn. Now she was able to accomplish many chores herself, and she understood that in their gentle way, they'd been teaching her all along.

"I've brought you the eggs, Miss Latah," said Carolina as she set the basket of brown eggs on the counter by the icebox.

Potato pie was sizzling in a black cast-iron skillet. Ice cubes floated in a glass pitcher full of amber-colored tea.

"Bless your heart," said Miss Latah. She leaned over and gave Carolina a casual kiss on her forehead. "Did those biddies in the henhouse behave themselves?"

"Yeah, they did. It was easy," Carolina said, rubbing tiny red welts on the top of her hand.

She heard Mr. Ray's boots banging up the porch steps. He and Lucas were talking and laughing as they sat down to untie their boot laces. They came inside and everyone sat together for dinner, the midday meal. Heads bowed and Mr. Ray said grace.

"Bless us, Lord, stranger and kin," he began.

Carolina looked at her plate but she wouldn't close her eyes. It was one thing to be polite. It was another to join in. She was still not on speaking terms with God.

The moment Mr. Ray said "Amen" she dug her fork into the buttery crust of fried potatoes and let the taste sit on her tongue, filling her senses. Everyone talked of the day in cheerful tones.

"What a sunshine-y blue-sky day—perfect for anything," said Mr. Ray.

Miss Latah smiled and nodded. She leaned over to Carolina.

"Won't that sow pig be in her glory when she sees this bucket full of garden scraps?"

Carolina held her fork in midair. That pig must surely weigh three hundred pounds. She'd seen up close how fast that pig could run. She'd heard it snorting and grunting, ready to plow down anything to get to its food. There was no way she could lift that bucket over the slatted boards of its pen and dump the contents into the trough.

"Would you please put these scraps in her trough on your way to the barn, Lucas?" Miss Latah asked.

"Yes, ma'am," said Lucas, scooping another slice of potatoes and onions out of the pan.

Carolina relaxed. She needn't have worried. No one ever pushed her too hard, not with chores, not with anything. They patiently waited until she was ready.

On the first morning that Carolina had awakened in the Harmony house, she'd peered into the kitchen from the stairwell. This was the third house she'd slept in this summer that was full of strangers, and she wasn't taking any chances.

Miss Latah greeted her with a big smile and a friendly "Good morning." She had breakfast waiting and heaped seconds on Carolina's plate without even waiting for her to ask.

While Miss Latah washed up the breakfast dishes, she had Carolina soak her bruised feet in a white porcelain pan that was filled with water and Epsom salts. After Carolina dried her feet, Miss Latah smoothed a soothing ointment over the cuts and gashes Carolina had gotten while running barefoot in the woods. Miss Latah sniffed and quietly spoke the names of certain plants, mostly to herself, trying to figure out what the sticky salve was on the foot coverings that Carolina had been wearing. Carolina stayed quiet and offered no part of her story.

Later that first day, Miss Latah untangled the knots from Carolina's hair. She took her time, gently coaxing out the knots without ever pulling too hard. All the while she'd spoken in gentle reassurances, letting Carolina know that everything was going to be all right.

Ever since that first day, Mr. Ray and Miss Latah had been patient, waiting for Carolina to tell her story. The first day nobody had asked anything. The second day, right during supper, the questions had come: where was she from; where was her family; how many days had she been lost in the mountains? Carolina had stared down at her plate, dragging her fork through the potatoes and gravy. Every time she looked up, they were staring at her, waiting. She figured she'd better give some answers.

She didn't know what made her do it, but she began making up stories as tall as Jack Tales. First it was a story about an uncle, and he was a hunter and they'd gotten separated while tracking deer. She had even pretended to call him on the phone, even had an imaginary conversation with the dial tone, even told everyone that he'd be coming for her any day now. That poor uncle seemed to run into one situation after another, and he never could find his way to come and get her.

Carolina tried telling her stories as convincingly as Auntie Shen, but after a while she saw the way Mr. Ray would lift his eyebrows and saw the look he'd give Miss Latah. She saw how Miss Latah would stare down at the table, folding and refolding a dish towel. She saw Lucas biting his lips to keep from grinning. Her stories were followed by a heavy stillness—it hung in the air—a stillness that eased its way into her skin and bones until her stomach was filled with shame. Their questions had slowly died out like the final drip-drip-drip of an afternoon shower. Carolina fooled herself into believing they didn't care to know anymore.

The midday meal was over. Carolina scraped the remaining tidbits of potato out of the heavy black skillet and then carried it to the sink, where Miss Latah was swishing dish soap into bubbles.

"Miss Latah," she began.

"What is it, honey?" she answered.

Carolina had been thinking it was time to tell the truth. Her story wanted to get out in the fresh air, run around and be free. She searched her mind for the words, but none of them sounded quite right. Miss Latah ran a dishcloth around one plate and then another. Carolina rinsed the suds off.

"Never mind," said Carolina.

She set the last plate to dry on the dish rack and headed straight for the kitchen door. She sat down on the porch and pulled her boots on and then set off toward the barn.

Wasps flew in and out of a nest under the eaves. A mouse scurried across the floor and into the hay. Yellow-winged flies had descended upon a fresh pile of manure.

Lucas was already hard at work. Carolina grabbed a wide shovel and shoved it under a dry mound of brown horse clumps. By the time they were finished, their clothes stuck to them like flypaper.

"Okay, I'm done," Lucas announced. "And I'm goin' swimmin'."

"Swimming!" Carolina was filled with new life. "C'mon. Let's go. I'll race you."

Lucas put both hands down squarely on her shoulders.

"Carolina, I like you fine, but today I'm goin' off for a swim with my friends."

She stared at him with her mouth wide open. She couldn't believe his rudeness. Hadn't she worked hard alongside him? Hadn't she laughed at his dumb jokes? Wasn't she standing there smelling like horse dung same as he?

Lucas hiked across the field. He looked back once to be certain she was staying put. Carolina folded her arms across her chest and stuck out her hip, but it didn't mean a thing to Lucas. He kept on walking.

The moment he entered the woods, she sprinted across the field and found the opening he'd ducked into. She could see him up ahead. Creeping along the edges of brambles and hiding behind the wide trunks of hickory and tulip trees, she followed him.

A large twig snapped under her boot, and she dropped behind a tangle of thorny brambles.

Splashing water and the whoops, hollers, and laughter of boys echoed through the trees. She watched Lucas join his friends on a high ledge of rock that jutted out over the surface of a wide creek. He peeled off his T-shirt and tossed it.

Carolina watched Lucas set his sights on a long rope that hung from a wide branch. He took a running leap off the ledge, grabbed the rope in midair, swung out over the water, and then he let go. Carolina heard him splash. She felt tingles on her arms as she imagined the feel of cool water.

One of the youngest boys, a skinny boy with a peach-fuzz haircut, was tussling with one of the older boys. Then he spotted her.

"Hey, some girl is spyin' on us," he said.

The three boys turned and all eyes were glued on her.

"This is our swimming hole. It ain't a place for girls," said the skinny boy. He seemed downright put out by her presence.

Carolina held her head high and pranced right past him out onto the ledge.

"I bet I can swim better than you," she said to the skinny boy as she stood on one leg, pulling off her boot.

"I bet you can't swim at all," he answered.

Carolina pulled off her other boot and heaved it into the weeds.

Another boy joined in with a loud bold voice. "Let's throw her in and see if she's telling the truth."

A third boy reached out and grabbed her arms, pulling her to the edge.

"Leave her alone!"

Lucas was suddenly in the midst of them, water dripping from his hair. He put himself between Carolina and the boy.

"Can I swing from the rope, Lucas? Please?" Carolina raised her eyes and put on her most pleading expression.

"What did you go and follow me for? Didn't I tell you not to?" he asked.

"Please, Lucas," she begged, putting her hands together as if she was praying.

"Do you want to crash back into this ledge? That's what will happen if you don't let go in time," he said. "I don't want you getting hurt. Go ahead now. Go home."

"I'll let go in time. I promise," she said. "I'm a good swimmer!"

"I bet she ain't," said the skinny boy. His face was so

close she could see a piece of grass stuck between his front teeth.

Lucas turned away from her as he put his hand against the boy's bony chest. In that moment Carolina saw her opportunity—a clear shot across the ledge. She ran.

Hands grabbed for her but none touched as she kept the dangling rope in her sights. Her feet left solid ground, her arms reached out, and a moment later she caught the rough hemp. Swinging out over the creek, she held on with tight fists.

"Woo-hooo!" she yelled. She was flying.

The rope slackened and she let go, taking a gulp of air. Down she went. A rush of bubbles brushed her legs, her belly, her arms, and then the cool water covered her head and she was under, down in the silence of the water world she loved. She stretched her arms out in front of her and kicked her legs like a frog, moving through the clear green water with her eyes wide open. At the reeds and cattails she surfaced faceup, feeling the water smooth her braids into long thick strands down her back. She glanced behind, surprised by how far she was from the ledge.

The boys were staring down at the surface of the water. Carolina wondered what they were looking at.

Lucas dove in. After a short while, his head popped up. "I can't find her!" he yelled.

She lowered down behind a clump of reeds, submerging herself up to her lower lip, and waited.

All the boys jumped in at once, a single mass of flailing arms and pumping legs. Water splashed high. They rose to the surface, looked around, and dove under again.

After a while, Carolina figured they'd suffered enough

and perched herself on a rock as if she was posing for pictures.

"Whatcha y'all looking for?" she yelled.

The skinny boy with peach-fuzz hair spotted her. She smiled back at him with mock sweetness, her prettiest *I told you so* smile.

At first the expression on Lucas's face was angry, but then he busted out laughing. In the time it took for Carolina to climb the embankment and run the length of their trampled footpath back to the ledge, all was forgiven.

"Well, I'll be darned, Carolina," Lucas said. "Nobody's ever caught the rope on the first try before."

She shrugged her shoulders with an air of pride. It seemed Lucas's comment was a direct insult to the skinny boy. He stood to the side with his shoulders slumped and a downcast expression on his face.

Carolina's long-sleeved shirt was stuck to her arms, so she peeled it off and stood there in nothing but her under-shirt and cut-offs, ready for another turn. She thought one of the older boys was eyeing the bumps that had recently sprouted on her chest, but she pretended not to notice.

Swimming and diving wore away the better part of the evening. By the time they were headed home for supper, Carolina had rope burns on both hands and up her arms, and a big broad smile plastered on her face.

As they trudged across the field, Lucas gently tugged one of her long braids. She turned her head to look up at him and he gave her a wink, as if they were sharing a secret.

Then it hit her—how he'd lied to his friends and told them she was his cousin. He'd told them she'd be visiting for a while. She'd heard him say it, heard him speak the words clear as a bell, and she'd pretended it was all true simply by ignoring it and jumping into the creek again.

Auntie Shen had a firm conviction about lying. She said a lie had no life to it; "it will vanish quick as haze on the morning meadow. . . ." She had said that once the light of truth shone down on a lie, it disappeared.

Carolina's brisk steps slowed to a crawl. It was only a matter of time before the bright light of truth shone down on all her lies. Auntie Shen had never taken a switch to Carolina, not ever, but Carolina was betting she'd want to if she caught wind of the stories that Carolina was telling.

Carolina felt as if she'd swallowed one of those tiny toads she'd seen on the creek bank, and now it was hopping about in her stomach.

Chapter 13

GOOD MEDICINE

"It's going to be another scorcher," said Miss Latah. "Let's get the garden work done while it's cool."

Carolina and Miss Latah walked to the barn to gather hoes and pitchforks. On the way Carolina was talking nonstop about the music groups she liked and demonstrating the twist. Miss Latah was telling Carolina about the dancing and singing that took place at a Green Corn Ceremony. Miss Latah pointed her toe and took a try at the popular dance, and Carolina began jumping about as if she was an Indian. Carolina looked at Miss Latah twisting back and forth, and Miss Latah looked at Carolina jumping about like a cricket, and they both broke into a fit of laughter.

Today had the promise of an easygoing day. Harmony Farm belonged all to them. At breakfast Mr. Ray had said it was a blessing that his left shoulder was hurt and not his right. A whole week had passed since the tractor accident, and, except for the sling he was wearing, one would hardly know Mr. Ray had been injured. Mr. Ray said he'd be able to shift the gears while Lucas steered. Lucas could hardly wait to leave for Asheville, since he'd be driving all the back roads. Mr. Ray said he'd have to take over when they got close to the highway, since the police could be particular about a boy driving without a license. They left directly after breakfast. They'd be home after supper.

Miss Latah strolled down the paths of her garden. She got downright giddy as she showed Carolina the yellow blossoms on the squash plants. She lifted wide leaves on the cucumber plants to reveal the tiny cucumbers taking shape on the vines.

Carolina could see that Miss Latah cared for her garden as much as she cared for her family. Miss Latah didn't let anyone take her work for granted either. Whenever Mr. Ray or Lucas spoke about working sunup to sundown to keep the farm going, she was quick to remind them what it took to put food on their plates. She said that without the garden, they'd all go hungry. Carolina had to agree. Miss Latah picked vegetables from the garden every day, and every evening at supper she had a flavorful dish to serve. Everyone went back for seconds.

"These weeds shoot up overnight," said Miss Latah, her hands on her hips.

She handed Carolina a hoe. "Corn roots grow close to the surface. Don't dig up the corn. Use the hoe to loosen the weeds."

It seemed easy enough until Carolina found out how stubborn weeds could be. She tugged on the stems and the roots tugged right back. She scraped and beat at those weeds with the corner of the hoe blade. She kept at it, feeling a sore spot growing between her thumb and forefinger. She chugged a swig of water from the milk bottle and looked over to the other side of the garden.

Miss Latah was humming. She pushed a pitchfork into the black soil with the heel of her boot, pulled up a clod of weed, and bounced it on top until the loose soil fell through the tines. Then she chucked the weed into the wheelbarrow. She did it all in one quick easy movement.

"You're having all the fun," said Carolina.

"Oh, so you think I've taken all the easy work for myself?" asked Miss Latah with a teasing tone to her voice.

"It sure looks easier," said Carolina.

Miss Latah laughed.

"It looks easy because I've learned how to work," said Miss Latah as she bounced another weed clump on the tines.

Carolina figured Miss Latah just plain hated hoeing. It wasn't fair that Carolina was the only one who had to suffer in this heat. The thought pestered her and she jabbed the edge of the hoe into the ground. Her blister was getting red and hot.

"Are we almost finished?" Carolina asked.

"The garden is never finished. We work the garden."

Miss Latah shoved the tines of the pitchfork into the ground so the tool stood upright, and then she gingerly stepped over feathery fronds of carrot tops that were tucked between straight shoots of chives. Miss Latah stood beside Carolina and listened to her complaints.

"I'll never be able to free the corn from these weeds. There are toooo many."

"Don't look at the whole patch. Weed around one stalk. When you're finished and happy with your work, move to the next one. That is working the garden."

Carolina tugged her hat down. She knew that if she gave up and walked away, Miss Latah wouldn't yell or make her feel bad. She'd continue working the garden. Carolina decided to try.

Carolina put down the hoe. She pulled weeds by hand until black soil was packed under her fingernails. Every now and then she'd look over what she'd done. She was amazed at her progress.

Soon the two of them were working side by side. They pulled up choke weed along with the spent pea vines that were drying up and turning yellow. Carolina watched Miss Latah reach her fingers into thyme and marjoram plants and pluck out tiny weeds as carefully as if she was coaxing out splinters.

Auntie Shen's garden was a big rectangle with long neat rows and plenty of space in between. Miss Latah's garden was planted in circles and squares, even zigzags. Green tomatoes and red ripe ones spilled over bright orange marigolds. Needlelike leaves of rosemary grew alongside massive circles of cabbage leaves. A crazy path wound in and around plants like one of those maze puzzles that Carolina liked to solve.

As the sun climbed higher in the sky, Carolina felt its heat on her straw hat. Beads of sweat rolled down her neck. The angry blister broke, leaving a half moon shape of tender pink skin.

Finally Miss Latah stretched her arms high. She breathed in deeply. She let her breath out in a loud *aaahhh*, and then she brushed her hands together and announced, "Enough for today."

"Those are sweet words to my ears," Carolina said.

She staggered out of the garden and swaggered like an old drunk until she was in the shade of the giant tulip tree, and then she fell onto the cool grass as if she was a dying soldier taking her last breath. She could hear Miss Latah laughing even after the screen door had slammed behind her. Carolina lay on her back with a big grin on her face.

While Miss Latah was in the kitchen, Carolina pumped the well until water splashed out over her hand, soothing the blister. She leaned her head under the water and then gasped as if someone had dropped ice cubes down her shirt. She leaned her head in the cold water again and let it stream over her neck and face. When she got up, her shirt was soaked. She refilled the milk bottle they'd been drinking out of and carried it back to the shady spot under the tree.

Miss Latah's arms were full when she walked out onto the porch. Carolina jumped up and grabbed the blanket that was tucked under one of Miss Latah's arms. She spread out the blanket, and Miss Latah set a woven basket and a plate in the center of it. The plate was piled high, covered with a dish towel.

Miss Latah bowed her head in a prayer of thanks. Carolina stared at the ground but like always did not close her eyes, still stuck on her silent refusal to join in. She waited respectfully for Miss Latah to finish. Then she pulled the dish towel off the plate.

"Cold fried chicken and biscuits," she said. "Boy, Lucas is going to be sorry he missed this."

Carolina crossed her legs in front of her and reached for a golden batter–covered piece. She took a big bite. Oh, she did appreciate Miss Latah's good cooking, and a picnic was an extra-special treat. Miss Latah reached into the basket and pulled out a warm red tomato. She sliced it up for them to share.

"Carolina, I'm going to walk to the medicine garden today. Would you like to come?"

On many evenings, she'd watched Miss Latah hike up into the forest. Miss Latah would come back with various herbs and roots and set them in the special room she had off the kitchen. In that room bunches of herbs were tied together and hung upside down from the rafters. Strange-shaped roots were kept in Mason jars, and leafy herbs soaked in bottles.

"Yes, ma'am," Carolina answered without any hesitation. Lucas had told her that his mother had a secret garden, and more than anything Carolina wanted to know where it was and what it looked like.

With her belly full and her thirst quenched, Carolina

climbed the hill with a fresh outlook. They entered a narrow path by way of soft lacy hemlock that brushed their hair as they slipped beneath its arching branches. They climbed higher still, making their way under the shade of tall beech and buckeye trees. It was cool and dark.

Miss Latah walked slowly up and down hilly slopes, her eyes focused on the woodland plants. She poked around moss-covered rocks. It looked like any other part of the forest to Carolina, except for the wooden markers that were poking up out of the weeds. Carolina walked directly behind Miss Latah. She was almost afraid to put her feet down for fear of squashing something.

"Ginseng!" exclaimed Miss Latah. Her face just lit up with excitement. "I've been hoping my transplant would take. Ginseng is not easy to find anymore. It used to grow all over these mountains. Indians and mountain folks have always valued it for its powerful medicine."

Miss Latah sighed.

"Then it became profitable to dig it up. Even people as far as China bought it. It seemed everyone was intent on digging up 'sang' and selling it for money. People got greedy. They picked so much that the plants died out. Now ginseng is a rare sight."

Miss Latah said she would come back in a month or so to gather the healing root when red seeds like berries sprouted in the center of the leaves. She'd plant the seeds in the surrounding soil and hope for its return.

"Can I trust you to keep this ginseng patch a secret?" Miss Latah asked.

"Yes, ma'am," said Carolina, "I won't tell anyone."

Dappled light fell on leaves and forest floor. A high ledge of silver rock glistened. Here in the deep woods, wood thrushes whistled beautiful melodies. Soft breezes gently brushed their hair.

Miss Latah stepped carefully through the forest duff, stooped over like an old woman. As she gathered she whispered prayers. Carolina followed, trying to figure what was so interesting about gathering green leaves and brown roots.

"Why do you pray so much?" asked Carolina.

"I am thanking the Great Creator," she answered. "So much has been given and in such abundance."

"What's so special about a bunch of ordinary weeds?"

"They may be ordinary, but they are good," said Miss Latah. "Look, this is Solomon's seal, good for curing sores. I'll make a poultice when we get home. It will soothe your blister. This is boneset for colds and cankers. Look at this jewelweed"—Miss Latah lifted the plant that had orange blossoms in the shape of tiny lanterns—"the medicine to cure poison ivy rash.

"All we need is right under our noses," she said, "but most people walk right by or trample them down without ever noticing."

Carolina followed Miss Latah down through saplings alongside a steep bank. Carolina recognized the green galax leaves. They were shaped like hearts. She had helped Auntie Shen pick bunches of them, so many they filled a burlap sack, and then they'd taken them to a florist shop in Boone and sold every one. Carolina wanted to tell Miss Latah about Auntie Shen. It didn't seem right to keep her a secret.

They heard the loud rushing sound of a waterfall. It fed a wide stream. They skipped across rocks and boulders, making their way to a large flat rock in the middle of the calmer waters.

"I could use a good rest," said Miss Latah.

They watched the water rushing over the side of a steep precipice. Along the outermost rocks, thin streams of water trickled down and spilled over ledges. A mist rose off the surface at the bottom, and then the water quietly flowed toward them over smooth stones and pebbles. Green trees grew along the banks and hills in graceful poses.

Around the large flat rock where they rested, the water was dark and deep. Miss Latah lifted her face to the sun. Her white blouse was open at the neck, revealing golden skin. Her long black hair cascaded to the rock, and it looked like a waterfall too, a black satin one.

Carolina lay back. The warmth of the sun shone on her face and the warmth of the rock seeped into her shoulders. She imagined that the life of a lizard must be divine.

"Miss Latah?"

"Uh-huh."

"How come you took Mr. Ray to the doctor if you already fixed his shoulder?"

"The joint was out of its socket. I wanted to be sure that I had repositioned it properly. The doctor took a picture of it with an X-ray machine, and we both looked at it," said Miss Latah. "Sometimes modern medicine is good."

Carolina peered into Miss Latah's basket.

"Can any of these plants make a stroke go away?"

"Plant medicine does not always offer easy cures."

"Then why do you have so many plants in your medicine room?"

"My grandmother taught me about the power that lies within certain plants and roots. Nature has a language of its own. It provides all that we need. She also showed me the healing touch in my hands. She taught me about the healing touch in my heart. Most important, she would say to me, is that these gifts come from the Great Creator. I learned. I continue to collect the plants and make medicine in good faith, and I rely on the Great Creator to perform the miracle to cure."

"Do any of the plants we collected today have powerful medicine?"

"Yes," said Miss Latah. "Prayer is also powerful medicine."

Carolina pulled off Lucas's old cowboy boots and placed them carefully on the rock. She dunked her feet into the cool water.

Carolina splashed her feet. She eased off the rock, lowering herself into the water until it soaked the legs of her shorts. Miss Latah stood and raised her arms over her head in a big stretch. Then she began making her way back to the bank. Carolina pulled herself up, grabbed the boots, and jumped from one rock to the next until she was across the stream.

Miss Latah was waiting. She kneeled down and crumbled a leaf on a plant that was blooming with delicate feathery spikes of white flowers. She held the leaves in her open palm.

"Can you guess the scent?" she asked.

Carolina sniffed.

"It's peppermint. Auntie Shen used to make me peppermint tea whenever I got a stomachache."

There was no way to take the words back. She'd gone and said them.

"Tell me about your Auntie Shen," said Miss Latah.

Carolina thought about how Miss Latah trusted her not to tell about the ginseng. Carolina thought about her daddy saying trust went both ways. She wondered what she could tell. What if Mr. Ray and Miss Latah were breaking the law? She figured there was probably a law against feeding a runaway and giving her a nice place to live. What if they ended up going to jail? If Miss Latah knew the truth, would she call the sheriff?

On a mossy patch of ground in the center of a circle of evergreens, Carolina looked inside herself as if she was peering into a basketful of secrets, wondering which ones were safe to tell.

When finally she began, she talked about the cats on Auntie Shen's porch and about their home on Blue Star Mountain and about Morning Glory Jelly Stand. Miss Latah listened and she did not interrupt, not even once.

"Auntie Shen is the best grandma any mountain girl could ask for."

Carolina spoke the words in a soft voice. It had been a long, long while since she'd had the chance to say those words to Auntie Shen. It had been a long, long while since Carolina had seen the sparkles dancing in Auntie Shen's eyes.

Telling the truth was a whole lot easier than trying to remember her made-up stories. Even still, Carolina thought it best not to mention the foster homes. She didn't dare confess that she'd run away. She wanted to tell Miss Latah about her mama and daddy and Caleb, but the words got caught in her throat.

"Auntie Shen had to go away for a little while, but she'll be heading back home pretty soon, I expect," Carolina said, no louder than a whisper.

Miss Latah was quiet for a long time. She picked at pine needles that had woven their way into the patch of moss and worked them between her fingers. Finally she spoke.

"When I was a child, I was forced to attend a boarding school for Indian children. I had to go far away from my family," she said. "It was an awful time, a very lonely time for me and many Indian children. The teachers at this school would punish us if we spoke our native language."

"What did you do?" asked Carolina.

"I learned to behave their way on the outside and to pray my way on the inside."

"Did you fool them?" asked Carolina.

"I suppose not," Miss Latah laughed, but it didn't sound happy. "I didn't want to be white. I am Cherokee. They spoke of a God that was cruel and punishing. Yet the Creator I knew was in the light and in the wind—beautiful and loving and free. I am grateful for my ancestors who came to my aid—their Cherokee prayers and songs lived in my heart. They live there still."

Carolina listened.

"My great-uncle was a man of great wisdom. When he was close to his last breath, I was with him," Miss Latah continued, "and he told me a story about a strong warrior woman named Cuhtahlatah who was brave in battle."

"Cuhtahlatah," Carolina repeated.

"He said I was brave in battle too and gave the name Cuhtahlatah to me. Latah is the name I gave myself when he died. I never again used the white name that had been forced upon me at the school."

"I want to be brave," said Carolina.

Miss Latah took Carolina's hands in hers.

"Pray for your Auntie Shen. I will pray too. Our prayers will be like great birds flying to Heaven."

Chapter 14 ·

BLUE STAR MOUNTAIN

A coyote had killed a lamb. Carolina and Mr. Ray were mending the break in the fence. She dragged a log post over the grass. Grunting from the weight of it, she struggled to lift it into the post hole.

"Here you go," said Mr. Ray.

He hoisted it up with his good arm, as easily as if it was kindling wood. Mr. Ray held the fencing in place and Carolina hammered in nails that looked like tiny horseshoes. Mr. Ray's shirtsleeve caught on the sharp edges of the wire fencing and ripped it from elbow to cuff.

"Law," he said.

They exchanged smiles. They both knew he'd hear it from Miss Latah when she discovered her mending had been in vain. He rested his hand on the post, his eyes scanning the length of fencing.

Carolina spotted a wasp slowly picking its way through the straw-colored hairs on Mr. Ray's tanned arm. One time she'd knocked a wasp's nest and was stung three times. Those stings had burned hot as fire.

"Mr. Ray," she whispered.

Her eyes were on the wasp; she hoped Mr. Ray wouldn't bump his arm and get stung. He followed her gaze, then leaned his head down.

"Take my cap and get a breeze goin' over him."

Carolina slowly reached up and pulled the cap off his head. Sure enough, the gentle breeze caused the wasp to lift off and take wing.

"Don't bother them and they won't bother you," he said.

"If you say so," said Carolina, thinking of her own experience.

Mr. Ray ran his hand over his head, scratching his scalp. His hair was like straw. It poked out every which way, except what had been matted down by his cap.

He took the lid off a bucket of grain and shook it. All at once, the sheep lifted their heads. They trotted after that bucket of grain, until Mr. Ray had gathered them all into a three-sided wooden shelter. Carolina had learned that the sheep felt secure when they were snuggled together but would panic and run if you tried to grab one out in the open.

Mr. Ray ran his right hand over each one. Some were friendly and would cozy right up to him. Others kept a wary eye. His fingers reached deep into their wool.

"Not too fat, not too thin," he said.

Carolina spoke to each ewe and ewe lamb by name while Mr. Ray checked the condition of their hooves. He said he couldn't have done the work without her. She was glad to know that Mr. Ray didn't think it silly in the least for her to talk to the sheep the way she did. In fact, he said he rather liked it.

They continued up the hill, looking for any more holes that might have been dug by the coyote. Tall weeds were entangled in the wire. In some places the wire sagged and the posts leaned far. Carolina feared for the safety of the sheep, and Mr. Ray assured her they were doing their best to protect them, but they couldn't stop nature at work—the fence going back to the ground, coyotes eating for survival, weeds growing fast in their season. The best they could do was pay attention to the daily work.

They reached the highest point in the pasture.

"Now, that's lovely," said Mr. Ray.

It was lovely. They had a bird's-eye view of the land laid out before them. They could see their own planted fields and the fields that belonged to their neighbors. They could see meadows green with alfalfa and meadows of gold and purple growing wild. The rows in a neighboring cornfield stretched out in long green stripes. Across the horizon blue lines marked the mountain peaks. They rose and fell like great humps, forming a chain across the entire line of sky.

"Mr. Ray," Carolina said, "can we see Blue Star Mountain from here?"

"Well, let's see. It's to the north. Blue Star Mountain is most likely in those distant peaks."

"Are you sure?"

"Aye," he said. "I used to hunt with a fella up that way."

She looked up at Mr. Ray. The collar of his shirt was frayed. His overalls were stained with farm soil and tractor grease. It didn't bother him in the least. He was shielding his eyes from the sun, taking in the view with a satisfied smile on his face as if he was the richest man in the world. Then his brow creased, but it wasn't from squinting into the sun. He was thinking hard about something.

"Carolina, are you ready to head back?" asked Mr. Ray.

"To the house?" she asked, confused by his question.

"Are you ready to head back to Blue Star Mountain?"

Carolina felt the beat of her heart picking up speed. It was exactly what she wanted. Since telling Miss Latah about Auntie Shen, she'd left herself wide open for all kinds of questions. The answers she gave were partly true and partly not, and it led to Mr. Ray and Miss Latah's thinking she'd run away from the place she loved most. She wanted to set things straight, but she'd made such a tangled mess, she didn't know where to begin.

Carolina looked down at the orchard next to the house. Apple, pear, and plum trees were gathered like ladies in fancy hats gossiping on the church lawn. Auntie Shen's church hat was a wide-brimmed straw one. In the summer she'd weave fresh flowers all around it before they headed to the Missionary Baptist Church. The church had bare wood floors and long windows all along the side, and a squared-off steeple came to a point right above the front steps. It was set back a ways on a little knoll off the dirt road. If folks happened to be strolling by during service, the gospel music flowing out the open doors would wash all over them.

Carolina figured her weavings of yarn and fact had gotten to looking as withered as the flowers on Auntie Shen's hat come Sunday evening. Carolina looked up at Mr. Ray. "I'm ready," she said.

They left the upper pasture and walked along a path that ran through the woods and around back to the house again. Carolina noticed a patch of star grass in bloom. In the past she would have walked right by, but Miss Latah had opened her eyes to a new way of seeing. Carolina noticed pale green lichen growing on the rocks in designs as pretty as Queen Anne's lace. Under tall trees with wide canopies boulders were covered in a carpet of moss. Carolina pressed her fingers in. It was soft, thick, and damp.

Mr. Ray had an observing eye too. He pointed out rings in the trunk of a fallen oak. They counted them, calculating how old the tree might be. He traced them with his finger.

"Look close," he said. "The rings show the seasons when this tree drank plenty of rain, when life was rich and good. It stayed strong so it could make it through the dry season, when life was hard," he said.

Later that evening, Carolina and Mr. Ray were out on the porch, catching a cool breeze. Carolina sat on the steps picking fresh snap beans out of Miss Latah's basket, breaking off the stems and tossing them into a cream-colored pottery bowl. Those were the ones for supper. The rest she was stringing up with a needle and thread. She didn't need to be told how. She'd done it plenty before. Auntie Shen called strung-up dried beans "leather britches."

Mr. Ray sat in a rocker. It was a strong chair, one he'd coaxed into shape out of twigs and small branches. He dragged his lips across a harmonica, getting warmed up to play a few songs. Carolina draped her strung-together beans over the railing and plucked the string on the banjo that Mr. Ray had made from a large gourd. She ran her fingers gently down the neck of it.

"No one makes banjos like that anymore," he said. "My great-granddaddy used to make them, though. I got it in me one day to try my hand at it. It doesn't sound the way I'd like, but it is fun to look at, isn't it?"

Mr. Ray handed Carolina a diddley bow, another old-timey instrument he'd made with nothing more than a straight piece of board, a nail, and some wire. He said he'd learned how to make this instrument from a banjo picker he'd met years ago. They'd worked together in the fields on a big farm in Tennessee. Carolina plucked the one-string instrument with her fingers.

"I can't make it sound like anything," she said.

"On the contrary," said Mr. Ray. "It's good playing. With practice, you'll play even better."

Carolina plucked the diddley bow some more, making high-pitched tinny sounds. Twing. Twang.

"How about trying your hand at a little tune," he said.

Carolina plucked the wire. Mr. Ray began to sing.

> *"It's a pretty good world this is, I say—*
> *It's a pretty good world this is!"*

Mr. Ray sang a song about folks making up stories and showing off and downright lying. The song was about hard times and getting on, and about how the Lord has His own plan and how everything works out for the best.

Carolina laid the instrument on the floorboards. "Do you really think this is a pretty good world?" she asked.

"Sure do," he said, "if a person makes up their mind that it is. Notice how some folks are happy all the time and other folks grumble like trouble is all they have?"

Carolina nodded her head.

"It's a funny thing," said Mr. Ray, "because trouble comes to everyone at one time or another. A person has to make up their mind to be happy."

"You made up your mind, didn't you, Mr. Ray?" asked Carolina.

"Aye," said Mr. Ray. "You can too."

The next morning fog was thick and damp and hung low in the valleys. Carolina watched Mr. Ray sip his coffee. She stared at his fork, watching him cut into the whites of his egg. She stared at his fingers as he dipped bread into the yolk.

"You and Mr. Ray will be heading off soon enough, Carolina," Miss Latah said. "Keep your shirt on."

Carolina stared at the Farmer's Almanac calendar on the wall. Today was Thursday, July 23. She couldn't sit still a moment longer. She pushed back her chair and went out on the porch to wait. She counted on her fingers to figure how many days she and Auntie Shen had lived apart. She figured it to be forty-six.

It was all set. Mr. Ray was taking her to Blue Star

Mountain. Carolina had been up and dressed before every-one. She peered through the screen door and saw Mr. Ray sit back in his chair and push his plate away. She watched him reach back and grab his cap off the chair post, then come out the door.

Miss Latah stepped out onto the porch behind Mr. Ray. She was carrying a small peach basket with the hand-me-downs from Lucas. Mason jars full of canned vegetables lay amid the clothing. "So they won't break," Miss Latah had said. On top of it all, folded up neatly, was the color-ful quilt from Carolina's bed.

"Good-bye, me dear wife," said Mr. Ray, and he kissed Miss Latah on the lips.

Miss Latah held his cheeks in her hands and kissed him back.

"Are you sure your shoulder feels strong enough?"

"To drive?" asked Mr. Ray, sounded offended. "It's fine, Latah. I promise I won't be trying to lift any steers along the way."

Miss Latah gave him an exasperated look, then leaned down and planted a kiss on the top of Carolina's head. Miss Latah put her arms around Carolina and held her for a long time. Carolina wrapped her hands around Miss Latah's waist and squeezed into that hug. When she looked up, she saw that Miss Latah's eyes had filled with tears.

"Your Auntie Shen is going to be mighty happy to see you," she said.

Lucas reached down and tugged one of Carolina's braids.

"Don't take any wooden nickels," he said.

Carolina believed she might actually miss having her braids tugged.

As Mr. Ray drove the truck down the drive away from the house, Carolina leaned out the window, waving her arm. Miss Latah and Lucas were standing on the porch waving back. Carolina was already looking forward to coming back to visit with Auntie Shen.

There was dense fog on the mountain roads. Mr. Ray drove slow and easy, picking his way around the curves. Slowly the fog evaporated and the sun broke through. The day was as clear as could be. Carolina's imagination took on fanciful colors, painted with wishes and hopes. She imagined Auntie Shen standing on the porch, drying her hands on her apron and stepping quickly down the steps with her arms open wide, ready to give Carolina a big hug.

Mr. Ray interrupted her thoughts. "I need to stop on the way and talk to a man about coming to shear some of those lambs."

"Can't Lucas do it?" Carolina asked.

"No, shearing takes experience, and Lucas doesn't have any," Mr. Ray said.

Mr. Ray said he couldn't hold a fidgety sheep with a lame shoulder. He didn't like hiring out either. The worst thing he could think of was a shearer nicking one of the lambs with the clipper. Nicking a sheep would be like giving a boy a crew cut and taking off a bit of his scalp.

Then he said, "I'll tell ya, it's times like these I wish I

was speaking with my brother. Now, he can take the wool off a sheep in two minutes."

"Why aren't you speaking with your brother?"

"He and the rest of my kin didn't take kindly to me and Miss Latah tying the knot, her being Cherokee and all. I'd about had it with my brother for making bad moonshine. Don't get me wrong. I got nothing against a fellow trying to provide for his family, but I am against making whiskey that could send a man to an early grave," he said, and then added, "Carolina, don't ever sip corn likker."

Carolina raised her eyebrows, thinking he was crazy for even suggesting it.

"Now I don't begrudge anyone a bit of pleasure, but whiskey has spirits and will overtake a body at the slightest opportunity," said Mr. Ray.

"Yes, sir," said Carolina, her mind filling with a memory of the men she'd come upon when she was lost in the wilderness.

"Does your brother make moonshine in the woods?"

"You mean, does he have a still?"

"If a still is a big barrel with a pipe coming out of its top and a fire under it," she said.

"That's a still, all right," said Mr. Ray. "The old-timers once had them hid all over these mountains."

"Did your brother ever shoot at anybody who came near his still?" she asked.

"Not anybody I knew well," he said. Then he changed the subject.

Hours went by. They covered a lot of winding roads. Every now and again they'd pass open fields with log cabins and unpainted outbuildings with roofs ready to fall in. Carolina was growing weary of the sound of tires on blacktop and the creaks and groans of the truck. She stared at the black hole in the dashboard where the radio used to be.

"Mr. Ray, I bet you could get a radio out of a junkyard truck," Carolina said.

Mr. Ray laughed.

"This *is* a junkyard truck," he said.

Carolina tapped a tune with her fingers on the dashboard.

"Mr. Ray, tell me the story of the love flute."

"Me dear wife has been telling stories about me, eh?" said Mr. Ray.

His face broke into a grin. He was fixing to tell a story. Mr. Ray was Scots-Irish, and whenever he was warming up to tell a good story, his speech took on an Irish brogue.

"Well, let's see. One day, near twenty years ago, I was strolling down the side of a long dusty road, kicking my toes into the dirt. I'd had a humdinger of an argument with my no-good brother and had it set in my mind to get as far away from him as possible. I remember a hawk brushed so close it could have knocked my hat, but when I looked up, I wasn't interested in the bird any longer. I was looking at her."

"You mean Miss Latah?"

"That I do."

"Did you think she was pretty?"

Mr. Ray looked far off, as if he was seeing it all for the first time.

"Her hair had a shine like the moon on still water. She was wearing a yellow summer dress."

"Did she think you were handsome?"

"From the look she gave me, she must have thought I was ugly as a possum. But fate kept bringing us together. I had no idea where she lived, and she wasn't about to tell me, so I guess the Lord himself was playing Cupid. I had a friend I used to hunt with. He said he learned from a Cherokee friend of his about an Indian tradition of courting with love flutes, so I kept after him until he drew me a likeness of one. I had to do some research on my own, of course, but then I used a piece of hollow river cane and made the finger holes fit my hand. I even carved the likeness of a hawk's head onto it. I carried it with me everywhere."

Carolina reached up and felt her daddy's carving, knowing his hand had been all over it. It was as close as she could get to him.

Mr. Ray was all fired up, telling his story.

"When I'd see Latah, I'd start to play. Once I followed her, playing that flute," he said, laughing a good hearty laugh from his belly. "Oooh boy! She gave me a look near struck me dead."

"But after a while," he said, giving Carolina a wink, "she smiled."

Carolina leaned her arm out the open window. She was thinking about how her own parents met. Her mama said she and some of her college friends had volunteered to work on the Appalachian Trail along the border of North Carolina and Tennessee. Her mama said she'd always wanted to see the Great Smoky Mountains, and so she went. Carolina's daddy said he'd just graduated college and was missing home, so he came back to roam the mountains. Her daddy said the minute he saw her mama, he suddenly became very interested in trailblazing. They worked side by side for weeks, clearing brush and marking paths. After that, they couldn't bear to say good-bye, so they got married instead.

Mr. Ray pulled up to a shack with rusting cars and trucks scattered around the yard. It looked as if a windstorm had lifted them up and crashed them back down again.

Mr. Ray walked up to the door and knocked. Carolina went with him. She could hear somebody moving about within.

The door opened a crack, and Carolina saw a woman who looked more tired than anyone she'd ever seen. It looked as if she hadn't combed her hair in a month.

"If you're looking for Sims, he ain't here," the woman said.

"Do you know when he'll be back?" asked Mr. Ray.

"No, I can't say," she said as she eyed Mr. Ray closer. "You Ray Harmony?" she asked.

"Is that you, Mabel?" he asked.

"I ain't been feeling too good," the woman said, as if she was making an apology for the way she looked.

Mr. Ray didn't say anything.

"This your girl?" the woman asked.

Mr. Ray slowly nodded his head.

"She's a pretty thing," said the woman, and then she started to cough. "You want me to tell Sims you stopped by?"

"You can tell him I've got some sheep needs shearing," said Mr. Ray. He turned to leave and then turned back around again. "Can I help you with anything before I leave?"

"Thankee for asking," said Mabel. "I'll get the boy to help." She quietly closed the door.

Mr. Ray slid onto the seat of the truck. Carolina slid in beside him.

"How do you know her?" asked Carolina.

"You won't believe it," he said, "but a long time ago we went to school together."

"How come she didn't ask us in?"

"Just feeling poorly, I suppose."

As Mr. Ray backed up the truck, Carolina spotted trouser legs and bare feet dangling from a branch in a tree down near the edge of the woods. Carolina figured it must be the boy Mabel had mentioned. He was just sitting there, swinging his legs to and fro.

Carolina turned around to get a better look, but he had pulled his legs up. There was nothing to see but the green leaves of the tree that offered a good hiding place.

Mr. Ray and Carolina traveled north for nearly two hours before they reached the back side of Blue Star Mountain.

Mr. Ray drove down paved roads and dirt roads and roads so rocky and full of ditches he could hardly get the truck through. He drove all over Blue Star Mountain. He finally pulled to the side of the road.

Carolina sat beside him on the back end of the truck. Mr. Ray broke a piece of corn bread in two, the last of the dinner Miss Latah had packed. With his whittling knife, he spread blackberry jelly across a large square and handed it to her.

"We've been driving in circles," he said. "I'm sorry to say that unless you can remember the way, we'll have to be heading home."

Carolina had always gone to Auntie Shen's with her parents—one road up from Boone and one road back down. She knew the path from Auntie Shen's to Miss Ruby's. She knew the way from Auntie Shen's to the jelly stand. But these roadways were unfamiliar. They'd even passed by places that were getting so dug up with bulldozers that there wasn't a tree or living thing left, just dirt, and not even fit for a garden. Mr. Ray shook his head and said something about rich men hiring developers to clear the land to put up fancy houses and ski resorts.

Carolina's heart sank. Here she was, probably close enough to spit, but she might as well have been as far away as the moon. Each bite of corn bread was like swallowing a mouthful of sand.

"What a sight that is," said Mr. Ray, pointing up the mountain to a giant rock protruding from the embankment. Its shape resembled the head of a turtle poking out of its shell.

"I remember!" Carolina exclaimed as she jumped down from the truck.

She headed up a steep slope. Mr. Ray followed as Carolina bushwhacked up the mountain. She remembered the turtle rock, and now she remembered a path that she had hiked with her daddy. Carolina trekked higher and higher until she was breathless. She came to a path hardly wider than a deer trail and followed it, knowing it would lead her in the right direction.

She moved swiftly through the trees, following the ridgeline, making out familiar landmarks. She was getting closer and closer. Then, suddenly, there it was—home.

Queen Anne's lace and black-eyed Susans grew in the grass, and jewelweed had grown waist-high. She heard the screen door squeak open. She heard it bang shut on the doorjamb.

Carolina shouted, "Auntie Shen!"

She didn't know if she'd laugh or cry as she ran up onto the porch. Her heart was fluttering like the wings of a bird as she burst inside.

Carolina stood still as a stone as she looked about. A spider had woven a silky web from the top corner of the window halfway down to the lock. Flies buzzed above the grease in the iron skillet. Carolina recalled pouring a bit of water into it so it would be easier to scrub. That had been on the very day she'd been forced to leave. On the table was a Mason jar. All the water in it had evaporated, and now the pretty flowers were nothing but dried-up sticks, thin as grass. Carolina didn't see a single cat about.

It was only wishful thinking that it was Auntie Shen's hand opening and closing the screen door. In truth, the house had never felt so lonesome and empty. The breeze blew the door open again, and again it banged shut.

Chapter 15

STORM COMIN'

Carolina stepped into her own bedroom and gazed over the animals lined up on top of her chest of drawers, all ready to walk into Noah's ark. She was home again, but not really. Without Auntie Shen, the house had an eerie stillness. The note she'd written to her was still there under the wishing stone. Carolina dropped the stone in her pocket.

When she walked back into the kitchen, Mr. Ray was standing in the doorway. She figured he was waiting for an invitation.

"It's okay, Mr. Ray," she said. "You can come in."

Mr. Ray reached down and picked up a gray kitten that was rubbing itself against the leg of his overalls. He held the kitten in the crook of his arm and gently stroked its fur. The kitten's purr got louder and louder.

"He's got his motor running," said Mr. Ray.

"This is Buzzy," said Carolina, "and he sure has gotten scrawny."

"Aye, he is a wee bit of a thing," he said, scratching the kitten behind its ears.

"Looks like he's the only one hung around to wait," she said, her voice low and quiet.

Mr. Ray put his hand on Carolina's shoulder.

"Let's go find your Auntie Shen," he said.

The truck headed down toward the hospital in Boone, the kitten curled up in a ball on Carolina's lap. Before they'd left the house, Carolina had packed up some of her own clothes and some of her books. They were stuffed into the peach basket that was wedged between the floorboards and the seat. Carolina's hand rested on the shoe box pressed against her leg. Inside it were some of her mama's best photographs.

"The hospital shouldn't be too hard to find," said Mr. Ray.

"They got a rule says I can't visit until I'm twelve years old," said Carolina.

"Stand up tall," said Mr. Ray. "You'll pass."

When they got to the hospital, the lady at the front desk said Auntie Shen wasn't a patient, and there was no evidence of her being admitted. Carolina loved Mr. Ray more than anything after the way he kept after the hospital workers, forcing them to search their records.

"Mr. Ray," said Carolina, tugging on his shirtsleeve, "maybe they should look under 'Ada McClaine.'"

The missing file turned out not to be missing at all. It turned out that Auntie Shen had been taken to a place called Shady Rest.

It sounded like an old folks' home to Carolina. *Auntie Shen must be miserable*, Carolina thought. The directions that the hospital worker gave them were not very good, but somehow Mr. Ray found it. The sun was easing down to the west when they pulled into a dirt parking lot.

There was a front desk at Shady Rest too.

Mr. Ray convinced the nurse who was guarding the place that he was Auntie Shen's long-lost nephew.

"And this is my daughter, Carolina," said Mr. Ray, "who is twelve years old."

Mr. Ray bent over and coughed and then straightened himself up again.

The nurse eyed them up and down. Carolina was still hearing the word *daughter*.

"Visiting hours have long since passed," she said.

Mr. Ray stood his ground and Carolina followed suit. Finally the nurse heaved a big sigh.

"Room two-twelve," the nurse said, and she let them pass.

Carolina walked beside Mr. Ray down a narrow hallway. There were rooms on both sides. She couldn't help glancing into them as she passed by. What she saw were lonely wrinkled-up faces, older folks slumped in their wheelchairs with nowhere to go and nothing to do. They looked so sad, as if the whole world had walked away and forgotten all about them.

When they reached Room 212, Carolina peered in.

There was Auntie Shen, bundled up in bed with a blanket under her chin, staring out the window. She looked so small. Carolina slipped her hand into Mr. Ray's as they entered the room. She walked to the other side of Auntie Shen's bed, got down on her knees, and looked into Auntie Shen's face.

"Carolina, is 'at you?" Auntie Shen's voice was weak and shaky.

"It's me," said Carolina in a soft voice. "This is Mr. Ray. I've been staying with him and Miss Latah, and Lucas too. He's their son."

Carolina talked about Harmony Farm and the sheep and the old hound dog.

"Are you rememberin' to feed the cats?" said Auntie Shen.

No matter how many times Carolina explained things, Auntie Shen stayed convinced that Carolina was still up on Blue Star Mountain. Auntie Shen kept forgetting why Mr. Ray was in her room. The nurse had warned them that older folks could get confused as it got late. It still didn't seem right.

The last rays of golden light were shining in the window. Mr. Ray stood beside Carolina and laid a hand on her shoulder.

"You best be going now," said Auntie Shen.

Carolina didn't answer. That big old lump had piled up in her throat again.

Mr. Ray gently patted Auntie Shen's hand, and when he did, she reached out and held his fingers. He bent from the waist, leaning down to listen to her soft-spoken words.

"You're taking good care of my girl. I can tell," said Auntie Shen, her voice barely more than a whisper.

Mr. Ray nodded his head.

"'At's good," she continued. "I'm getting stronger every day. I'll be out of here soon."

Auntie Shen suddenly looked up at Carolina and winked at her. "We've got jellies to make, haven't we?"

Carolina smiled then. The weight of the world that had been bearing on her suddenly fell away. Auntie Shen had come back to her old self.

"Yes, we have lots of jellies to make," said Carolina.

Carolina and Mr. Ray were walking down the hall when Carolina remembered something important.

"I'll be right back, Mr. Ray," she said.

Carolina ran into Auntie Shen's room. She leaned down so they were eye to eye.

"I brought the wishing stone, Auntie Shen," Carolina whispered. "I think you know how to work it better than I do."

Auntie Shen smiled. "Let me see it."

Carolina held out the two-colored stone. It was almost white with a black line going all the way around it.

"Put it under my pillow," said Auntie Shen. "I'll make the wish for us both."

The sky was black with silver stars when Carolina and Mr. Ray began the long drive back to Harmony Farm.

All Carolina could see was the road in front of them, illuminated by the headlights of the truck. The gray kitten was sound asleep, sprawled out on the seat between them. Carolina's thoughts were on Auntie Shen. She was remembering the times when she was very little and getting sleepy. Her eyes would start to itch, and Auntie Shen would say the sandman was filling her eyes with dreams. *Close your eyes and let them be sweet dreams he's bringin'.* Carolina felt the sandman coming now, filling her eyes so heavy with sand she could hardly keep them open, and finally she gave in.

She woke up with Mr. Ray gently calling her name. She felt herself being lifted up into strong arms and then realized Lucas was carrying her to the house as if she was a baby. She was so tired, she just rested her head on his shoulder. She was home. The yellow light in the kitchen was on and Miss Latah was standing on the porch, waiting to greet them.

The next day a wind kicked up and blew the treetops to a slant. Black clouds were threatening to storm. Carolina was setting the table for supper.

Squares of corn bread were piled high in a woven basket in the center of the table. Butter was melting in creamy mashed sweet potatoes. On the stove, rabbit stew simmered in a broth of summer vegetables. The savory scent of meat and herbs steamed up, creating a moist cloud in the kitchen. Carolina sat at her place and watched Miss Latah sprinkle rosemary and thyme into the stew.

She watched Mr. Ray through the screen door as he untied his muddy boots with one hand and set them on the floorboards of the porch. He smiled at her as he came through the doorway. Lucas was right behind him. Miss Latah placed the last bowl on the table and sat down, completing the circle.

They all reached out and held one another's hands. Everyone bowed their heads. Carolina felt Miss Latah's hand, warm from handling hot dishes, and Mr. Ray's hand, calloused and rough from the fields. Mr. Ray began the prayer as he always did.

"Dear Lord, bless us all, stranger and kin," he began.

He continued, expressing his heart, grateful for their many blessings. Carolina was filled with a sweet feeling. Harmony Farm was her haven, and her heart was filled with its sweetness.

"And we thank you, Lord, for bringing Carolina to our family. Amen."

Carolina stared at her plate. It didn't feel right anymore, keeping her eyes open when everyone else was praying. She closed her eyes and said a silent *Amen.*

The conversation came around to the business of sheep.

"I've hired Sims Farley to shear the lambs we're keeping," he said.

She wondered what Mr. Ray meant when he said *lambs we're keeping.*

"I was on the phone with Sims this morning," he said.

Carolina spread honey on her corn bread and took a big bite.

"Sims said he and Mabel have been caring for a nephew. He said his sister, Lily Jean, had been caring for the boy over to White Oak, but he was too much for her."

Carolina stopped chewing.

"Seems his sister is running a foster home," Mr. Ray continued.

Carolina washed the corn bread down with a gulp of milk.

Mr. Ray took a bite of stew. Carolina watched him chew real slowly, as if he was chewing on his thoughts too. She waited for him to continue.

Finally, Mr. Ray spoke again, "He said one of the kids run off on her, a girl about ten, a redhead."

Carolina saw the way Mr. Ray looked at Miss Latah.

She saw Miss Latah look back at him with eyes that were fierce.

"Maybe the child had good reason to run away," said Miss Latah.

Mr. Ray put his fork down. He laid the words out gently, as if he was shearing a sheep, being careful not to make a mean cut.

"Good reason or not, running away because it's too hard to make things right is just keeping things wrong," he said. "Sims said they got the police out looking for her."

Miss Latah's chair scraped on the floor as she pushed it back. She set her plate on the counter by the sink and stepped out on the porch, quietly closing the screen door behind her. Carolina's eyes were on Miss Latah's back. Miss Latah stood still, staring into the distance.

"Hey, Carolina," Lucas said.

Her body tensed up.

"Are you going to eat that last piece of corn bread?"

"No, you have it," she said. "I'm full."

Mr. Ray tapped Lucas on the knee. "How about you and Carolina help your mother by washing up these dishes?"

"Yes, sir," Lucas replied.

Mr. Ray pushed his chair back and walked out onto the porch. He put his good arm around Miss Latah and kept it wrapped around her as they headed down the steps. Carolina watched them as they strolled across the farm-yard.

Carolina dragged a soapy cloth around and around a plate.

"When I was a youngun I helped a dog run away," said Lucas.

"Why did you do that?" Carolina asked.

"I was tired of watching that little pup get beat by his owner," said Lucas as he dried a plate and set it on the shelf. "One day, I mustered up my courage and unleashed that hound from his chain. At first that pup stayed put like he was too scared to move, as if the spirit of his master was still holding him."

"Then what happened?"

"Something must have clicked inside him, for he took off real sudden like he'd heard a gunshot. He tore out of that yard. I remember watching him take off toward the woods. How my heart cheered him on."

Lucas took another plate out of the dish rack. "I didn't think I'd ever see that little pup again, but I did. He seemed to show up everywhere. I swear, that pup was following me, so I brought him home."

He leaned down close to Carolina and pointed to the old hound dog lying asleep on the porch. His name was Homer. His brown fur was going gray around his eyes.

"Didn't the owner come looking for his dog?"

"Yep. That ol' codger dragged that poor pup away more than a few times." Lucas laughed. "And Homer kept running back to me."

"How could he run back if the owner kept him chained up?"

Carolina saw Lucas grin as he set the last plate in the cupboard.

"He was lucky. He had me helping him out."

Carolina smiled at Homer sprawled out on the porch. She'd never paid him much mind before now. What that poor dog had been through. She decided she wouldn't get so mad at him when he chased Buzzy into the barn.

Chapter 16

SQUARE DANCE

No one had made mention of Sims Farley since last night at supper, and Carolina was relieved of it. Her mind was on the excitement of today. They were all going over to the next county to attend a square dance. Miss Latah said a square dance was one place no one ever brought up old grudges. She said dancing was just about the most fun a person could have.

Carolina felt the gentle tugs on her scalp. She could see Miss Latah in the reflection of the mirror. Her fingers worked quickly, weaving long strands of sweetgrass into Carolina's braids. Sheer white curtains billowed out in the breeze and brushed against Carolina's knees. As she gathered the fabric in her hands, she looked out the window and saw Lucas closing the barn doors and slipping the latch over.

Carolina's hair had grown so long it nearly reached her waist. Her daddy had said it was the color of sunset because it sparkled with red and orange and yellow light. It had been cut only twice in her whole life.

The first time was when she'd gotten hold of her mama's sewing scissors. She was only three years old at the time. Carolina remembered feeling so proud to be able to open and close the handles. She remembered hearing the crisp snip, snip, snip as she cut away her hair. She remembered being surprised by her mama's gasp, her hand covering her open mouth.

As her mama had told the story, Carolina cut away until only short tufts of hair stuck straight up on her head like spikes. Her mama had done the only thing she could do. She'd grabbed her camera. Carolina and her mama had pulled out that picture every time they'd needed a good laugh.

The second haircut happened after she'd fallen asleep with bubble gum in her mouth. What a sticky gooey mess of tangles she had. Not a comb or a brush could get through her hair. The gum would not pull apart either, so Carolina cut it out with the scissors. She left a big gaping hole where hair should be. So she did her best to shorten the rest of her hair to make it all match up.

This story had made her daddy chuckle on that day so long ago. Carolina and her daddy had sat side by side in matching barber chairs and gotten neat trim haircuts. Carolina had looked like a boy, and she'd felt as free as one too. She'd loved running through the woods without her hair getting caught on the briars. She'd loved going for days without picking up a brush or comb.

Miss Latah finished her braiding.

"There," she said. "You look like a Cherokee princess."

Carolina held a small mirror in front of her so she could see her hair in the big mirror behind. It sure did look pretty. Being a girl suited her fine.

Carolina's new outfit lay over a chair. Miss Latah had taken all the stitches out of one of her prettiest dresses and used the material to sew a skirt for Carolina. She had sewn a white blouse too and stitched on a piece of embroidery, a wildflower design, all along the neckline.

Miss Latah tied back her own hair with a blue ribbon. Mr. Ray put on a clean white shirt. Lucas spent a lot of time trying to tame the cowlick in his hair.

Carolina sat in the front of the pickup truck between Miss Latah and Mr. Ray so she wouldn't get her hair windblown. When they finally reached town and pulled down Main Street, it was lined with farm trucks, old cars with rusted fenders, and a brand-new Pontiac. It was easy to see that the white building with GRANGE HALL painted in black letters was where the action was taking place.

Carolina and Lucas followed Miss Latah and Mr. Ray as they all headed over. They passed by women all caught up in conversations. Boys were chasing each other in a game of tag and practically stepped on their toes as they raced around the side of the building. Mr. Ray tipped his hat over and over again, politely greeting other farmers he knew. Inside the grange hall couples were gathering in groups.

"Look," said Miss Latah to Mr. Ray, "there's a square we can join."

Mr. Ray and Miss Latah stepped into place with three other couples and made a square. Auntie Shen had taught Carolina square-dance steps, and the two of them had danced back and forth across the porch until they loosened the floorboards. She figured the dancing these folks were setting to do would be a whole lot harder to learn.

Up onstage a farmer was all dressed up in clean overalls. He placed a fiddle under his chin and dragged the bow across, real quiet, getting warmed up. The man next to him was plucking a banjo.

A woman stood before the musicians. The music began. She called out to the dancers, "All join hands. Go forward and back. Turn your partner right hand round. Back by the left—now don't get lost. Now two hands round and do-si-do."

All manner of country folk, rich and poor, young and old, danced together, and everyone seemed to be having a good time. The dancers circled around and linked arms. It looked as if they were working a human puzzle. The music, the laughter, the feet shuffling across the floor, and the conversations taking place on the side made it a festive party. Carolina smiled as she watched Mr. Ray spin Miss Latah around and around. She was glad his shoulder had healed up so quickly. He barely ever wore the sling anymore.

Men and women and boys and girls stood side by side in long lines, and a different dance began. The music beat faster and faster. Boots stomped the floor. Tiny flecks of dust rose up and were lit by the last rays of sunlight shining through the tall windows. When the dance stopped, the dust fell like a veil, covering them all.

On the other side of the room, a woman danced with a baby on her hip. A big burly man was stomping his big boots and having himself a time. It was Mr. Jim and Miss Abigail! When it was over, Mr. Jim wiped the sweat from his brow. He was laughing. He held his baby girl in one arm and put his other arm around Miss Abigail's tiny waist, and they headed outside.

Carolina made her way around the crowd to the wide-open doors. She saw them cross the street and walk along a green meadow, where lightning bugs were blinking on and off. Carolina followed, watching their little girl run from Mr. Jim's arms to Miss Abigail's outstretched ones. She stepped quicker to catch up.

"Hello, Miss Abigail," said Carolina, feeling breathless. It seemed her heart was beating about as fast as the music coming from across the street.

Miss Abigail's mouth opened in surprise. She started speaking in that squeaky voice of hers. "Carolina? Why, look at you, pretty as a picture. How are you these days?"

"I'm fine, thank you."

"We heard it didn't work out at the reverend's house," Miss Abigail said in a quiet voice, her hand half-covering her mouth.

Carolina suddenly remembered it was Mr. Jim and Miss Abigail who'd started all her troubles by talking to the church ladies.

"When we brought it up to the church that you were in

a fix, we never expected those old biddies to take matters into their own hands," said Mr. Jim.

"Sheriff said he hauled you off to some foster home," said Miss Abigail. She looked up at Mr. Jim. "I never did care for Clayton."

"Well, it looks like you're doing fine," said Mr. Jim. "I sure would like to meet the folks you're living with. We'll take word back to the church and give them the good news."

Carolina's throat squeezed up tight.

It felt as if she'd stepped in a trap. All she could think about was getting free.

"Uh, well, sure," Carolina stammered. "We'll have to do that. I best be getting back now. I'll let 'em know you're wanting to meet them."

Carolina didn't say good-bye. She didn't turn around when they called her name. She ran. She darted past the wide doors of the grange hall and scurried around to the back. She ran past a couple of boys climbing a tree. She ran past a group of kindergarten girls who had a party dance of their own going on.

Carolina took cover in a stand of trees behind the building. There was a little stream meandering there. Carolina scooted down the bank and sat beside it. She figured Mr. Jim and Miss Abigail hadn't meant to bring her trouble, but here it was. She remembered what Mr. Ray had said. *"They got the police out looking for her."*

She could hear the little girls singing and dancing. She climbed up the bank and watched them move round in a circle, all holding hands and singing "Pawpaw Patch" and

"Bluebird, Bluebird, Through My Window." They hadn't a care or worry in the world.

"Hey, where you been? I've been looking all over for you."

It was Lucas.

"It's too hot inside," said Carolina, making up an excuse.

"I've got some change in my pocket. How about I treat us to a couple of bottles of Grapette?"

Carolina had noticed the old general store on their way through town.

Carolina nodded.

Once they were in the general store, Lucas reached in and fished around in the ice and water in the cooler and pulled up two Grapettes. He snapped the bottle cap off one of them, using the metal bottle opener attached to the wall, and handed it to Carolina.

"Thanks, Lucas," she said. Carolina let the purple soda linger on her tongue, it tasted that good.

Lucas plopped down two dimes for the sodas and another dime for the deposit, five cents each, which they'd get back as soon as they returned the bottles. The storekeeper left the dime right on the counter, as it was easy to see they'd be draining their bottles right there in the store.

Lucas burped and then laughed.

"C'mon, Carolina," he said. "You're going to dance with me." He grabbed her hand and she ran along with him. She didn't have any choice. His grip was strong and he moved fast. They reached the hall and Lucas pulled her into a group of dancers just as the caller began to shout.

"Birdie in the cage. Three hands around. Birdie hops

out and crow hops in. Crow hops out and circle again. Swing your partner and on to the next."

A gray-haired grandpa linked his elbow with Carolina's, and she was twirled around. Then her arm was linked with a smiling teenage boy, and she was sent in another direction and then another boy was spinning her around. Around she went, bumping into one partner after another, being twirled every which way. All the while she was looking out for Mr. Jim and Miss Abigail. Lucas took hold of her hand and put an arm around her waist and spun her around and around until all she saw was a blur of colors.

When the dance ended, Lucas gave his attention to a pretty girl who was smiling at him. *Probably wanting him to ask her to dance*, thought Carolina. She scooted behind a group of women resting in folding chairs. They were full of gossip, cackling away like a bunch of hens in the farmyard. Carolina pushed her back to the wall, staying out of sight.

When the fiddler had put down his instrument and the grange hall was clearing out, Carolina saw Mr. Ray wiping the sweat from his brow and Miss Latah next to him, taking off her shoe and rubbing her toes. Mr. Ray spotted Carolina and waved his arm, motioning for her to come along. Outside, the warm air of a hot summer night made a good night for business at Mom and Pop's Ice Cream & BBQ.

It seemed the whole crowd was strolling down the street to get barbecue. The storekeeper and his helper were cooking it up in a big vat right outside the store. Picnic tables

had been set up and covered with red and white check-
ered vinyl tablecloths. Some of the folks who'd been dancing were now bringing out their own fiddles and guitars
and banjos, and it was turning into a real party.

Carolina wasn't taking any chances. She pretended she
had a stomachache and headed back to the truck as fast as
she could. She crouched down low. Carolina figured she
was just like the man on the television show *The Fugitive*,
wrongly accused, always staying one step in front of the
law. She laid her head on the seat, wishing she had another Grapette.

Chapter 17

TRANSISTOR RADIOS

HARMONY FARM was newly painted in black letters across the faded green paint on the door of the truck. *Lucas has good penmanship,* thought Carolina. She opened the door and jumped up onto the passenger seat. She and Miss Latah were taking a trip into town to get supplies. As she rolled down the window, she could see Miss Latah strolling across the yard carrying a split-oak basket she'd woven together herself. She was dressed in a blue skirt, starched and ironed, and a white sleeveless blouse. A braid ran down the length of her back.

"Ready to go?" asked Miss Latah with a smile.

"Ready!" said Carolina, grinning back.

The road curved in S shapes. Carolina leaned to the

right, then held the armrest as she leaned to the left. The truck groaned as Miss Latah downshifted, and they headed down the steep mountain road. Trees grew up the sharp grade to their left. To their right, the land dropped off abruptly. Carolina's ears popped.

Around another bend, a valley opened before them; a landscape of mountains and trees. Miss Latah slowed nearly to a stop in order to make a sharp turn onto a narrow road. It was an old road, the pavement patched together in squares of gray and black. They passed by a simple unpainted house with a long porch. It was set on a grassy hill near a meadow. Beyond it were a springhouse, a barn, and a shed that might have been a smokehouse. Carolina spotted an outhouse tucked into the trees.

It reminded Carolina of Blue Star Mountain. She and Auntie Shen had been living the way mountain folks used to live. They knew how to make do with little or nothing. Auntie Shen had grown up with only one sister, but caring neighbors made her feel as if she'd grown up in a large family. She said that folks knew how to take care of themselves. Everyone grew vegetables in their gardens and fruit in their orchards and knew how to preserve it all so they'd have something to eat come winter. Trees were cut down for firewood so people could stay warm. The cow provided milk, the chickens provided eggs, and the pig provided bacon and sausage. There wasn't a thing wasted. Auntie Shen still used a pig's head to make souse meat. She acted as if it was the best-tasting stuff in the world. Carolina thought it looked downright disgusting and refused to taste it.

As they passed by the little farm, Carolina saw two horses grazing in a fenced pasture. One was cream colored with a white tail, and the other was chestnut brown. Miss Latah meandered along the winding road, one hand on the wheel and the other resting on her basket. They passed modern houses made of brick, long skinny trailers, and shacks that looked ready to fall down.

Finally they pulled down a dirt driveway. Blue paint was peeling off the tiny house. The grass in the yard was a foot high. Daisies grew along a piece of decorative picket fence that still held a bit of white paint. Cheerful yellow petals reached their faces above the weeds, as if determined to speak well of earlier days.

"I thought we'd stop in and check on Miss Bertha. I've been doctoring her for arthritis," said Miss Latah.

Miss Latah knocked loudly on the front door.

"She's a bit hard of hearing," she explained.

It took a while, but the door finally opened. There stood a plump woman wearing a light green button-up house-dress and pink scuff slippers. When she saw Miss Latah at the door, her face lit up as if she'd just spotted the presents under the Christmas tree.

"Cum mo ih," she said. Her smile was all gums, like a newborn baby's.

Miss Bertha shuffled on into the kitchen. Miss Latah and Carolina stepped inside and followed. Immediately Miss Bertha put a kettle on the stove to heat water for tea. She set a plate of biscuits on the table next to a cup that held a full set of teeth. She reached in and stuck those teeth in her mouth, and just like that she could talk.

"There, now I can speak clearly," said Miss Bertha, "and

the first thing I want to know is the name of this sweet child."

It seemed like nothing more than a friendly visit at first, but then Carolina could see that Miss Latah was taking stock of Miss Bertha's health. Miss Latah spoke in a soft and gentle voice, and Miss Bertha answered every question like a student answering her teacher. Miss Latah brought out packets and jars from her basket.

"You can brew this up just like you do your tea," said Miss Latah. "It will take the ache away."

"How's it taste?" asked Miss Bertha.

"Well, you might have to drink it fast," said Miss Latah.

The two of them started to laugh.

Miss Bertha smiled. "I'll do it 'cause you tell me to. I trust ya."

When their teacups were empty and only a piece of biscuit was left on the plate, Miss Latah pushed back her chair. It was time to go. Carolina could clearly see that their visit was much too short for Miss Bertha by the way she followed them to the door. Miss Bertha kept remembering one more thing she had to say, as if she could hold them there in the doorway forever. Finally, Miss Latah promised to come back in a few days.

Miss Bertha seemed to relax a bit. She stayed in the open doorway as Miss Latah backed the truck onto the road. Before she drove off, Miss Latah reached her arm out the window and waved. Bertha stood at the door with a big smile on her face, waving back.

"What was in those jars you gave her?" asked Carolina.

"Oh, a little partridge berry to ease the soreness in her joints," she said, "and some root tea."

"Miss Bertha really likes you. I can tell," said Carolina.

"I like Miss Bertha too. She had her feathers ruffled when I first come to call. She only let me in because her daughter was the one who brought me." Miss Latah used a gruff voice to imitate Miss Bertha. " 'I don't want no Indian touching me.' " She laughed and then her voice softened.

"Now we get along just fine."

Miss Latah headed down back roads, admiring the scenery as they made their way toward town. She was looking out over the land and pointing things out to Carolina. Carolina was more interested in Miss Latah's face.

She had a broad nose and golden-brown skin. The sun shone bright in the windshield and made Miss Latah squint, and Carolina saw how tiny creases formed near her eyes. Carolina looked at Miss Latah's hands on the steering wheel. They were as rough and calloused as Mr. Ray's. Carolina figured Miss Latah had probably never worn fingernail polish.

Carolina had looked at the covers of magazines all lined up in racks at the grocery store. The women on those covers were posed in ways that showed their bosoms. They had fair skin and most had blond hair. They wore the latest fashions. Carolina's mama would never buy gossip magazines. She said she wouldn't waste her money. She said *true beauty is on the inside*. Now, looking at Miss Latah, Carolina was beginning to understand what her mama had meant. Miss Latah had true beauty—inside and out.

"I still can't believe you met my mama," said Carolina.

"That sure was a surprise to see those pictures you brought out of the shoe box," said Miss Latah.

Carolina's mama had sometimes sold pictures to the newspapers; pictures of ordinary folks doing their every-day ordinary things. Her pictures seemed to tell a story. One picture showed a boy turned around on a tractor. He was laughing as if somebody had just told him a good joke. That boy turned out to be none other than Lucas himself. Turned out Carolina's mama had gotten a flat tire a spit-ting distance from Harmony Farm. Mr. Ray said he'd changed her tire that day, and that was how she'd ended up with that picture of Lucas. Lucas had only been twelve years old then. Now he was fifteen.

"Maybe we could go and visit Auntie Shen," said Carolina, "and you can bring your medicine basket, and you'll have something in there that can help her get better."

Miss Latah stared ahead for a few moments before she answered.

"We'll go see your Auntie Shen," said Miss Latah. "There is no medicine better than to see the face of the one who loves you."

Carolina smiled.

"Can we go today?" asked Carolina.

"No, not today," said Miss Latah, "but soon. I promise."

They passed a gas station and bumped over the railroad tracks on their way into town. Main Street had traffic lights and buildings on both sides. They passed by a playground, and Carolina looked out the open window at children her own age swinging on swings and going down the slide. Miss Latah drove on at a slower speed and they passed a hardware store, a women's clothing store, and a barbershop that had a red, white, and blue sign that slowly twirled the colors in a spiral. Carolina was beginning to wonder if Miss Latah was going to drive straight through town without stopping. At the far end of Main Street, where the stores were separated by grass and vacant lots, there was a big building that looked more like a barn than a store. The sign said DOTTIE'S—GENERAL MERCHANDISE AND CAFÉ. Miss Latah pulled into the parking lot.

Dottie's was a big store with lots of aisles and little rooms full of merchandise. There was a big barrel of crackers near the cash register, and there was a big barrel of pickles too. There were shelves of clothes, boots, rakes for gardens, hunting rifles, bug spray, and Pond's cold cream. There was a feed and granary store out back. The café was filling up with people hungry for lunch. Miss Latah glanced down at the list she'd written on the back of an envelope.

"I'm going to roam around a bit while I gather the supplies I need," said Miss Latah. "You can go your own way if you like."

She handed Carolina a dime. "Go ahead and treat yourself to a candy bar too."

Carolina looked around. A cardboard sign and a display of transistor radios caught her eye. She gingerly held one of the tiny radios in her hand. They looked just like the ones she and Mattie had seen in the newspaper advertisement.

Carolina read the words on the cardboard sign.

Portable radio—$6.88
Compact!
Room-filling sound through 2¼" speaker!
10 transistors, 1 diode!
Complete with leather carrying case and battery

She got lost in her thoughts, wondering how she could earn six dollars and eighty-eight cents.

She heard a loud voice coming from within the café. It startled her. When she looked up, she knew why. It was Sheriff Nash, otherwise known as Cousin Clayton. He just seemed to show up everywhere. He was bragging to a man she figured was a deputy officer, talking about a prisoner who'd escaped custody and about being hot on the criminal's trail.

Carolina looked around to figure an escape route. She could head out to the truck, but then she'd have to walk right past the register, right smack-dab in the middle of everything, right out in the open where everyone could see. The sheriff and his deputy stood up, and she saw the sheriff pat his belly. They were headed her way. Carolina kneeled down and shimmied over to the hunting caps, pretending to be all taken up with choosing the right one. A row of camouflage-print hunting jackets and long pants were hanging from an iron bar. She slipped between the heavy jackets and pushed her back against the wall. She barely breathed.

The bell above the glass doors sounded a tinny ding. Was it the sheriff going out or another customer coming in? Carolina moved the last jacket forward a tiny bit, just enough to catch a glimpse.

"Carolina, you come out of there right now."

It was Miss Latah.

"Shhh," Carolina hissed. "They'll hear you."

Carolina dropped the jacket and pressed her back to the wall again.

There was just enough space between the jackets to see the expression on Miss Latah's face. Carolina figured Miss Latah was thinking that she'd gone plum crazy. Then Carolina saw Miss Latah reach down and casually hold a price tag in her hand, as if she was seriously considering the purchase. The sheriff and his deputy stepped so close by, they practically touched Miss Latah's shoulder.

"I could sure use a new huntin' jacket," said the deputy with the sheriff. "That other one a'mine used to be my granddaddy's, and I tell you, it is gettin' threadbare."

Carolina saw the officer's hand reach in and grab the sleeve of a jacket.

"We ain't got time to be dressing you up in a new outfit," said the sheriff.

"I know," said the deputy. "I was jest—"

"Yeah, you were jest," laughed the sheriff. "C'mon. We got a criminal to catch."

Miss Latah whispered into the hunting jackets, "They're gone."

All the way home Miss Latah stared straight ahead and didn't say a word, although it was painfully clear to Carolina that she was doing some serious thinking.

Carolina was doing some serious thinking too. How that sheriff kept turning up was beyond her. Then she remembered Mr. Ray's comment that a person brought trouble on himself.

At suppertime, Carolina was getting bored listening to Mr. Ray and Lucas talk about how to fix the rusted tractor in the barn. Then the conversation turned to shearing. That got her attention.

"Sims Farley should be coming the first of August to shear the ewe lambs. I'm still not keen on hiring him, but we need the help," Mr. Ray said, and then he heaved a sigh that made his shoulders drop. "Lord knows he needs the work."

Mr. Ray continued, "He'll be staying on a few days extra to do the slaughtering."

Slaughtering. The word hurt like getting hit with a stone. It wouldn't let go.

As soon as Carolina had the last dish dried and on the shelf, she dashed out the screen door and ran up to the sheep pasture. Mr. Ray was planning to kill some of the lambs. Wandering in the midst of the lambs, she wondered how he could do it. Would it be Cassie? Beth? Oh, she hoped he wouldn't take Ramona.

The lonesome whistle of a freight train sounded in the distance. She'd never paid the sound much mind before. Now it moaned in such a sad refrain, she couldn't help listening. Carolina headed in the direction of its call.

The long pointed leaves on the cornstalks were already getting dry, and they rustled in the breeze as she walked along the neighbor's cornfield. She was thinking about how Mr. Ray had saved Roamer, the hound dog. She'd seen Mr. Ray stand and brush Sadie's mane and tail until not a single burr was tangled in her hair. He loved his animals. Didn't he love the sheep too?

The thought occurred to Carolina that she and Auntie Shen had always been mighty happy whenever another family shared the meat from a hog they'd butchered. *That's different*, thought Carolina. *Who cares about hogs?* Lambs were sweet as babies.

The train's whistle blew again, louder this time. She figured that if she wanted to see the engine, she'd better move. She cut through the woods, raced through an open meadow and another stand of trees. The engine was rounding a bend in the track, winding through the trees like the head of a black snake, its body a long line of freight cars trailing behind it. They were all shapes and sizes. Some had turned orange from rust. Some looked like big wooden boxes.

"Fifteen, sixteen, seventeen," Carolina counted aloud, and then she gasped. A face appeared. It was there and then it was gone. A man in one of the boxcars was getting a free ride. She wondered where he was going. Finally the red caboose passed by. She waved to a man who was leaning on an iron railing at the tail end of it. He smiled and waved back.

Carolina stood on the rails until she could no longer feel the vibration. Stepping from one wooden tie to the next, she got to thinking about the sheep shearer named Sims Farley, and that led to thinking about Russell. It all added up. It made sense. Carolina remembered when Mr.

Ray had first talked about Sims. She remembered the part about Sims's having a sister named Miss Lily Jean and her being a foster mother. She remembered the part about the boy's being their nephew and his moving out of Miss Lily Jean's house and in with Sims and Mabel. It had to be Russell. Who else could it be?

The track forked. On one set of tracks three freight cars had been left there, just begging to be explored. Carolina climbed up a steel ladder attached to the side of one and stood on the platform. A large hole at the back of the freight car reminded her of a rabbit hole, only it was just her size. Carolina peered inside.

"Hello!" she yelled, and her voice echoed inside.

She climbed into the dark chamber. Its metal walls and floor were hard and cold. She wondered if hobos hid inside these holes when they wanted to ride the train for free.

Miss Latah turned the page of the old Farmer's Almanac calendar to August and tacked it back on the wall. It was the beginning of the last month of summer vacation. Mr. Ray said he was expecting Sims Farley to come by.

All through the day Carolina was filled with an uneasy anticipation. She was sitting in the straw at the open doors of the barn loft, just letting her legs drape over the edge. She was staring down at a patch of daisies growing up out of the weeds. When she looked up, she saw the truck pulling into the lane.

The back of the truck had wood boards on both sides. She figured it was rigged up for hauling goats and sheep. It came down the lane so fast that dust balls swirled behind it. She heard the engine rumbling as it was coming around the barn, and then there it was, parked right beneath her. She could see down into the back of the truck bed. It was heaped with yellow hay.

Sims got out and stretched his arms over his head. Carolina took in every whisker on his face. She watched him scratch his skinny belly. She saw Mr. Ray and Lucas come out of the barn and stroll on over to meet him. They must have been working together on that rusted tractor again.

Carolina felt like a bird in a tree, watching everybody below without anybody noticing her. She watched the man shake hands with Mr. Ray, and she leaned down a bit, trying to hear what they were talking about. Their conversation was mostly about the weather and such, the usual stuff folks talk about when they're getting warmed up to each other. Lucas stood near Mr. Ray.

Carolina pulled her legs up and sat cross-legged as she spied on Lucas. He kept putting on such a serious expression, as if he was trying to act all grown up. Then the three of them headed over to a small shed.

Something moving down in the back of Sims's truck caught Carolina's attention. It looked like a mess of dark fur moving about in the hay. It was too small for it to be a cat and too big for it to be a mouse. Then Carolina saw that the dark curly hair belonged to a head. She saw the boy rise out of the hay and peer between the cracks of the boards along the side of the truck. It wasn't hard to figure out that he didn't want anybody to know he was hiding in there. Carolina's eyes were glued to him, just waiting for him to turn his face so she could see for sure. The boy lay down again and buried himself in the hay. He was lying on his back, completely covered except for his face, and he was staring right up at Carolina.

Russell.

His face broke into a big grin.

Chapter 18

SOW IN A BUCKET

"You are the answer to my prayers," said Russell. He was at the top of the ladder, staring at Carolina. That big grin was still plastered on his face. It deepened the dimples in his cheeks. His blue eyes were full of mischief. His hair had grown long and was covering his ears.

"Hey, Russell." Carolina swallowed her worry and put on a smile.

"You up here spying down on everybody?" asked Russell.

"I was," she said.

Russell climbed over the ladder and into the hay.

"This *is* a good place to spy." He stood at the side of the doorway and took a cautious look out over the farm. "It's a good place to hide too."

Russell laid out his sad story. He said that his life had gone from bad to worse the day Uncle Freddie and Miss Lily Jean came back from the lake. He said Miss Lily Jean was actually worried about their leaving Carolina behind. Uncle Freddie said he was sick and tired of looking after foster kids, and he'd get rid of all of them if it wasn't for the check they got every month from the state.

"They didn't get paid to look after me," said Russell, "since I'm kin, so Uncle Freddie had me packing that very day and drove me over to my Uncle Sims's."

Russell said his life went from worse to miserable. Miss Lily Jean was nuts, but Uncle Sims was mean.

"Then just two days ago, something good happened," said Russell. "I saw my brother on the news," he continued. "He was getting off a plane with other soldiers and I'm fixing to go to California and find him. I just need to hide out here for a little while. You got to help me, Carolina."

Russell's voice got real sincere. "I won't tell nobody about you either. I promise. You can trust me."

About as much as I can trust a fox circling the henhouse, Carolina thought.

"Okay, Russell," Carolina said. "I'll help you, but you have to stay out of trouble."

Staying out of trouble was not something Russell had much experience with.

Not more than an hour after he'd arrived, Carolina heard Miss Latah scream from within the barn. So did Mr. Ray. They reached the barn doors at the exact same moment. Miss Latah was standing inside, looking offended. A

239

dead mouse was hanging from the rafters, and Miss Latah was vigorously brushing the top of her head. It was obvious that she'd bumped right into it.

"Carolina, do you know anything about this?" she asked.

"No, ma'am," she answered.

Mr. Ray was pressing his lips together, trying not to laugh. Miss Latah grabbed her hoe and walked right past him, her head held high. Mr. Ray looked over to Carolina. Carolina shrugged, pretending she didn't have a clue.

"Why don't you help Miss Latah by taking those scraps in the kitchen down to the sow's pen?" asked Mr. Ray.

Carolina thought it best not to argue under the circumstances.

The bucket of scraps was set down near the kitchen sink. Carolina was already wishing that Sims and Russell had never showed up. Already she was doing the one chore she could always count on Lucas to handle. She hauled the bucket outside and headed over to the sow's pen. She had barely reached it when her heart just about lurched out of her chest.

The gate to the pen was wide open. She quickly looked in at the thoroughly tromped ground that had grown muddy. No sow. Carolina looked all around, afraid she'd turn suddenly and see it ready to charge her, but she didn't see it anywhere. Carolina dropped the bucket and ran. She found Lucas in one of the old outbuildings they'd set up for the shearing.

"Lucas," she said, breathless from running, "the sow's got loose."

"I'll be right back, Sims," he said.

Lucas sprinted through the farmyard and past the pen with such long strides, Carolina could hardly keep up. They passed the vegetable garden. It looked as if it had been flattened by a hurricane. The old sow had rooted its nose down half the rows and tore up the other plants as it ran through.

"Law!" yelled Lucas.

The old sow was trotting down a dirt path, rutting its nose to the ground and eating everything in sight. Miss Latah, flushed from the heat and her own temper, was chasing it, smacking its butt end with her hoe. Carolina jumped up and down, waving her arms at Mr. Ray, who was headed to the shearing shed. He saw what was happening and came running.

"Carolina, grab a bushel basket out of the barn," ordered Mr. Ray, "and hurry."

By the time she was running to catch up with them, the sow had picked up speed. It was steaming forward like a freight train, making its way toward the sweet potato field. Lucas was sprinting behind it. He suddenly leaped into the air, attempting to tackle that muddy old sow, but he slipped off as if he'd landed on grease.

Carolina saw it all happening as she headed toward the scene, taking all the shortcuts she knew. The bushel basket bounced along at her side. That fat sow could really run. To her surprise, it veered off course. It turned around.

It was headed right for her.

"Carolina, hold that basket out!" Mr. Ray shouted. "Catch it!"

Carolina figured Mr. Ray had lost his mind. Three

hundred pounds of snorting flesh was running toward her, and he expected her to catch it in a bushel basket? She held her ground as the old sow trotted forward.

"Ohhhhh," she said. Her knees got to shaking. Her arms got to shaking.

"Ohhhhh, noooo," she cried as the sow lifted its head, grunting and sniffing the air.

The sow's strong snout with those flaring nostrils was all Carolina saw as she pushed the basket forward. The sow stopped in its tracks, its head buried in the dark space. Carolina didn't dare move.

Mr. Ray came up beside her. He took the basket with his good arm and pushed forward. The sow backed up. Carolina stared in awe and amazement.

That was how the four of them walked back to the pen—the sow in the bushel basket stepping backward; Mr. Ray pushing the basket forward; Lucas on one side, covered with mud; and Carolina on the other side, feeling as if she was part of the circus. Miss Latah was marching toward them. She was throwing up her hands and giving an inventory of how many tomatoes and how many beans and how many peppers the old sow had consumed. She shook her finger at the rump of the beast.

"I ought to serve you up for bacon this very evening!" she yelled.

The moment the sow was back in the pen and the gate securely fastened, Mr. Ray turned to Carolina. "Well, that was something," he said. Then he started to laugh. Finally, he took a deep breath, took his cap off, and brushed back his hair, then walked off.

Carolina climbed over the side of the ladder and plunked down in the hay. Russell's grin grew wider and wider until he began to chuckle.

"Russell, did you open the sow's pen?" she asked.

Russell was laughing so hard he was holding his sides.

"You did do it," she said, "It wasn't the least bit funny."

"Carolina, it was hilarious," he stated, replaying the whole scene, hardly able to finish his sentences.

At supper, everyone was still laughing about the old sow. It looked as if everybody was in good spirits. Sims had plenty of stories to tell too, and it seemed like Mr. Ray was enjoying the company of another man.

After helping Miss Latah with the dishes, Carolina swiped two biscuits from the counter. She climbed into the hayloft. No Russell. She searched the farmyard, swatting flies as they tried to land on the biscuits. In a dark and shady spot near the edge of the woods was an old abandoned shed. Its roof was caved in and the wood walls were breaking apart and working their way back to the earth. That was where she found him.

Russell and a rooster were having a standoff. Russell and the rooster held their stances, as if they were ready to duke it out to see who was boss.

"What are you up to now?" Carolina said.

Russell ran up a hillock of compost soil. He turned to her, flexing the muscles in his arms as if he was the strong man in the circus, not noticing that the rooster was right behind. It suddenly leaped up, pecking at the cuff of

Russell's blue jeans, sending Russell into the air, yelling and kicking. He landed facedown in the black soil that held a mash of decaying melon rinds and vegetable scraps.

Carolina's laughter spilled out of her as if from a bottomless well. She just couldn't stop. Russell lifted himself up. The color in his cheeks turned red as a beet as he glared at her.

Carolina offered to bring the blankets out to the barn for Sims to sleep on. She wanted to be sure Russell had a blanket too, not that he deserved it. When no one was looking, she grabbed two hard-boiled eggs from the refrigerator and a big square of corn bread. She pulled a ripe tomato off its stem in the garden as well as a handful of string beans from their vine. She figured Russell had to be starving by now.

Russell had rearranged the bales of hay and made a little fort to hide in. He sure was grateful for supper. He gobbled it down as quickly as she handed it to him.

"Carolina," said Russell, his voice hushed, "that silo out there is haunted."

At first Carolina thought he was getting ready to play a trick on her. Then she saw that Russell really was spooked. Carolina couldn't help herself. She seized the opportunity to get even.

"It *is*," she said. "Come with me. I'll show you."

Russell hesitated.

"Unless you're too scared," she said as she scooted down the rungs of the ladder.

"I ain't scared of nothin'," said Russell. He nearly stepped on her fingers as he followed her down.

Her voice was barely a whisper as she tiptoed around the circular structure. Russell was right behind, listening to every word.

"Once upon a time, near one hundred years ago, an old Indian sitting by his campfire was swooped down upon, grabbed up, and *caught* up by the sharp talons of a giant white owl," Carolina began.

"Those talons cut into the belly of that Indian until he was just about dead. When the owl landed, the Indian somehow managed to escape, but the next night"—here Carolina paused for effect—"the owl caught him up again. This time"—Carolina took a deep breath and then exclaimed—"he *killed* him!

"The Indian didn't know he was dead. He was still a-runnin' away from that giant white owl. He didn't know it was his ghost a-runnin'. That's how scared he was."

Carolina looked over to Russell to see how the story was going. He was looking at her with wide eyes. Carolina continued.

"The ghost hid in this silo, *this very one*, right here, and here he stays, nursing his wounds."

Carolina brought her voice to a whisper. "Hear that Indian a-moanin'?"

She continued with the Indian's sad story, taking on faces and gestures she'd learned from watching Auntie Shen. Carolina heard the pigeons in the empty silo cooing in their nests. The pigeons did sound like a person moaning, and she could see that she had Russell convinced. The wider his eyes grew, the more intense her storytelling became. When she was satisfied that she had him scared good, she broke into a big grin.

"Have a good sleep, Russell," she said.

Thoroughly pleased with herself and intent on her self-congratulations, she didn't pay heed to the arguing going on around the side of the springhouse. Then she heard angry words. Carolina peeked around the corner to see what was going on. It was nobody but Sims Farley, sitting there by himself, having an argument with an imaginary person.

He tilted his head back and took a swig from a thin amber-colored bottle. Then he started talking again to the imaginary person in front of him, using words that would have been cause for soap in Carolina's mouth if Auntie Shen had heard her use them.

Sims started waving the bottle around as if he was trying to make a point to that imaginary person. He reached into the pocket of his shirt and took out a cigarette. He struck a match against an old marker stone leaning against the barn, and the match flamed up. He lit his cigarette and then he threw the match. It lit a patch of dry grass on fire.

"Hey!" Carolina shouted. She ran forward and stamped it out.

Sims Farley looked over in her direction and his eyes were nothing short of evil.

"Come over here, girl," he said.

Carolina didn't move a muscle.

"Come on over here," he said louder. "I ain't gonna bite ya."

Carolina took three baby steps closer.

"Now what y'all yelling 'Hey' at me for?"

"You're goin' to burn the building down if you're not careful."

He just laughed and shook his head.

"Well, ain't you the little guard dog."

Sims broke the red tip off his cigarette and put it out between his fingers.

He opened his shirt pocket and dropped the cigarette into it.

"There," he said. "Now don't be telling tattle tales on me, little girl."

Carolina felt as scared as if she'd come upon a copperhead snake.

"Go on now. Git," he said, and moved his hand at her as if he was throwing something.

Carolina didn't need to hear it twice. She took off at a run, heading toward the house. Her feet couldn't move fast enough. She smacked right into Lucas in front of the barn.

"Hey, where's the fire?" he said.

"I . . . uh . . . ," she stammered.

Before she could say a word, Sims appeared.

"Hey, Sims," said Lucas. "My dad said for me to come and fetch you. He says to come on over to the porch and set for a while. He says to bring your fiddle."

"That'll suit me fine," said Sims, and off he went, shoulder to shoulder with Lucas, as straight and sober-looking as could be.

Carolina headed up to the hayloft to find Russell.

Russell was sitting with his back against a bale of hay.

Carolina plunked down beside him. They could hear the music playing from the porch. Lucas was playing the banjo. Sims was playing the fiddle. Mr. Ray was singing.

"Russell, remember that night you caught the lightning bug for me?"

"You mean the night I gave you a *diamond* ring?"

Carolina and Russell laughed as they replayed the memory, each having their own favorite part.

Music had been coming out the doors of the Blue Moon bar, and Pammy, Joey, and Buck were running about the yard trying to catch lightning bugs. Carolina was following one blinking glow of light along the fence when Russell's hand suddenly reached out of the darkness and snapped it up. While it was still aglow, he pinched its light.

He stuck the bug light on Carolina's ring finger.

"There you are—a diamond ring," he said.

Carolina had waved her hand around as if she was a famous rich lady.

She'd let Russell hold her hand and lead her away across the backyards of the neighborhood. They spied on an old man and his wife eating dinner in their kitchen. They spied on a family that was roasting marshmallows on a metal grill. It was as if Carolina and Russell had turned invisible.

They had run down back streets until they reached the railroad station. Russell pulled Carolina back into the shadows. A man and woman strolled by, so close Carolina could have reached out and tapped the woman on the shoulder. The man kept trying to hold the woman's hand, but she kept pulling it away. Russell poked Carolina in the ribs, and she had to cover her mouth to keep from laughing.

"Now here we are," said Russell.

"Together again," said Carolina.

"Law, it's hot," said Russell. "I'd give anything for a swim."

"There's a creek just through the woods," said Carolina. "It's a great swimming hole."

Russell's face lit up. Dimples creased his cheeks. His blue eyes sparkled.

"Let's go," said Russell.

"Not yet," she said. "Lucas's friends might be there."

She told him there was no telling what they'd do if she and Russell showed up. Those boys acted as if the creek belonged to only them.

"Okay," said Russell. "We'll go after everyone's gone to sleep."

Carolina looked up to a round full moon. It was shining bright, lighting the farmyard in a blue twilight glow.

"Okay," said Carolina. "After everyone goes to sleep."

That night, on the night of a moonlit swim, Carolina was kissed by a boy for the very first time. They were sitting side by side on the ledge. Russell slid his hand closer and placed it on top of Carolina's. She glanced his way without raising her head, just caught a look out of the corner of her eye. His expression was so soft and thoughtful that she had to turn away.

"Carolina," he said, "I've been meaning to tell you

something, and well, what I've been meaning to tell you is, you're the best friend I've ever had, and, uh . . . I like you."

Carolina felt the pink flush rise up in her cheeks, and she went shy.

"I like you too," she said in a soft voice.

"Friends to the end?" he asked.

Carolina looked up and smiled.

"Friends to the end," she said.

Then just like that, he leaned forward and touched his lips to hers, just stayed there a moment, and then moved away. It was as sweet as the butterfly that once alighted on her hand in the meadow. The butterfly had stayed there, opening and closing its wings, trusting her.

Carolina went to sleep that night with the most wonderful feeling. She woke up with it too. Just before dawn, while the stars were still shining bright, she met up with Russell just as they'd planned, along a line of birch saplings at the edge of the woods.

Russell had taken the ax from the barn. He said he was fixing to build a lean-to because he needed a safer place to hide; he was getting jumpy. Twice now he'd nearly run into Sims. "If he finds out that I got here by hitching a ride in his truck, he'll beat me to a pulp." Russell told her Sims had a real mean streak. He told her about Sims's drunken fits and about how Sims would beat him with a switch for no reason at all. "All Sims wants me to do is be a servant boy to Mabel. I'm sick of it. That's why I come here. Besides, I saw you and Mr. Ray the day you stopped by. I was climbing a tree when you pulled up."

After seeing Sims's strange behavior behind the barn, Carolina had every reason to believe Russell's stories. She was making sure she stayed clear of Sims too. Right now, she was staying clear of the ax.

"Where did you learn how to make a lean-to?" she asked.

"I haven't lived in town all my life," he said.

Russell started hacking away at any old log and tree that happened to be in front of him. Carolina had to wonder if he really had lived in town his whole life. Staying far away from the ax, she pointed out a fallen tree that had landed on a wide boulder.

"I bet this is the place you're going to build, isn't it?"

Russell eyed the spot. "Yeah, how did you know?"

Carolina dragged over some of the stick-thin saplings Russell had already taken the ax to, leaning them up against the fallen tree and the rock. Then she crawled beneath them.

"You'll have lots of room in here," she said.

Russell was getting the idea. He added more long sticks to the structure, and then they added smaller branches and twigs. When it was good and tight, they covered it with moss and leaves and ferns. They worked together well into morning.

"I've got to go now, Russell," she said.

"What for?" he asked.

"Everyone will be wondering where I am. I've got to get to my chores."

"Chores? This ain't your farm," said Russell.

"Miss Latah will be expecting me to bring her the eggs from the henhouse," said Carolina.

"Let her get her own eggs," said Russell. "Stay here."

"I *have* to do my chores, Russell," she said with a stronger tone to her voice.

Russell looked genuinely hurt.

"How much are you getting paid for being their little farmhand?" he asked.

"I don't get paid," said Carolina. "No one gets paid. We work together . . . as a family."

"Well, you ain't family. Did they say you were?"

"No," said Carolina in a small voice, "not exactly."

"That's because you're not," said Russell in a loud voice. "They're just keeping you around for free labor. Can you think of any other reason?"

"They keep me because they . . ." Carolina's voice trailed off.

She was about to say "because they love me," but she didn't dare. She knew Russell would laugh out loud. She'd have to defend it.

"I have to go," she said. She started running through the trees.

"See what I mean!" he yelled after her. "You're not their farmhand. Their *slave* is more like it."

Carolina hurried through the brush and trees. Her legs picked up speed as if they had a mind of their own. By the time she was in the open field, she was in a full run, the hot air choking her throat, her face damp with sweat.

She could see Lucas up in the sheep pasture. Some of the ewe lambs looked as if they'd just come back from the barbershop. They looked awful scrawny next to the sheep that still had their wool on. Lucas was leading one of the lambs out of the pasture, and the word *slaughter* came into her mind again.

Carolina's mind was a nest woven with worries as she entered the henhouse. She couldn't make Russell's words go away. Maybe he'd said those things to her because she'd hurt his feelings. Maybe he just didn't want to be left all by himself. Or maybe, just maybe, she was fooling herself with thinking that Mr. Ray and Miss Latah and Lucas cared about her. Was it all just wishful thinking?

Carolina reached under a hen.

A sharp beak jabbed her hand.

"Ow!"

She drew her hand back fast. The egg flew up into the air. Carolina tried to catch it, but it hit the floor. Splat! Chickens raced wildly from all directions, descending on the broken egg. It was gone in an instant. Carolina drew in her breath. She'd never seen the hens go crazy like that before. She held the rest of those eggs in a firm grip as she collected them. By the time she was finished, she'd been pecked so many times her hands looked as if she had a bad case of chicken pox.

She stepped out of the henhouse. The sun was hot and the air was close, humid. She held the wire basket with both hands. It was full to the brim. She stepped gingerly across the yard, being careful that none of the eggs dropped. All the things Russell had said filled her mind again, and all kinds of bad feelings started coming on.

As she stepped up onto the porch, she figured she was a lot like one of those eggs. She seemed sturdy enough at first glance, but if truth be told, her happy existence was wearing thin. Yes, she thought, she better be careful. One good crack and her whole big lying mess would spill out and she'd be done for, just like the egg on the henhouse floor.

"Oh good, you've brought the eggs," said Miss Latah.

The pottery bowl and the canister of sugar were on the kitchen table along with a sack of flour, cocoa, baking soda, and butter.

"Are you making a cake?" asked Carolina.

"Yes, I am," she said. "Today is Mr. Ray's birthday."

"Can I help?"

"Of course you can. Thank you for asking. Here, rub a little lard on these cake pans and then sprinkle them with flour. You can shake the extra right into the sink."

Miss Latah hummed as she creamed butter and sugar. Carolina was wishing she'd known about Mr. Ray's birthday. She would have made him a gift.

"What are you giving Mr. Ray for his birthday?" Carolina asked.

"Chocolate cake," said Miss Latah in a matter-of-fact tone.

"Is that all?" asked Carolina.

Miss Latah smiled and said, "Is that all? Why, it's his favorite."

"I wish I could give him something," said Carolina.

"You are. You're giving it right now, by helping with this cake. And he'll love you for doing so. You can ice it too. Decorate it any way you like."

"And he'll be happy with just a cake?" asked Carolina.

"He'll be the happiest man in the world," said Miss Latah.

"What did you get for your birthday?" asked Carolina.

"Why, don't you remember?" Miss Latah asked.

She stopped stirring and put down the bowl. She reached over and put her hands on Carolina's cheeks and gave her that soft look again. Carolina was puzzled.

"I got you," she said.

Carolina figured she must be holding a big question mark in her expression because Miss Latah began to explain.

"Sometimes you get something you never knew you wanted," she said. "When we stumbled upon you in the meadow, Mr. Ray and Lucas and I were celebrating my birthday in my favorite way. We were going blackberry picking. What a surprise to see you sitting there in the grass. You were our gift from the stars."

Miss Latah took two eggs from the wire basket and handed them to Carolina. Carolina gave each of them a good crack and opened them up. The yolk and the white fell over the cream and sugar in the bowl. Miss Latah stirred it round and round with a wooden spoon and started humming again. Carolina hummed right along with her. She didn't feel so fragile anymore.

Chapter 19

TRAPPED

Carolina ran a swirl of blue icing all around the edge of Mr. Ray's cake. She did the subtraction in her head. Today was August 3, 1964. Carolina calculated, *1964 minus 1924 is forty.* She used almost two whole packs of birthday candles, sinking them into the icing without ruining her decorations, and then she was finished.

She counted the squares on the Farmer's Almanac calendar that was tacked to the wall by the icebox. Not including today, her birthday would be in twenty-eight days. She'd turn eleven. She squeezed her eyes shut and sent out an early birthday wish that she and Auntie Shen would be together.

Celebrating Mr. Ray's birthday blew away Carolina's

worries. He just couldn't say enough about the pretty cake decorations. Why, he said he didn't have the heart to cut into it, it was so pretty. Carolina's heart swelled. They all stayed up late into the night singing the same songs their great-granddaddies and -grannies used to sing. They sang the tunes that Doc Watson was singing in dance halls all over the state.

Lucas picked that banjo of his well into the night, until Carolina thought his fingers would bleed. It turned out that Sims was a mighty fine fiddle player, and it was plain to see that Mr. Ray had taken a real liking to him. When no one else was looking, Sims raised his eyes and gave Carolina a stare that put a bad feeling all through her. It was a warning and she knew it. Carolina stuck to Miss Latah like glue.

The following morning Carolina dragged herself out of bed at the crack of dawn. She had to find Russell. Her eyes itched as if she had sand in them. Still, she couldn't sleep with all these thoughts of Russell in her head.

She figured he'd be starving to death by now, and she had a big slice of chocolate cake to give him. Russell wasn't in the loft. His blanket was gone. Carolina tiptoed through the barn. She didn't know where Sims had found a place to lay his head, and she didn't want to find out either. She headed to the lean-to in the woods.

Fog was thick. Shades of gray surrounded her. The sky was gray, the ground was gray, and she couldn't even see across the length of the farmyard. She'd have to go by way of the creek. Carolina followed it to where it trickled down over the rocks and behind the moss-covered boulder, where she and Russell had built the lean-to.

Russell *was* half-starved, judging by the way he swallowed big bites of the cake.

"Having a good time without me last night?" His eyes held hurt and anger mixed together. "Some friend you are," he said softly.

Carolina didn't know what to say. It was true she'd had a lot of fun at the birthday celebration and forgotten all about bringing Russell a piece of cake until now.

"This lean-to looks real good, Russell," Carolina said, trying to change the heart of the conversation. She'd also spotted the ax leaning on its side at the far end. It wouldn't be long before Lucas went looking for it.

Russell was determined to wallow in pity. "There ain't a thing to do out here. Remember all the fun we had sneaking around at night at Miss Lily Jean's?" he said.

Carolina did remember. It had given her a thrill.

Russell swallowed the last bite of cake. "The bugs tried to eat me alive last night," he said. "I'm heading back to the barn today." He turned his back to her and pulled his blanket tight.

Carolina crawled out from under the saplings that made the pitch of the lean-to. Then she slowly reached her hand in and pulled the ax toward her. It moved across damp leaves without making a sound.

She ran back by way of the creek again. Light was beginning to illuminate the fog, and everyday things like stumps of trees took on shapes and shadows that got her mind imagining faces and limbs. She nearly dropped the ax when she saw what looked to be a monstrous haint ahead.

Stepping slowly, peering forward into the mist, she saw a big black circle. She crept closer. It was the wheel of the tractor. It looked as if someone had tried to drive that tractor right into the creek.

Carolina ran. She had to tell Mr. Ray and quick. That tractor could move right on down the bank, right into the water. The fog seemed to open a path as she ran, as if she was moving through a tunnel, always seeing about four feet in front of her eyes.

Mr. Ray was on the porch, trying to tie up his boot laces with one hand.

"The tractor is falling into the creek. It's stuck in the mud now, but it looks like it could roll in any minute," Carolina said all in one breath.

"Blast it all!" Mr. Ray took his hat and whacked it against the porch post.

It was the first time that Carolina had ever seen his temper flare. The blood in her veins suddenly turned all lumpy, just began sputtering through her arms and legs. It bumped through her chest and into her stomach too.

"Carolina, I have seen the twisted bodies of farmers killed by their tractors. Now, we had a real close call, you and I. It was a miracle we didn't get hurt bad. For you to take it upon yourself to drive the tractor down to the creek, why, that's senseless. I've a mind to—"

Mr. Ray stopped midsentence and set his mouth tight.

Carolina just stood there with her mouth hanging open

as if she was catching flies. Here she was trying to do the right thing and she was getting accused of causing all the trouble.

"What are you doing with that ax?" asked Mr. Ray.

Carolina just stood there, as still and dumb as a doorknob, looking guilty as sin.

"Carolina, my patience is wearing thin," said Mr. Ray.

He didn't need to say more. Those few words spoke the story like a whole book, and Carolina took it as a warning. Miss Latah, who'd been listening on the other side of the screen door, walked out and touched Mr. Ray on his shoulder.

"Ray, you're accusing her. Let Carolina defend herself."

"Latah," he said. "We've been caring for this girl as if she was our own, and up till now, I've been going along with it."

"Ray," said Miss Latah. She had a pleading tone to her voice.

"It's going to bring the law down on us, and you know as well as I do, that's the last thing we need."

Mr. Ray pushed the screen door open, walked inside, and then barreled out again, letting the door slam behind him.

"I'm going to the barn for Sims," he said. "Tell Lucas to meet us down by the creek. Tell him to drive the truck, and tell him he better bring the chains."

Miss Latah's face held so much sadness that Carolina couldn't bear to look at her.

"Mr. Ray's just hurting today," said Miss Latah. "A farmer needs two strong arms to do his work, and he's been

260

trying to make do with only one. He just won't give it time to heal proper."

Miss Latah turned to walk back into the kitchen, and then she turned around and said, "Best to stay out of his way for a while."

Carolina sat amid the ewes and lambs under the shade trees. Wind was tumbling down over the ridge, sweeping the fog away and blowing through the strands of her long hair. She figured Mr. Ray thought she was nothing but trouble. The dark cloud of doom moved on the breezes and brushed over her.

On her last birthday, she'd wished for Mattie. She'd made a wish to go back to Blue Star Mountain. She'd wished for Auntie Shen to get well. Last night, Carolina had made a secret wish that Harmony Farm was home.

Wishes don't ever come true.

Carolina and Russell spent most of the day up by the railroad tracks. He took a penny out of his pocket and put it on the track. When they heard the train whistle, they hid in the trees and waited for the long line of freight cars to pass. The penny was still on the track. It was flatter than a pancake.

At suppertime Carolina was plenty thankful. She'd eaten handfuls of blackberries through the day, but hunger was growling for meat and potatoes.

"Set a place at the table for Sims too, Carolina," said

Miss Latah. She didn't say a word about Carolina not showing up for dinner at midday. Carolina noticed the eggs on the counter. Lucas must have collected them.

Carolina wished she could set a place for Russell. He was hungry too. Carolina chose five plates that didn't have any chips in them, and she laid them so the designs were all facing the same way. She folded the napkins and laid a fork out straight in the center of each one. On the other side of the plate she laid down a knife and then a spoon. She filled glasses with water and put one above each knife and spoon. Then she sat in her seat and waited for Miss Latah's praise.

Carolina's thoughts returned to Russell. He was back in his hiding place in the hayloft. She'd have to sneak food past Sims if Russell was going to eat. Keeping Russell a secret was wearing Carolina ragged.

Loud footsteps pounded up the porch steps. Carolina sat still and quiet as she watched Mr. Ray untie his boots. He heaved a weary sigh and stepped inside.

"Evening, ma'am," said Sims, who walked in right behind Mr. Ray.

"Evening," said Miss Latah, and then she turned back to her cooking. She didn't even notice how nice the table was set.

Carolina folded her hands and bowed her head when Mr. Ray said grace. She'd started closing her eyes again. She thought about adding a few words of her own, not for anyone to hear, just a silent request from her to God, but before the words came, Lucas interrupted.

"Carolina, pass the butter, please," he said.

Lucas had been spending all his time with Sims the last couple of days. He didn't seem to miss her company a bit. Carolina remembered a day at school when no one picked her to be on their team for kick ball. The boys just began playing without her, all because she'd decided to be friends with Mattie. She figured Lucas liked Sims better than her.

She cut into a piece of okra that had been breaded with cornmeal and fried to a crisp. To her dismay, it was gooey and slimy on the inside. She dragged it around on her plate, creating a green trail in the cornmeal. The smells that had made her mouth water were now making her stomach feel queasy.

"May I be excused?" she said quietly, looking up at Mr. Ray.

He looked up from his plate, holding his fork in midair, his mouth full.

"I have a stomachache," she said.

Mr. Ray nodded.

Carolina plodded up the winding stairs that led from the kitchen up into Miss Latah's sewing room. Up until tonight it had felt like her room too. Now she wasn't so sure. She'd barely slept a wink on the night she and Russell took their swim in the creek. Last night she'd stayed up past midnight, celebrating. Now a fearsome tiredness was taking hold, and there was nothing she could do to stop it. Carolina lay on her stomach. She was too tired to even take off her sneakers.

Sleep wouldn't come. Her thoughts jumped from one thing to the next. It seemed the only friend she had left was Russell. She needed a friend right now, needed a friend this very moment. She'd have to climb out her window if she wanted to find him, and more than anything that was what she wanted.

Carolina tiptoed over the porch roof. She could hear everyone talking and the sounds of supper in the kitchen below her; dishes being passed along the wooden table, forks on plates, and spoons dipping into pottery bowls, going for more. Carolina walked to the very edge, where she knew she wouldn't be seen, and jumped off, landing a bit too close to Miss Latah's flower garden.

"Russell?"

Carolina spoke softly, calling her friend's name as she climbed the ladder up to the hayloft. Russell turned around all of a sudden, as if she'd scared him.

"It's just me," she said.

"Where's my supper?" he asked.

"I'll have to sneak back into the kitchen later," she said. "Everybody's still at the table."

Russell gave her a confused look.

"I pretended to be sick and snuck out my window. I wanted to be with you."

Russell smiled.

"What do you have behind your back?" she asked.

"Nothing," Russell brought his hands forward and made a display of it, turning his palms up and turning his palms down.

Carolina laughed. "I want to see." She quickly reached behind him, but Russell was quicker. He lay down on his back as if he was covering up something. Carolina laughed again and tried to tickle him, but Russell held her arms.

"I think I hear Sims," he said.

Carolina stopped, listened.

"I'll be back later," she said, and headed back down the ladder.

It was too early to go back to the house. She realized now that she'd have to sneak in the same way she'd snuck out. She ran through the meadow toward the woods. The air was still and humid. By the time she reached the edge of the wood, her shirt was soaked with sweat.

Carolina lay down and closed her eyes, just to rest, but as she lay there, the sandman of sleep sprinkled dreams in her eyes.

In her dream, she was running with her daddy. They were jumping from one blue mountain peak to the next, over puffy clouds the color of snow. The mountains rose and fell like waves in an ocean, blue with whitecaps. They jumped to peaks so high their heads nearly touched the stars. Her daddy reached up and pulled down the Milky Way. He draped it around her shoulders, and she snuggled into it as if it was a white shawl. The other stars became angry with them for taking pieces of their light without asking. The tiny twinkling stars grew larger and larger until they were giant fireballs, and Carolina and her daddy were surrounded by the hot blaze. The mountains disappeared, the sky disappeared, her daddy disappeared, and all that remained was hot, crackling light.

Carolina woke in a sweat, her heart pounding. She smelled smoke. She jolted upright. The sky above the farm was lit up orange. She heard a crackling, a sound like branches breaking and falling in a storm.

The barn is on fire!

As Carolina ran down to the farmyard, she saw flames shooting straight up through the roof. Mr. Ray and Lucas looked like black silhouettes against the fiery light. They were struggling with Sadie. The horse reared up on her hindquarters, scared senseless. Lucas grabbed hold of her halter, trying to lead her away as she fought to go back into the barn.

Smoke was billowing up into the hot air. Giant flames licked wildly at the wooden boards of the barn. They lashed up at the sky like a whip.

Carolina searched the farmyard for signs of Russell.

She saw Miss Latah frantically spraying a hose at the barn. The spray of water looked pitifully small, like spitting on a campfire.

Chickens were running over the grass, squawking and screeching. She saw Buzzy duck under the floorboards of the porch and then dart out the other side and take to the field. Her kitten was safe.

Out in the pasture, Homer sat on her haunches near Elsie the cow, who was lulling and mooing. The sheep ran together from one corner of the fencing to the other, back and forth, bleating loudly. Carolina caught a glimpse of the old sow. She was headed up into the trees.

Where was Russell?

Carolina ran to Miss Latah.

"Carolina, stay back!" yelled Miss Latah. She started toward the house, dragging the hose behind her. "I have to wet the house down. It will catch fire too."

"Miss Latah!" Carolina yelled.

"Carolina!" Miss Latah yelled. "I told you to stay back."

Where was Russell? Was he trapped in the hayloft?

Mr. Ray and Lucas were still struggling with Sadie. Miss Latah was spraying water over the side of the house, as frantic as the sheep.

Russell's going to be burned alive!

Carolina ran around to the back of the barn, cutting a wide swath between her and the flames. Even still, her skin felt hot as fire. The smoke scorched her throat. An explosion went off behind her. She turned. Flames blew through the boards, sending them shattering and splintering over the ground where she'd just run.

Russell!

She felt a hand clamp down on her, felt a thumb press into the soft flesh under her arm.

"Ow!" she yelled.

It was Sims. He had the front of Russell's T-shirt wadded up in his hand and was dragging him across the ground. Russell was flailing with his arms, trying to break free. Sims had him lifted up by his T-shirt, and Russell was forced to walk on the toes of his sneakers. Russell's face was black with soot.

"I seen you two sneaking around, been watching you the whole time," said Sims. "Thought you'd get away with it, did you? Now everyone's going to be let in on what lying troublemakers you are."

Carolina tried to move, but Sims squeezed her arm tighter. Russell had a fighting look in his eyes.

"Let me go. We have to help!" Carolina screamed,

barely hearing her own voice over the roaring flames and the sound of wood crashing into splinters.

"Help with what?" laughed Sims. "This barn is burning to the ground!"

"Let me go!" yelled Carolina.

"I'll let you go," said Sims. "I'll let the both of you go— straight to reform school. I know you're the girl 'at ran away from Lily Jean's, and Russell, you ain't been nothin' but trouble since the day you were born. Reform school is where the two of you belong. You know what that is? It's jail for kids, that's what it is."

"We didn't start the fire!" yelled Carolina. "You did. You're the one with the cigarettes."

An evil look spread across Sims's face. "Who they going to believe, little girl?"

Russell kicked. Russell punched. His T-shirt ripped down to his belly as he escaped Sims's grip. Carolina reached over and bit Sims's hand.

Russell took off running at a clip. Carolina was right behind him. She didn't think. She just ran. She stayed close to Russell's dark shadow, cutting around the outbuildings and down along the edge of the clearing until they were running through the neighbor's cornfield. Carolina pumped her legs to keep up, racing between the tall stalks and feeling the sting as sharp-edged leaves cut into her bare arms.

"Where are we going?" she yelled.

"We're going to hop the train," said Russell.

"Are you crazy?"

"No, I ain't crazy. You got a better plan?"

The sky above held an eerie orange and green glow. Black smoke rose up like a cloud. Carolina's sneakers pounded over the hard ground, and a familiar mix of fear and excitement coursed through her veins. She was running away again, but this time it was different. This time her heart thumped along behind, dragging its feet, wanting desperately to stay.

Where the cornfield ended, the woods began. Carolina and Russell ducked into the trees and ran over a rock-strewn path that led to the field growing wild with grasses. They trampled through, kicking up insects that rose like dust.

They reached the embankment and scrambled up to the tracks. Finally they collapsed on the railroad ties. Carolina coughed on phlegm and smoke, trying to catch her breath. She felt a dampening chill filling her lungs and making her throat burn. Her cough was loud and hoarse. Russell extended his hand. Carolina reached for it, and he pulled her up.

Russell meandered ahead of her as carefree as if he was on his way to his favorite fishing hole. He even started a sprightly step from one railroad tie to the next. Carolina lagged farther and farther behind, the distance between them growing wider and wider. She turned and stared at the sky. It was lit like a torch. *The whole barn must be ablaze by now,* she thought.

Harmony Farm was going up in smoke and flames, and Carolina's last bit of hope was burning down to ash and soot.

"C'mon!" yelled Russell.

She paid him no mind. She was thinking about Mr. Ray. *Would he have believed me?* She was thinking about all the hay that he and Lucas had brought in from the fields. Now it was burning up like kindling sticks. She should have told him about Sims and his cigarettes. The devil of blame blew down the tracks in a cold wind. Goose bumps rose on her arms. Carolina shivered.

All through the night Carolina trudged along the tracks. Russell pretended he was a hawk, running down the tracks with his arms outstretched. He pitched stones into the trees. He tapped the rails with a long stick, playing a tune.

Carolina dawdled far behind him, listening to an eerie silence interrupted by strange echoes from another time, catching faint glimpses of a life that had once been there but was no more. She was remembering walking through the rooms of her home on the day she knew for certain it wasn't going to be her home anymore. She and Auntie Shen had been there only to pack up Carolina's belongings.

Caleb's blocks had been scattered on the floor. He used to build tall towers just to knock them down. Her daddy's gray lunch box had been on the floor next to the icebox, the same place he used to set it down every evening when he got home from work. Her mama's photographs had been laid on a table, out of Caleb's reach. She had the same lost feeling now as when the landlord had said another family would be moving in.

Carolina stumbled, tripping on a steel spike that had worked its way up through the railroad tie. She felt her knees scrape against jagged rocks. She picked herself up and brushed the pebbles off her knees. She stood perfectly still, suddenly aware of the silence.

Carolina took a few cautious steps forward. Rock ledges rose up like two giant shadows on both sides of the tracks. In the sky above, wisps of clouds rolled over the moon in a ghostly white mist. She turned around in a complete circle.

"I know you're out there, Russell!" she yelled. "You're not scaring me one bit."

A shiver ran up her spine as she felt eyes on her back. She moved forward. Searching the black edges along the rock that hemmed her in, she hoped for a glimpse of his white T-shirt.

"Agggghhhhh!" Russell jumped in front of her, hollering at the top of his lungs.

Carolina screamed.

Russell laughed and laughed.

"Aw, man, I got you good," he said. He jumped up and pumped his fist in the air. "Yeah, I got you good."

Dawn's first light illuminated a thick hazy fog. They walked on, as if through a cloud, their skin and hair damp.

"Hey, look," said Russell. "A trestle bridge."

He stood at the steel girders. The fog was so thick they couldn't see to the other side. Russell disappeared into it.

Carolina walked across the steel rail as if she was on a balance beam. She peered at the space between the wooden boards. The spaces were wide enough to swallow her whole leg if she slipped. Black water churned in an angry roar far below.

"Look at that wild river," said Russell.

She could see it through the wide dark space between the boards. The river crashed against jagged boulders, rolling onto itself in white spews of fury. It made her dizzy. She thought she'd tumble. Carolina leaned her hand against the girder and forced her eyes up. Looking straight ahead, she let out a slow and even breath.

"Hurry up!" Russell was only a voice coming out of the fog.

"Who died and left you boss?" she yelled back.

"Stay if you want to," his voice yelled again. "The train will be along soon enough and slice you into bits, and then you won't be going anywhere."

She took another deep breath and moved forward, her body tense and tight, balancing on the rail until finally she stepped onto solid ground.

"You ever hop a train before?" asked Russell, as laid-back and easy as if he was asking her if she wanted corn-flakes or chocolate puffs.

"No," she answered.

"You got to be quick. You can't be afraid. You got to stay away from the bums on the train too," said Russell. "Just follow me. I know what I'm doing."

The railroad tracks were as lonesome as could be. There wasn't a soul around but the two of them, and their tempers were wearing thin. They got to kicking up rocks onto each other's legs and speaking in harsh tones. Carolina felt the scrape on her knee tightening into a thick red scab.

The distant rumbling of steel wheels brought them to attention. The train was coming! They could hear the toot-toot of the engine whistle and the clickity-clack of freight cars.

Positioning themselves behind the trees, they waited. The train slowed to a crawl as it approached a sharp bend in the track and finally came to a halt. The engineer climbed down from the engine and walked slowly up the length of track to where it crossed an old dirt road. He lit red flares and then began his walk back to the engine.

"Grab the ladder," said Russell. "We're not tall enough to jump up into an open car. Our legs would whip under. We'd be fed to the wheels."

"What?" she asked.

"We'd get our legs cut off," said Russell.

The thought of several tons of steel slicing her in two was far worse than her fear of an ax. Carolina ran beside Russell. She pumped her arms, moving her legs faster and faster until she was beside the train.

Russell grabbed hold of the ladder attached to the railroad car and swung himself to the bottom step. He raced up and over onto the railroad car.

Carolina grabbed the ladder and felt the hot metal in her hand; then the train moved in a violent, sudden motion. Her hand slipped and her foot slid off the rung. She screamed. Then she felt a strong force, felt her body being lifted, felt her feet hit solid on the rung of the ladder as the train picked up speed and the rails beneath her became one silvery sliver of liquid. Auntie Shen had told Carolina many stories about angels saving people, and now Carolina knew those stories were real. She believed it as sure as she was breathing.

"I knew you could do it," said Russell. He had a big smile plastered on his face.

She climbed up and over the ladder. They stooped down and crawled into the hole at the back of the freight car. It was just like the one she'd explored near Harmony Farm. It was loud!

Steel wheels screeched as they rolled along the tracks. Carolina covered her ears with both hands. The motion knocked them back and forth until she was sure her shoulders were turning black and blue.

When she couldn't stand it any longer, she poked her head out the opening. Trees blurred by in a haze. Wind caught her hair and whipped it into her face. She felt as if she'd been plunked inside the story she'd made up to scare Russell. Here she was, being carried along on this train the same as that old Indian had been carried along in the talons of the giant white owl, and there wasn't a thing she could do to stop it.

Chapter 20

STARS

Carolina and Russell suddenly fell forward, catching themselves with their hands pressed against the hot metal compartment as the train's brakes screeched on the rails. They poked their heads out of their cavelike hiding place.

"I'm getting out of this tin can." said Russell.

He wasted no time. He scooted out and was down the ladder as quick as a chipmunk. Carolina was right behind, running along the length of freight cars. Hands suddenly appeared from a boxcar, and Russell was pulled up into it. Carolina was next, her belly scraping over the edge as she held on tight to the hands pulling her in.

Scrambling on her knees across the wooden boards blackened with grease and dirt, she saw that there were five rough-and-tumble boys in the boxcar. A teenager older than Lucas was in there too. He had long straight hair that hung way down past his shoulders. He was leaning against a backpack. There was a man too. He had a wild-eyed look like a dog has when it's never let off its chain. The train lurched forward, and Carolina fell back on her rear end.

Russell hunkered down with the other boys. They were all in high spirits. They said they'd been riding the train all day—taking a joyride. Carolina noticed the teenager with the long hair kept real quiet, pretending he was taking a nap, but she could see that he was taking in the conversations. Every now and again, he lifted his eyes ever so slightly. The big man scared her. She didn't dare look in his direction, but the temptation to do so was coming on something fierce.

A heavyset boy asked Russell where he was headed. Russell told him he was meeting his brother and started talking about Vietnam and how his brother was a hero. The boys gave him their full attention. His talk led to all kinds of stories about guns and fighting, and the boys started getting fired up and in a wrestling mood. The teenager with the long hair said a few words to set them straight about war, but they ignored him. He closed his eyes then and leaned on his pack, even though Carolina could tell he was still listening.

It wasn't long before the boys were determining their pecking order. Carolina was reminded of the roosters on the farm, strutting about and clawing the dirt. Russell was doing his best to prove that he was the toughest. He reached in his pocket and pulled out a pack of cigarettes.

He looked at Carolina and smiled. "Sims won't miss one pack."

She turned her eyes away and looked out on the green landscape out the wide-open doors. The train was headed west, going over the mountains. A field opened the view to blue peaks and sky, a scene as pretty as a painting, but her thoughts were on the barn. In her mind she could still see it burning. An uneasy feeling began to work its way into her chest. She picked at a splinter lodged in the palm of her hand, making it throb. When she looked up again, Russell was blowing a thin trail of smoke. He grinned at her.

"Hey, Carolina," he said. "That fire sure put on a good show, didn't it?"

Russell really had all the attention now. His vivid descriptions of the barn blazing got the boys to laughing and heehawing about it. The more he talked, the faster Carolina's blood boiled. She felt her fists balling up.

The temper within her took on a life of its own. Carolina flew into Russell, beating him with her fists. She cried out over and over.

"Why did you do it? Why did you do it?"

The yells and hollers of the other boys echoed in the car as they egged on the fight, hoping for it to continue. Russell didn't fight her back. He held her hands, laughing, as she struggled to break free. She slipped from his grasp and socked him square in the eye. He grabbed her hair and she flailed at him. Suddenly the big man, who'd been nothing but a shadow till now, lurched forward. He grabbed Russell's arm and twisted it so it was against Russell's back.

"Leave the girl alone," the man said in a low gravelly voice.

The man forced Russell's arm up his back. Tears flooded Russell's eyes.

The man let go and went back to his corner. Russell stared straight ahead. The heavyset boy chuckled, and another boy joined in. Russell flashed a dark look toward Carolina that said he hated her more than anyone in the world.

Train wheels rumbled along the track. The day wore on. The hot sun turned the car into an oven. A lot of the boys had taken off their shirts and were using them as pillows. The big man sat in the darkest corner. Carolina wondered if he was really sleeping or wide awake with his eyes closed. Carolina's lips were dry as a desert. She struggled to keep her eyes open, but the heat wore on her. Despite her best efforts, her eyes shut and her head bobbed forward.

Brakes screeched. Carolina's head jerked up. The sun shone into the car, casting strange shadows. She was sure she'd never been hotter or thirstier in her whole life. She rubbed her eyes.

The big man and the teenager were gone. The boys were still there, and every one of them was staring at her. She ignored them. Carolina reached up and felt for her necklace. The knot in the cord had worked its way down next to the pendant. She held the catbird carving, and as she pulled the knot up to the back of her neck, her fingertips touched stiff choppy ends of hair. For a moment she stayed in a sleepy state of confusion. Then she saw the mean grin on Russell's face. She saw her braids dangling from his fist.

He began to swing them around and around. Laughter rang out and echoed against the walls of the boxcar. The screech of train wheels braking and skidding across steel rails drowned out Carolina's cry.

She crawled to the opening of the car. The gravel and weeds along the tracks came into focus as the train slowed to a crawl. Up ahead was a black tunnel.

Jump, Carolina. Jump.

She didn't hesitate.

She jumped. She figured she'd clear the gravel and land feetfirst on the grass. Instead she landed hard on her belly like a sack of flour. Her only thought was escaping those steel wheels, and as she scrambled forward, she began to tumble, falling head over heels down a steep embankment. Weeds and brambles did nothing to break her fall.

When the ground around her stopped moving, she pushed herself up from the dirt. The caboose was already well down the track and entering the tunnel. The clickity-clack of steel wheels on tracks became a distant hum. Then all was quiet except for the soft rustling sound of something moving in the underbrush.

It was a lone catbird hopping about under the twigs and green leaves of a chokecherry bush. It jumped up from one tiny twig to the next. When it reached the uppermost branch, it chirped out a *mew* much like a kitten. Then it took flight.

Carolina climbed back up the embankment. She slipped

on loose gravel and felt the scab rip away from one knee. Standing on a railroad tie between two gleaming rows of track, she saw the black tunnel before her. She turned in the other direction. Nothing but tracks as far as her eyes could see through a land of beautiful mountains and green trees.

Carolina took a step. Then she took another. She was heading in the opposite direction of the friend who had proved to be no friend at all. With each step she felt the weight of his betrayal, like a hard pebble falling down to the bottom of her heart, landing silently on top of the heap.

There were more railroad ties than she could ever count. She wanted to lie down and give up. Then she heard Mattie's singing voice, heard it as clear as if she was standing beside her. It was a rhyme Mattie would sing whenever Carolina started feeling sorry for herself.

> *"One, two, three, four, five, six, seven.*
> *All good children go to Heaven.*
> *Seven, six, five, four, three, two, one.*
> *Carolina sucks her thumb."*

Carolina stepped along with the rhyme playing in her head. She hopped from one wooden tie to the next without hitting the jagged stones between.

> *One, two, three, four, five, six, seven.*

When she got bored with that rhyme, she started another. This time she sang out loud.

"Clickity, clickity, clack.
Chickety, chickety, chop.
How many times before I stop?
One, two, three, four . . ."

She picked up a broken branch lying across the track. It was straight and solid, a perfect walking stick. She tapped it against the steel rails; five, six, seven, eight . . . At step forty-six she tripped and fell against the stones, ripping the scab on her other knee. Dark red blood seeped up and ran in a red trickle down her shin.

She flopped down right in the center of the tracks and stretched her legs straight out. The sun bore down on her. Her nose and cheeks ached with sunburn. She looked ahead—miles of train tracks. She looked behind—miles of train tracks. She imagined tea, a gallon jug of it, with ice cubes floating at the top and sugar stirred into it all.

A low panting sound brought her attention to the present moment. A shiver tingled up between her shoulders. Carolina sucked in her breath. A shadow was cast on the ground before her. *Painter cat.* She watched the shadow grow larger and larger as the panting got closer and louder. Carolina figured she was a goner.

Its shadow and her shadow became one. She felt the hot breath on her neck. Then she felt the beast's tongue on her ear. It was licking her.

It was the most pathetic-looking dog Carolina had ever seen. It seemed to be a mix of everything. It was curly-haired on top and straight-haired on the bottom. Its fur grew in ragged patches of brown and white and black. Its long tail was full of burrs and weeds. Its ears were two stubs sticking straight up.

"Hey, pup!" Carolina cried out. "Where did you come from?"

She reached out to give the dog a scratch behind the ears, and then he sprang at her, knocking her onto her back, and then she was caught in a flurry of big sloppy dog kisses. She could feel its nose and tongue wetting her cheeks and arms and legs. It sniffed her all over as if she was made of milk and sugar. Carolina wrestled with it, rubbing its ears and its belly until it was dancing with that long burr-covered tail steering its backside. Finally they were both worn out. The dog curled its entire body onto her lap. It fixed its big brown eyes on her, as if it was waiting for what was next.

"I plan to follow this track until I come to a town," Carolina said as she gently rubbed a soft patch of fur behind its ears. "You want to come?"

The dog gave a little yip and its tail got to thumping with fresh excitement. Carolina and her new all-weather friend set off down the tracks. Having a friend along gave her new energy, and she started to skip from railroad tie to railroad tie.

> "What shall I name my little pup?
> I'll have to think a good one up.
> A, B, C, D, E, F, G . . ."

The dog trotted along beside her. It reached up every so often and licked her hand.

Carolina missed the railroad tie.

"Okay, pup. Your name starts with Q," she said.

She took three more steps and then she knew.

"Your name is Queenie."

Queenie looked up at her and barked.

The sun had been bearing down on them for hours by the time Carolina and Queenie finally stepped off the railroad tracks and strode down the back streets of a good-sized town. They took a detour into a backyard garden and drank from the hose, which had been left on, grabbing cherry tomatoes from the garden on their way out.

They sauntered down the sidewalk along Main Street, looking at the displays in the store windows. Carolina stopped at the plate glass doors of Woolworth's Department Store.

"You stay here, Queenie," she said, and stepped inside.

A large fan was whirring. Carolina strolled down an aisle full of hair ribbons and barrettes, toys and dolls, transistor radios, and record singles called 45s. She casually flipped through the selection: Bobby Darin, the Supremes, the Beach Boys. At Bob Dylan she stopped. Her mind flooded with thoughts of her daddy. She pushed the records back into place, trying to push away the hurt of missing him.

Woolworth's Luncheonette took up almost a whole wall. A waitress was wiping the long gray counter. She had big eyes and blond hair pulled back in a ponytail. Carolina read the menu tacked on the wall.

Extra Rich Ice Cream Soda	25¢
Deluxe Tulip Sundae	25¢
Super Jumbo Banana Split	39¢
Milk Shake	25¢
Coca-Cola, Large	10¢

The waitress kept checking her watch and looking out the window. Carolina wondered if she was waiting for someone.

Ham Salad Sandwich	30¢
Egg Salad Sandwich	30¢
American Cheese Sandwich	30¢
Bacon and Tomato Sandwich	50¢

Carolina shoved her hands into the pockets of her shorts, expecting to find a dime. There was nothing but a hole in her pocket. She leaned her elbows on the counter. "May I have a drink of water, please?" asked Carolina. She lifted her elbows so the waitress could continue wiping a wet sponge across the counter. The name tag pinned to the waitress's blouse said GEORGIA.

Georgia grabbed a glass from under the counter and filled it at the sink.

"There you go," she said, and placed the glass down on a tiny square napkin.

Carolina gulped it down without stopping once. She plunked the glass on the counter and let out a long breath.

"I'd say you were a mite thirsty," said Georgia.

Carolina hopped up onto a red vinyl–covered stool and watched Georgia refill glass sugar containers from a giant bag of sugar. She watched her balance one ketchup bottle on top of another. Then Georgia popped open silver napkin containers and placed more white paper napkins inside. Carolina stared at the upside-down ketchup bottle until a red glop dropped into the upright bottle.

Georgia was checking the time on her wristwatch again and peeking out the window, looking upward as if she was searching the sky.

"Who are you waiting for?" Carolina asked.

"Not who, what," said Georgia.

"*What* are you waiting for?"

Georgia smiled and said, "You'll have to wait and see."

There was a long mirror behind the counter. Carolina was startled by her own reflection. She looked like something the cat had dragged in backward. Her skin was covered with a fine layer of black dust and soot, and her freckled nose and cheeks were bright red with sunburn. She tried not to look at her hair, but she couldn't help it. It stuck out at all different lengths, the longest strands above her left shoulder and the shortest above her right ear. She hardly recognized herself. It crossed her mind to grab a napkin and wipe her face, but she let the idea go, figuring it wouldn't make much of a difference one way or the other.

There was something more to her reflection; something that didn't have anything to do with dirt or hair. It was as if she was looking at someone she didn't know. It wasn't just that her braids were missing. It was as if *she* was missing.

Carolina pushed off from the side of the counter, making the stool spin. She tucked her knees under tight and held the toes of her sneakers against the base. She pushed off again and again and again, whirling faster and faster and faster.

"Hey," Georgia said, grabbing Carolina's shoulders in a firm grip.

Carolina stopped in one quick jolt, but her brain kept going. The aisles, the counter, the walls, and Georgia spun by in a blur.

"It's closing time. If you're not going to buy anything, you'll have to get going."

The kaleidoscope of colors stopped whirling, and Georgia's face came into focus.

"Sorry," said Carolina.

"Your momma isn't with you, is she?" Georgia asked.

Carolina shook her head.

Georgia hesitated a moment, staring up at the ceiling with her head resting in the palm of her hand, as if she was trying to figure out fractions. She looked back at Carolina.

"Do you like ice cream?" she asked.

Carolina nodded her head.

"What's your favorite flavor?" Georgia whispered.

"Strawberry," Carolina whispered back.

Georgia went behind the counter and filled a large silver container with ice cream and milk. She hooked it under a blending machine that stirred and whirred. When Georgia unhooked it, it had made a thick frosty shake that Georgia poured into a tall glass. She stuck a straw in the center and set it down on the counter. Carolina's cheeks sucked on that straw so hard, they caved in. Georgia laughed and handed her a long-handled spoon. Carolina dug in.

Then Georgia made a ham sandwich and placed it on the plate at the very end of the counter, in front of the stool farthest away from the window. "Here, set down here," she said. "It's almost time."

Carolina hopped from stool to stool, sliding her glass along the counter until she was seated in front of the ham sandwich.

"Almost time for what?" she asked.

"You'll see," Georgia said.

The first bite landed in Carolina's stomach and warmth radiated through her like a warm ember. It felt as if she had been holding her breath for three solid days and had finally been granted permission to let it out. Carolina sipped her milk shake and took bites of her sandwich. The giant fan attached at the ceiling blew a breeze against her bare arms.

"This counter sure is shiny," Carolina said.

"It sure is," said Georgia.

Carolina slurped up the last of her milk shake, making a noise so loud it let the whole store know about it. Georgia grinned at her. She came around the counter and draped her arm around Carolina's shoulders.

"Here it comes," she said.

The sun was setting in a clear sky. Carolina faced the window, wondering what she'd see, but mostly liking the good feeling that came from having Georgia's arm around her. Then the red-yellow rays of star-fire burst into the Woolworth's big plate-glass window. Tiny flecks of silver caught the light, and the whole length of the counter glittered like a million brilliant stars.

"Isn't that the prettiest thing?" Georgia said in a soft voice.

It was in the way she'd said it that Carolina knew that up until this very moment, Georgia had been keeping this secret all to herself. If Carolina could have made time stand still, she would have, but in less than a whole minute, the sun had sunk lower on the horizon. The glittery counter turned back to a dull gray.

"Closing time," Georgia announced.

Carolina waved as she headed out the door. "Bye, Georgia. Thank you."

"Bye, honey. You have a nice evening."

Carolina stepped outside. She looked down the street to her right. She looked down the street to her left. Queenie was nowhere in sight. Carolina strolled across the street to a small park. No Queenie. She plopped down on a swing and sat with her head in her hands. She squeezed her eyes shut, wishing for the dog to come around the corner and start licking her hand.

"It's getting late. Shouldn't you be getting on to home?"

Carolina opened her eyes and saw a pair of blue Keds. She looked up and saw Georgia standing right in front of her.

Carolina was about to say, "Yes, I think I will," and pretend home was somewhere she could go to, but when she tried to speak, that big old lump was in the way.

"You don't have a place to go to, do you?" asked Georgia.

Carolina shook her head.

Georgia kneeled down close to the swing and spoke softly. "I ran away once when I was your age," she said.

Carolina watched Georgia stare off into the sky as if she was doing fractions again. Georgia sighed. Finally, she spoke again.

"You can come home with me, if you want. It isn't safe to be out alone all night."

Carolina nodded her head and smiled.

Georgia's arm fell over Carolina's shoulder as if it was the most natural thing in the world, as if they'd known each other forever.

It turned out that the train had taken Carolina all the way into Tennessee. Georgia lived in a trailer park on the out-skirts of town. There were petunias planted in front of a white trailer that had a blue stripe going all the way around. A cement block had been placed near the front door. They stepped up onto it, then took another big step to get inside.

There was a tiny kitchen with a small white icebox and a white stove and a chrome-edged table and two matching chairs. The living room had a pale blue chair with arms worn through to the stuffing. Instead of a sofa there was a jumble of big pillows, and a low table was covered in framed photos.

Georgia held three jars filled with bubble bath crystals. She opened each one.

"Lavender, rose, or gardenia?"

Carolina sniffed each one. "Lavender," she said.

Under a warm blanket of white lavender-scented bubbles, Carolina's head bobbed back and forth under Georgia's strong fingers. A shampoo had never felt this good. She relaxed as if she was under a spell, feeling the gentle massage on her scalp.

"I'm learning how to be a beautician at Vivi's Beauty School," said Georgia.

Carolina was barely listening, paying more attention to the squishy sound of soap lathering up in her hair like mounds of whipped cream. Georgia attached a long rubber tube to the faucet. The water came out the other end in a shower spray. Carolina squeezed her eyes tight while the shampoo and water fell over her face and neck and back.

"You have more rings around your neck than a raccoon has on its tail," said Georgia. "This necklace has got to come off."

Carolina grabbed her catbird and held tight.

"I didn't say I was going to take it," said Georgia. "Just wash it, that's all."

Carolina had never taken it off, not since the night her daddy had given it to her. She lifted the leather cord over her head and held the carving in her hand. It was black with dirt. She swished it in the soapy water until the catbird came to life again.

Her daddy had carved it as good as anything he'd ever made. It looked so real, she could imagine it singing. She admired the delicate cuts in the wings and the tail. He'd carved an eye that was as perfectly round as a marble.

Carolina dressed for bed in Georgia's baby-doll pajamas. She made a nest of blankets and pillows in the living room, then turned to the photos. Carolina tried to guess which pictures might be Georgia's mother and father and which pictures might be brothers and sisters. One picture showed Georgia in a bathing suit with a man's arms wrapped around her. Carolina picked up the picture and looked closely at the man's face. He looked so familiar.

She quickly put the picture back in place as Georgia emerged from her bath. Her hair was wrapped in a towel twisted up like a big turban. She plopped down in the pillows next to Carolina, dropping a bag of fuzzy pink and black rollers, then handed Carolina a mirror with a long handle.

"Hold it steady," Georgia instructed.

Carolina tried to hold the mirror still in front of Georgia, but she was so fascinated watching Georgia section off her hair that she needed constant reminders. Georgia's face held a look of complete concentration as she combed the sections smooth and then rolled the strands around the fuzzy rollers.

"When I save enough money, I'm going to buy a television," said Georgia with a mouthful of bobby pins. "For now we'll entertain ourselves with girl talk."

Carolina listened intently, learning about first kisses and what to wear on dates and how a car can tell you a lot about the boy who drives it. She learned that Georgia's boyfriend had gone to school to be a police officer, and now he had a good-paying job. She learned that Georgia had no intention of getting married until she had her own beauty shop, which she called a *salon*. Georgia talked about plans and goals and dreams.

After she pinned the last roller in place, Georgia turned to Carolina. "Okay, your turn," she said. She took the comb and began combing out the tangle of knots in Carolina's hair.

"The grandmas love for me to do their hair," Georgia said. "They always ask for me special. I take my time coaxing out their tangles. The other girls yank and pull like they've forgotten somebody's head is attached to that hair."

Carolina felt the gentle tugs on her scalp as the comb straightened tangles. She felt the comb scrape gently at the nape of her neck. It was a strange sensation. She was used to feeling the comb and brush moving down her back. She remembered the gentle touch of Miss Latah's hands as she wove sweetgrass into Carolina's braids. She brushed those thoughts away, telling herself it didn't matter.

"You're going to be the best beautician ever," said Carolina. "I bet word will get around and you'll have the busiest beauty shop—I mean *salon*—in town."

"Do you really think so, Carolina?"

"Sure do."

"Oh, you're the best girl ever."

Georgia put her arms around Carolina's shoulders and gave her a little squeeze at the same moment that she planted a kiss on her cheek. She continued to comb and lift up Carolina's hair.

"Well, I must say that whoever cut your hair should not be allowed to even *carry* a pair of scissors," said Georgia.

Carolina swallowed hard. She pinched up her face and tried biting her lip, but still tears flooded her eyes. That big old lump in her throat was refusing to go down.

"I'm sorry, sweetie. I didn't mean to hurt your feelings," said Georgia.

"Why did he have to cut my hair?" Carolina whimpered her angry words, then coughed, choking on them as they pushed that big lump right out of her throat.

The thin shell around her heart cracked into a million pieces. All the hurts she'd been damming up inside spilled out like a river, and tears poured down like rain. They trickled over her cheeks as her words flowed. She told Georgia about the car accident that had killed her mama and daddy and her sweet baby brother, Caleb; about how much she missed them; about how she had been living with Auntie Shen and then been forced to leave; about the foster families who didn't care for her a bit; about how she kept running away. Finally she told her about Russell.

"He said he was my friend," Carolina said.

She let Georgia pull her close, and she lay still in Georgia's comforting arms. She looked at their nest of pillows. Tissues were scattered like downy feathers. She took the tissue Georgia handed her and blew her nose. It felt tender and sore, as if she'd been rubbing it all night with sandpaper.

She took a deep breath and heaved a big sigh, then began to tell Georgia about the Harmony family. She told her how kind Miss Latah was and how Mr. Ray made her laugh. She told her how Lucas had treated her like a little sister.

"I wish I could go back and start all over," said Carolina.

"Wishing won't make it so," said Georgia. "You can't unscramble eggs."

Carolina was all tuckered out. Her body sank into the plump cushy pillows. Georgia reached up and turned out the light.

Chapter 21

HEAVEN

Carolina began to dream.

Silver lights trickled across the Milky Way and cascaded down from a brilliant star in a smooth silvery ribbon like a waterfall. Carolina saw that the star was not a star. It was an opening in the night sky, and Mattie was sitting on the edge of it. She smiled down at Carolina and kicked her legs, sending glittery sparkles splashing across a black velvet sky. They sprinkled down onto Carolina like snow, and the tiny flecks of light illuminated her pajamas like the glow of lightning bugs. Carolina looked up again and her friend was gone, but she heard Mattie's laughter. It tumbled down the silvery ribbon waterfall like tiny bells.

The stars of Orion's belt, which were not stars, were getting larger and larger as the constellation drifted down from the heavens. Closer and closer they came and brighter and brighter they grew, until she could see a brilliant blue light within. She reached up, grabbed on to the edge of the lowest star, and jumped. Leaning against the edge as if she was balancing on the top rung of a farm gate, she peered in. On the other side was a lush green meadow illuminated by a light more brilliant than the sun. Red and yellow and white and blue and purple flowers grew in wild masses, their blooms glittering in that magnificent light. Carolina arched her back and lifted her arms high above her head as if she was preparing to dive, and in one fluid movement she let her body drop forward.

It was a long, soft, floating fall. Butterflies with giant iridescent wings flew around her. They alighted on her pajamas, in her hair, and on her arms and gently held her up. Carolina landed in the meadow of rainbow flowers with a soft thump. She opened her hand, and a tiny yellow and blue butterfly settled in her palm. It slowly opened and closed its wings, then flew up in an ever-widening circle and joined other butterflies in a flight that looked like dancing. The perfume of so many wildflowers made her giddy, and Carolina skipped over the meadow, rising and falling as if she was bouncing across a white fluffy cloud. She came to a silver-blue stream. It meandered through the meadow, rippling and trickling over amber and amethyst stones, making music.

An angel appeared before her.

"Blessings are flowing," the angel said.

"Is this Heaven?" asked Carolina.

The angel was gone as quickly as she had appeared. Only a flicker of light remained. It was moving across the meadow on wings as small as a butterfly's. Carolina ran after it.

"Wait," Carolina cried, "where is my daddy?"

The tiny flicker grew larger and larger, until it was a great silver circle that had both the reflective qualities of a mirror and the transparency of a window. Carolina pressed her face against the warm surface. It felt as soft as her mama's cheek, and she peered dreamily at what lay beyond. It was a field of tall golden grass, and a little boy was running. It was Caleb!

Carolina called to him, but he did not turn. Then she saw her mama. She was skipping behind Caleb and waving to someone high above. Carolina's eyes looked up to a ledge high upon a mountain, and she saw her daddy standing on the edge of a great stone. He was smiling, looking down on her mama and Caleb playing in the meadow. Carolina banged on the silvery surface, but her fists made no sound.

Carolina's heart broke to pieces. Had they forgotten all about her? Didn't they miss her at all? She leaned her head against the glittering circle, wanting to feel her mama's soft cheek again. So comforting was the touch of the circle that she didn't notice the surface was melting and getting larger. She fell into it as easily as if she was being lowered into a bath, only she landed in the golden meadow. She called out. "Mama! Caleb!"

She ran through the grass, shouting, looking in all

directions. She climbed the ledge until she was at the very top. Fields and mountains were laid before her. She saw three figures. Their arms and legs were moving in a curious way. Carolina smiled. They were dancing.

"Wait!" she cried. She took a running leap and jumped.

Landing on her feet perfectly, she immediately broke into a run. She ran faster and faster through the meadow, leaping and hopping like a deer, and when she was almost upon them, the three figures turned around.

It was Mr. Ray and Miss Latah and Lucas.

Miss Latah was holding the corners of her apron, which was full and round with a great harvest. She let the apron drop open, spilling hundreds of blackberries that tumbled over the meadow. Dark ripe berries bounced across Carolina's feet, and sweet juice splashed onto her legs. She felt weak. Carolina reached for the berries, but she could not pick them up. Her hands and her fingers would not move.

The angel appeared again.

"Blessings are flowing," said the angel.

The angel opened Carolina's hands for her and dropped blackberries into them. She lifted Carolina's hands to her mouth so she could eat them. The angel gave her more and more and more. Carolina's hands were never empty. She ate until purple juice dribbled down her chin and she was filled with their sweetness.

"Take me to my family," Carolina pleaded.

The angel's hand touched Carolina's forehead. It was a warm hand with a strong yet tender touch. Then the angel spoke. It sounded like the rush of many wings, like when a flock of birds suddenly turns and flies directly over-head.

"You are loved," said the angel.

Carolina opened her eyes. She was wide awake. She lay quietly, listening to Georgia's soft rhythmic breathing. She sat up and, as her eyes adjusted to the darkness, saw that two curlers had come undone from Georgia's hair. Carolina moved her blanket aside. She tiptoed across the room and slowly opened the door, which squeaked on its hinges.

Outside, a roadway wound in a circle, trailers parked alongside it. In the center was a grassy clearing. Carolina stood in the middle of it, wildflowers, grass, and weeds reaching as high as her knees. It was just before dawn. The Big Dipper was standing on its handle. All the constellations had rearranged themselves while the world was sleeping.

Carolina tried to remember her dream, but only glimpses of it remained and led her to thoughts of her daddy. So many times, they'd gazed at the stars on black moonless nights. She'd been held in his arms in the wee hours just before dawn, sleepily listening to her father as he told her stories and pointed out how the stars had traveled during the night.

Her daddy told her of ancient astronomers who had drawn pictures of the stars and had given them names and stories. He said it was as if those men had breathed life into the sky. There were the Seven Sisters, Cassiopeia, the Gemini twins, and Taurus the Bull, and there was Orion, alive and moving in the sky.

As she got older, her daddy had explained that it wasn't really the stars moving. It was the earth spinning, turning night to day and, on the other side of the planet, turning day to night. It was the people who were being rearranged. Earth was in a constant spin, and everyone on the planet had no choice but to move along with it. Even so, the stories of the stars caused her to wonder.

She looked at the brightest stars, the only constellations still visible in the early light of dawn. She thought about her strange dream. It made her wonder if stars really could be "openings" in the sky, gateways to Heaven, worlds where angels lived.

Somewhere in the distance, a rooster crowed. Carolina thought of Mr. Ray, Miss Latah, and Lucas. She figured they would be rising from their beds now, heading out to do morning chores. She missed them. Her heart ached for them.

She thought of all the times she and Lucas had started the day with a race across the farmyard, slapping their hands on the side of the barn. Now those days were gone, and so was everything that had been good. How could she ever make things right again? She thought about Auntie Shen's warning her about the light of truth shining down on a lie. Carolina figured she'd told so many lies, the light of truth must have just burst into flames.

Carolina sighed. She'd really messed things up for good now. *Are they wondering where I am?* She had a terrible feeling that maybe they were glad she was gone.

Chapter 22

FAITH

Carolina sat at Georgia's kitchen table and shook the box of chocolate puff cereal. The last sugary crumbs fell into her bowl. All that crying had made her hungry. It was as if she had been hiding in a dark closet and the door had slammed on her, locked itself tight, and was holding her captive. Then Georgia came along and, easy as pie, unlocked the door and threw it open. Carolina tipped her bowl and drank the sweetened milk.

"This is the smallest dress I could find," said Georgia. She'd been rummaging around in her closet trying to find something clean that Carolina could wear.

The dress was bright yellow with a black collar. Carolina slipped it over her head and the sleeves fell off her shoulders. Georgia tried to hike up the length of it with a black belt, but it still fell to Carolina's ankles.

"I look like a bumblebee," said Carolina.

"Well, maybe if we . . . um," Georgia mumbled as she fidgeted with the dress, then stood back and looked Carolina over. She pressed her lips together, but it didn't help. Her laughter came up in spurts and sputters, and suddenly the two of them were laughing together.

"I don't mean to be picky, but I'm not going anywhere dressed like this," said Carolina.

Finally they were headed into town. Carolina had on a pair of lime green capris and a green top to match. The pants and top hung baggy and full on Carolina, but it was better than looking like a bumblebee.

When Carolina and Georgia walked through the doors of the beauty parlor that was connected to Vivi's Beauty School, four pretty girls with pink smocks were waiting for them. April had dark brown hair curled up in a flip. May had blond hair all piled up on her head like a beehive. June had bangs and a ponytail, and Fran had red curls that fell all around her face and down her back. They were Georgia's best friends, and they'd come over the moment she'd called. Carolina was suddenly surrounded by them. They fussed all over her.

They had Carolina sit in a pink-cushioned chair. Georgia stepped on a bar that made the whole seat rise. The radio was blaring and the girls were arguing over which station to play. April wanted Motown and May wanted country.

Fran finally settled the argument and put on the popular Top 40 station. The announcer was talking about the British Invasion, and then he introduced a brand-new group straight from Liverpool, England: the Beatles.

Carolina felt like a princess sitting on her throne as she soaked up the attention of the beauty-shop girls. A book with pages and pages of hairdos lay across her lap. Most of them were very fancy. Some were downright hysterical. The beauty-shop girls leafed through the pages in the book and all the latest modern teen magazines too. They pointed to this one and that one. Carolina scrunched up her nose. She put her hands over her eyes. She laughed right out loud at some of them.

Georgia stood nearby. She'd put on a pink smock too. After taking her curlers out that morning, she'd puffed her blond hair out full in what she called a *bouffant*.

"Keep looking," said Georgia. "She's bound to find something she likes."

"Oh look, here's a picture of Sandra Dee," said April. "Oh, I just love seeing her in the movies."

"She looks like Georgia," said Carolina.

"She sure does," said Fran.

"You should see Georgia's boyfriend," said June. "He's as dreamy as Bobby Darin."

May piped up, "How about this style?"

Carolina looked at the model on the page. She was standing in the sand, tossing a beach ball, and a blue ocean was in the background. The model's hair was short like a boy's, only she had long bangs. Carolina imagined herself on that sand. She could picture herself throwing that beach ball in the air. Short hair looked fun. "That one." Her finger landed on the picture.

Carolina heard the swish and click of the scissors moving around her ears and along the nape of her neck. She felt Georgia's fingers lifting her hair and felt the comb on her scalp. She remembered her barbershop haircut as having been quick and tidy, but today she was being pampered. Georgia finally put down her scissors. A thin layer of tiny red and gold hairs encircled the pink chair.

"Okay, close your eyes," said Georgia.

Hairspray touched the sides of Carolina's face in a cool mist. It filled the whole shop with a perfume smell. April handed Carolina a giant-sized mirror with a pink plastic handle. May and June swirled her chair around. Carolina moved the mirror so she could see the back of her head. She looked at herself from the left side. She looked at herself from the right. Fran stood near, holding her breath.

"I love it!" said Carolina.

"She loves it!" Georgia and the beauty-shop girls shouted all at the same time.

"Let's go down to Miss Thelma's and pick out something pretty for Carolina to wear," said May.

April, May, June, and Fran strolled down Main Street, their high heels clicking on the sidewalk. Georgia and Carolina followed in their sneakers. They all were talking and laughing, even waving to folks on the other side of the street. Everyone they passed by suddenly started to smile, and Carolina felt as if she was part of a jolly parade. Everyone on the street seemed in a better mood because they were there. They walked through the doors of Thelma's

Thrift Shop and immediately began combing through the racks.

Carolina emerged a half hour later dressed up as if it was the first day of school. They'd all chipped in and bought Carolina a sleeveless baby blue blouse, a skirt with blue and white and green stripes, and white sandals. She even had on a new pair of underwear with *Tuesday* embroidered on the edge. The other six days of the week, each a different color, were held in a paper bag. She wished they hadn't talked her into the bra. She kept folding her arms across her chest, certain that the whole world was staring at her. April fastened a tiny yellow bow in Carolina's hair with a bobby pin.

"There, now the look is complete," she said.

"Let's celebrate," said May.

Their jolly parade continued down the sidewalk and into a diner. April, May, and June slid onto a big cushy seat on one side of the table, and Carolina, Fran, and Georgia slid onto the seat on the other side. Fran reached into her purse and handed Carolina three nickels for the jukebox that was set at the end of the booth.

Carolina turned the knob and the metal pages inside flipped over, each flip revealing more of her favorite songs. Carolina picked H7 to play "He's So Fine" by the Chiffons, L3 to play "Love Me Do" by the Beatles, and B15 to play "The Times They Are A-Changin' " by Bob Dylan. She plunked in her nickels and pressed the buttons. "He's So Fine" began to play at the same time as the waitress started scribbling down what they wanted. Georgia ordered Cokes and cheeseburgers for everybody.

Carolina was dipping her cheeseburger into a mound of ketchup when she noticed Georgia smiling and wiggling her fingers in a little wave. Carolina turned around to see whom she was waving at and nearly choked. She swung forward and sank low in her seat.

"Hey, Georgia," said the young police officer in a voice as slick as a peeled onion.

"Hey, Bobby," Georgia answered him in a voice as sweet as candy. "Come on over and meet this pretty little girl we've dolled up."

Carolina had no way to escape. The window was on one side and Georgia and Fran had her pinned in on the other. Carolina stared down at her cheeseburger, glancing up only enough to see for certain. It *was* Bobby, the skunk who'd pretended to be her friend and then dropped her off at Miss Lily Jean's.

"Carolina, honey, don't be shy," said Georgia. "I want you to meet my boyfriend."

Boyfriend! Carolina held the cheeseburger in front of her face. A blob of ketchup dropped onto her plate.

"Aw, come on. Georgia didn't chop you up that bad, did she?" Bobby said.

April reached across the table and gently pushed Carolina's hands down.

Please don't recognize me, thought Carolina.

"Better keep an eye on her, Georgia. She's a head turner," he said.

"She sure is," said May.

Bobby leaned down and spoke to Georgia, "We still going to the drive-in tonight?"

"Pick me up at eight," said Georgia, "and don't be late."

He put his police cap over his heart. "On my word of honor," he said, and then he gave her a wink.

The bell over the door rang out as he left the diner. Carolina let out a long slow breath. It seemed as if no matter how far she ran, trouble was always a step behind.

"We'd better get back," said Fran. "Vivi will have our hide for sure."

"Go ahead," said Georgia. "I'll catch up."

April, May, June, and Fran slid across the red vinyl seats and headed on their way. Carolina watched them through the window. They sashayed up the street, their full dresses swishing from side to side. Thin fabric belts that matched their dresses were wrapped around their waists so tight the girls looked like Barbie dolls. They were beautiful. They were happy. They were in charge of the world.

Carolina checked her hair in the reflection of the window. She liked her new self. Georgia slid onto the seat across the table from Carolina. She took both of Carolina's hands into her own.

"You look like a brand-new girl," said Georgia. "I guess you're ready for a brand-new life now."

"A brand-new life?" asked Carolina.

"Sure," said Georgia. "Now that you won't be going back to Harmony Farm, you'll have to start all over."

"Start all over?" asked Carolina.

"It's a shame you won't get to see your Auntie Shen ever again," Georgia continued, "but you know, I've been thinking. You could stay right here with me and pretend to be my little sister."

"Never see Auntie Shen again?" asked Carolina.

Georgia nodded her head. "I'm afraid so. There's just no other way."

Carolina considered what that might be like, to simply start over with Georgia. *What would it be like to have a big sister?* She looked over at Georgia, who was fishing through her purse, taking out coins. Her skin was the color of a peach, with a pretty pink glow in her cheeks. Georgia looked up and smiled at Carolina, and her bright green eyes were full of light. So was her smile. Carolina bet Georgia had never told a lie in her life. She wondered how saying yes to something so easy could be so hard.

"Georgia, do you think they'll believe me if I tell them the truth?" Carolina asked. "If I go back to Harmony Farm, do you think they'll even want to talk to me?"

Georgia looked as if her feelings had been crushed. Her shoulders rose a little bit as she released a sigh.

"My mind's made up," said Carolina, and then she repeated Mr. Ray's words. "Running away because it's too hard to make things right is just keeping things wrong."

"Are you sure you can do that?" asked Georgia. "Aren't you afraid to go back?"

"Yeah, I'm scared, a little, but Mr. Ray says a person can do just about anything once they make up their mind to it," said Carolina, "and I've made up my mind."

Georgia took Carolina's hands in hers and gave a little squeeze.

"Bless your heart," said Georgia. "I guess I can scrape up enough money to get you a train ticket. This time you'll ride in the passenger car."

"Let's go now," said Carolina, practically hopping out of her seat.

Georgia looked at her wristwatch.

"Miss Vivi is going to have a fit if I don't get back soon," she said.

"Please, Georgia."

Georgia looked up to the ceiling as if she was doing fractions again.

"Okay, but we better make it quick," she said.

They stepped out onto the sidewalk. Bobby was leaning against the police cruiser. He let out a long whistle as Georgia walked by. Georgia pretended she didn't like it, but Carolina saw her smile.

"Hey, you two," he said. "Where are you off to in such a hurry?"

"Never mind," Georgia said in a flirty voice.

Bobby caught up to them. Carolina saw the look of recognition come over his face. He put two fingers under Carolina's chin and lifted her face until they were staring at each other, eye to eye.

"Well, I'll be," he said. "Carolina Campbell, do you have any idea how many people are out looking for you?"

He turned to Georgia.

"I don't know where you're headed or what you're doing, but this little girl is coming with me."

Georgia gave him a look that said she didn't take orders.

"I mean it, Georgia. This one's a runaway. I've got to take her in. A little ten-year-old kid can't be running all over the countryside by herself."

"I'm not little. I'll be eleven in twenty-five days," said Carolina.

No one was listening.

Georgia was standing firm with her hands on her hips. "For Heaven's sake, Bobby, you can see that she isn't all by herself. She's with me. Besides, she'll be on a train for home soon enough." She took Carolina's hand. "So you see, Bobby, everything is all set."

Bobby's face flushed beet red. Carolina just heard the word *home*.

"Georgia, I'm the law and I'm in charge. I say she's coming with me."

Bobby took hold of Carolina's other hand.

"She's coming with me," said Georgia, pulling Carolina closer.

"No, she's coming with me," said Bobby as he tugged Carolina in his direction.

Georgia pulled her back. Carolina felt like a rope in a game of tug-a-war. Georgia and Bobby tossed words above her head.

"I don't know why I ever even looked at you, Bobby. Why, you're just plain mean," said Georgia.

"Aw, c'mon, Georgia. Don't talk like that. I'm only doing my job," said Bobby.

"Well, what are you going to do? Arrest me and throw me in jail?"

"No, of course not. Georgia! Aw, man," said Bobby. "You know what? Maybe I *should* take you to jail. I'll take you both down to the station right now."

Georgia and Carolina sat in the backseat of the police cruiser. Bobby turned on the siren. Carolina could see the reflection of the round red light flashing in the store windows as they sped down Main Street.

Georgia had won the argument hands down, and now they were getting a police escort to the train depot. Bobby said only one train a day left this station. If they didn't make this train, they would have to wait until tomorrow. Carolina knew that would leave plenty of time for Bobby to change his mind. Ten minutes was all she had. Ten minutes would determine the direction of the rest of her whole entire life. The train was rolling into the station just as Bobby pulled the cruiser into the parking lot.

"Hurry!" Carolina shouted.

Bobby turned around to face them.

"Georgia," he said, "I don't know about this. I could have my badge taken away. I've been thinking about it the whole way over, and I'm going to have to take Carolina down to the local station to straighten this whole thing out."

He turned and faced Carolina, "Don't worry, kid. Everything will turn out all right."

"No!" Carolina cried. She yanked on the door handle and Georgia held her hand.

"Maybe Bobby's right," said Georgia in a soft voice.

Carolina couldn't believe what she was hearing. She looked over to the tracks. The train was pulling in.

"I have to go back," Carolina pleaded.

She saw the doors of the passenger train opening. She saw the conductor stepping onto the platform.

"Please," cried Carolina, blinking back tears. "Please, let me go."

On the train platform, the conductor was bending over,

lifting a heavy suitcase with one hand and helping an elderly woman onto the train with the other.

"I don't feel right just sending you off like you were a letter," said Georgia.

"I can do it," said Carolina. "I'm brave."

The conductor stepped back inside the train. He was leaning out, taking a final glance to his left and a final glance to his right.

"The train is leaving," cried Carolina. "We have to hurry."

Carolina pushed the door open. She took off at a full run. She saw the train doors shut tight.

"Wait!" screamed Carolina.

Bobby and Georgia caught up with her as the train rolled away from the platform. Carolina stared after it, watching it head down a straight stretch of tracks. All her newfound hope shriveled up inside her.

Chapter 23

ANGELS SINGING IN THE STARS

AUGUST 5, 1964

At the end of Carolina's journey, another was about to begin. Carolina stood beside the sign at the edge of the road. HARMONY FARM.

"Are you sure you don't want us to come with you?" asked Georgia.

"No, I have to do this on my own," said Carolina.

"Now, if things don't work out, we'll be right here waiting for you," said Bobby.

Carolina nodded. Then she took the first step and headed down the lane.

Sadie was grazing in the pasture. Elsie was grazing beside her. They were good friends, plow horse and milk cow. They looked up at her as she passed, as if to say *Welcome home*, and then lowered their heads to the grass again. Carolina walked with steady steps toward the house.

A big gaping ash pit surrounded by singed grass and weeds was all that remained of the barn. Not even a board was left, just a large rectangle of black dust. The metal silo looked lost without it, but there it stood, the faithful sentry. Carolina thought back to the fiery inferno, remembering the silhouetted bodies of Mr. Ray and Lucas struggling with Sadie.

During the ride back from Tennessee, Carolina had imagined this moment many different ways. She had filled her head with happy thoughts and had seen herself skipping right across the porch and knocking on the door with a pum-pum-pum-pum-pum-pum, pum. She'd imagined happy smiling faces ready to greet her.

Even Georgia and Bobby had agreed with her. After the train had left the station, Bobby had suddenly had a change of heart. He'd dried Carolina's tears and announced to no one in particular that a police officer's first job was to take care of people. Carolina smiled, thinking about how Bobby had turned out to be a friend after all. She figured that what Bobby had done ranked right up there with the biggest surprises of her life. She just about fell over when he said he was going to drive her all the way home, all the way back to North Carolina. Even Georgia wasn't about to leave her side. Georgia said Miss Vivi wasn't as strict as everyone made her out to be. She'd understand about Georgia's sudden absence. Bobby and Georgia acted as if there was nothing more important than getting Carolina home, and now here she was.

Now that the big moment had come, Carolina's stomach was doing flip-flops. She remembered Mr. Ray's angry face and Miss Latah's sad expression. Would Lucas walk away from her? She remembered Sims's mean *"Who are they going to believe?"*

Carolina turned and headed up the rise to the sheep pasture. The ewes were good listeners. She'd talk it over with them first.

Goldenrod and blue cornflowers bloomed along the fencing. A few sheep trotted over and others followed, curious and wary at the same time. Carolina reached into the square of wire and put her fingers into the wool of one who seemed to want his head scratched.

She gazed back at the house and yard, and there was Lucas, stepping out of the henhouse with a basket of eggs. She watched him take the porch steps two at a time, saw the screen door slam behind him. He emerged only moments later, and then he sauntered off toward the apple trees. She knew where he was going. It was his daydreaming place. She'd seen him with his legs stretched out in the "king's cradle," a wide branch that grew out and then up from the trunk of an evergreen. She'd seen him with his arms crossed up behind and his head resting in his hands, enjoying being lazy.

Carolina continued up the hill alongside the pasture until she was at its highest point. She could see the field that she and Mr. Ray had cleared. The stony red clay soil was now a pale green. The seeds they'd planted shortly after the accident had sprouted.

Harmony Farm was getting along fine without her. Maybe she really had been nothing but a heap of trouble. They might even have been glad to be rid of her. Then she remembered Lucas tugging on her braids and Mr. Ray throwing back his head and laughing at her jokes. She thought about the way Miss Latah would look at her with those soft eyes and say *"It'll be all right."*

Carolina shook the stones out of her sandals. She brushed the grass off her skirt and noticed a large stain. She figured it was the peach juice that had dribbled down her chin and arms. They had stopped at a farm stand along the way, and Bobby had bought a whole dozen. They all had leaned against the police cruiser and eaten three peaches apiece.

A dark cloud moved in front of the sun and cast a shadow over the land. It looked as if a thunderstorm was brewing. Carolina could see Georgia and Bobby still standing by the police cruiser at the head of the lane. She figured she couldn't stay up here with the sheep forever. She had to admit she never much cared for hiding, not even in a game of hide-and-seek. All she ever wanted to do was stand up and shout "Here I am!"

Her sandals barely made a sound as she stepped up the porch steps. She peered through the screen door. The kitchen was quiet. She knocked on the wood frame and waited. She knocked again, louder this time. No answer. She pressed her face against the screen.

"Hello!" she yelled.

A breeze stirred the wind chime. Its soft tinkling music

mingled with the buzz of a bee. There was neither hide nor hair of anyone, not even the dog. She leaned over the railing, where a hummingbird was whirring above a wild rosebush, and scanned the side yard. She looked to the vegetable garden and looked farther over to the clothesline. She didn't see a soul.

She sat down on the top step and slumped forward, her elbow on her knee and her chin in her hand. Wasps were flying in and out of a hole in the wood under the eaves. Back and forth they went, in a steady hum, following each other's scent as if they were traveling back and forth along a winding road. She heard the faraway sound of a tractor. *Mr. Ray must be making his way back home.*

The thought of facing Mr. Ray made butterflies in her stomach. They started beating their wings and flying in a wild frenzy. Carolina tapped her fingers on her knee, filling her mind with a little tune to calm them.

Elsie bellowed a deep lulling moo. The first rumblings of thunder tumbled in the clouds. A sound like a bell rang out, like a tiny Christmas jingle bell. She cocked her head and listened. It wasn't a bell at all. It was Miss Latah, and she was laughing. Carolina hastened around to the back of the house. She could hardly believe her eyes.

Miss Latah was coming down the path from her mountain medicine garden. Her arm was linked into the arm of another, one who walked along at a slower gait, one who used a cane to support each step. Her hair was whiter than Carolina remembered, and her dress hung loose over her thin frame. Even so, she was singing. She was singing and laughing right along with Miss Latah.

"Auntie Shen!"

Carolina ran, her worries blowing away like seeds from a milkweed pod. She didn't stop until she entered Auntie Shen's open loving arms. Carolina wrapped her arms clear around Auntie Shen's waist and buried her cheek in Auntie Shen's dress. She felt the kisses that Auntie Shen was planting, felt them land in her hair and on her forehead. Carolina felt Auntie Shen's gentle hands on her cheeks and raised her face to her. Auntie Shen was looking at her full-on, like she was drinking her in.

"I jest love ya to pieces," she said.

Carolina's face was wet with tears. Ever since that big old lump had popped out of her throat, her eyes were spilling over about as regular as the winding creek down by the hickory trees.

Auntie Shen patted Carolina's back, saying, "It's all right. You're home now."

Carolina followed the line of Miss Latah's gaze. Walking up the hill toward them was Mr. Ray. He had his face set tight, his lips pressed together. He looked down and wiped his eye, as if he had a piece of dust in it. When he looked up again, his face broke into a broad smile, and then she knew. She'd been forgiven.

In the week that followed Carolina and Miss Latah fixed up a room for Auntie Shen off the kitchen. Miss Latah stitched up pretty curtains. Carolina framed some of her mama's photographs and placed them on a small chest of drawers, and Auntie Shen hung her favorite stitchings on the wall. Auntie Shen said it looked *"right invitin'."*

Mr. Ray started building extra shelves in the pantry for jelly jars.

On August 31, 1964, Carolina stood in front of her birthday cake holding Buzzy in her arms. Carolina closed her eyes and silently said thank you. Seemed her wishes had already come true.

On that very day Mr. Ray and Miss Latah asked Carolina a question that was sweeter than the icing on her cake. She began to write her name as Carolina Harmony, seeing how it looked on paper. Auntie Shen and Carolina wrote it in longhand and then they printed it and then they wrote it in big balloon letters. They decided it looked all right. Carolina said yes.

Carolina, Auntie Shen, Mr. Ray, Miss Latah, and Lucas all drove down to the county courthouse. Mr. Ray and Miss Latah signed legal documents that had lots of words on long white paper. They said it wouldn't be long before they could all stand together as a family and listen to the judge proclaim Carolina's new name. She would be adopted, the legal way. Lucas would be her older brother for real.

It seemed change was happening everywhere. Blue Star Mountain was fast becoming an attraction for people who wanted to ski and for people who wanted to build fancy houses. It just about broke Auntie Shen's heart to see how all those pretty ferns had been bulldozed away. Mr. Ray and Miss Latah locked up the door to Auntie Shen's mountain home, and to everyone's surprise, Auntie Shen smiled and said she wouldn't miss the outhouse.

It wasn't long before Auntie Shen began writing letters to everyone she'd ever known. She put the word out from Boone to Asheville, telling folks that the Harmony family needed their neighbors. The grandpas and the grannies she wrote to were quick to put the bug in the ears of their sons and daughters.

Auntie Shen said something was valuable amid all that ash and soot, something that couldn't be seen or held, something that would rise up out of it and enter the hearts of these folks. And sure enough, it did.

They came from three counties for an old-fashioned barn raising. Auntie Shen was tickled pink.

"This is livin' proof, Carolina. The old mountain ways are alive and kickin'."

Carolina saw the truth of it in the hammering and sawing, the sweat on the brows of the men, and the commotion in the kitchen as Miss Latah cooked and baked alongside women who might never have spoken to her before.

Miss Ruby was one of the many cooks in the kitchen. She and Miss Latah were fast becoming friends. Miss Latah really understood how Miss Ruby felt about the Civil Rights Act and agreed it was helping everyone. Carolina figured some changes were good ones. It seemed people were standing up for what they believed and were putting away old judgments. They were trying on a new way.

Carolina carried a pan of baked apples and sweet potatoes out to the yard, where borrowed tables and chairs had been set up. Tablecloths of all colors made the yard look like a giant quilt. The sun was shining in a bright blue sky. Maple leaves were tinged with scarlet. Puffs of cloud drifted lazily above them all.

Everyone gathered at the tables, and soon bowls of food were being passed from one to another along with lots of stories and jokes. Laughter rang out. Carolina looked around at all the white faces and black faces and red faces, some young, some old, all different and yet in a way all the same. Miss Latah and Miss Ruby were sampling each other's pie, Auntie Shen was holding a baby on her lap, and Mr. Ray was all fired up and telling one of his stories. Lucas was showing considerable interest in a pretty girl across the table, who was smiling right back at him.

Toward dusk, men and women reached for fiddles and banjos and guitars and dulcimers, and the music began. Mr. Ray reached for his fiddle too. His shoulder was completely healed up.

"This is life at its best," said Auntie Shen. She began playing her dulcimer, singing a gentle hymn about turning eyes to clouds of great glory, her voice soft but strong.

Carolina thought about the twists and turns her life had taken this summer and the people she'd met along the way. All the good and all the bad had somehow blazed a trail that led her home. *It's all right if a family takes on a whole new shape and form. It's good and right as long as they truly love you.* Carolina knew for certain Mr. Ray and Miss Latah loved her, because they kept her even when she made mistakes.

In the hour before dawn on a frosty October morning, Carolina and Auntie Shen were sitting on the top step of the porch, talking in soft voices. Carolina was going on and on about how she'd hit it off with a group of girls at school, how her teacher was as kind as Georgia and as serious about books as Mrs. King. Yes, sixth grade had promising possibilities.

They gazed up at the starry sky. Orion had returned. He was now making his way to the western horizon. Carolina pointed to the three stars that made up Orion's belt as she told Auntie Shen about her daddy's telling how he'd be heading there on his way to Heaven. She showed Auntie Shen the stars that glimmered off Orion's sword. She pointed to his arm raised high. They traced the stars down to his legs. Orion was in motion.

"I'd say he's on his way, headin' off for new adventures," said Auntie Shen.

Carolina pulled the quilt up higher on Auntie Shen's shoulders, and they snuggled closer. They wondered aloud if stars really could be angels lighting the way for souls on their way to Heaven. Auntie Shen said all she knew was that Carolina was doubly blessed with a father in Heaven and a father here on earth.

Carolina admitted to having been so angry with God that she'd stopped speaking to Him. Auntie Shen said a seed of faith must have sprouted in Carolina's heart much like a bean seed breaks through hard ground.

"Sometimes the heart does the praying for us," said Auntie Shen.

Carolina trusted that.

Stars faded and the sun rose over the mountains. Its brilliant light touched the tips of the trees. Dew sparkled in the grass. Auntie Shen pointed to a catbird moving in and out of the spindly brown branches of a honeysuckle bush. It flitted up through leaves that were turning yellow, then flapped its wings and flew to a branch high in the tulip tree. Carolina's eyes followed it as it left its perch and took to the sky, disappearing into the clouds.

Acknowledgments

Delving into the lives of characters in a story requires much uninterrupted time. I am deeply grateful to my husband, Peter, for offering me this gift of time, as well as for carefully reading early drafts, driving and hiking all over the Blue Ridge Mountains with me, and sharing his knowledge of the natural world.

Many, many thanks go to my agent, Stephen Fraser, who loved the book from the beginning, and to my editor, Michelle Poploff, who, with keen insight, asked the questions that challenged me to dig deeper. Her editorial guidance and direction brought about my best work. I give huge thanks and big hugs to Christine Cuccio, Barbara Perris, and Colleen Fellingham for their patience and diligence in copyediting all my additions and changes, as well as to Orly Henry, editorial assistant, who kept the ball rolling like a seasoned pro.

My heartfelt appreciation is warmly extended to Patricia MacLachlan, an author whose stories have touched my heart over and over again.

Librarians, musicians, square dance callers, lawyers, museum workers, and fellow writers provided assistance in a myriad of ways. I thank you all from the bottom of my heart.

To my children: Justin, Rob, and Christina. Thank you. You are my cheerleaders.

This is a work of fiction, and the names, places, and events are inventions of my imagination. Yet it is my sincere hope that this story captures the loving, fiercely loyal, independent spirit that lives within the folks blessed to have been born and raised in the western mountains of North Carolina. I thank the divine muse for bringing me this story.

MARILYN TAYLOR MCDOWELL has been bringing children and books together for more than twenty-five years, volunteering as a school librarian, a cultural arts chairperson, and a storyteller, and working as a teacher and as the proprietor of a children's bookshop. Marilyn makes her home in North Chittenden, Vermont. This is her first novel for children.